THE TALE OF THE HIDDEN VILLAGE

Crimson Smoke and the Emerald Flame

K.C. NORTON

RILEY ROOKHOUSE

Cover illustration by Hannah Elizabeth, HannahElizabeth.ca

Cover lettering by James T. Egan, BookflyDesign.com

Managing editor: Diane Callahan, QuotidianWriter.com

Copy editor: Angela Traficante, LambdaEditing.com

Sign up for notifications of upcoming releases by Riley Rookhouse at RileyRookhouse.com

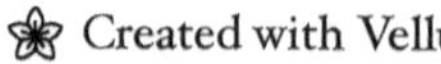 Created with Vellum

Dedication

Ami – we all knew this one was going to be for you.

And for those who are struggling to find themselves, we see you.

Chapter One

My first experience of the world, even before I saw it, was a voice. "Hell after hell," it growled. "Never taken me so many tries before. Downright embarrassing."

I opened my eyes and took in the scene around me. I could not make out where the voice had come from, since there was nothing in my immediate vicinity but the skeletons of trees and an immense boulder standing upright to my left. The light was failing, and the landscape was made of only silhouettes. In the beginning moments of my existence, I stood robed in near-darkness, believing that the whole world was gray. An unnatural light shone on the horizon, in the opposite direction of the setting sun, and my initial thought was that I must go to it and begin asking questions at once, but I could not think *why*.

A sudden movement beside me startled something in the branches above, and I glanced skyward in time to see one of the trees shudder as a handful of small black birds took flight.

"Come along then, Crimson," grunted the stone at my elbow. "Let's see the bastard get away from me *this* time."

I was impressionable and easily led—I had just been born, after all—and it was natural to follow the stone as it moved through the thicket. It was much taller than me, and quite broad, but its stride was nearly silent as we walked through the fallen twigs and drying leaves.

This did not alarm me. I, too, left no mark of my passing.

We made our way through the dusk-soaked landscape toward the golden light ahead, which became brighter as we drew near. It was accompanied by a terrific clamor: loud voices, the dull thump of pewter on dead wood, and the skillful plucking of a lute beneath the din.

There was another sound as well, one that hissed like a lullaby in the background, although I did not understand its source until we reached the edge of the woods. When we did, I stopped, my eyes fixed on a vast, flat, reflective surface, which seemed to trap and refract the light of the stars and the twin moons climbing through the still-gray sky.

What is it? I wondered.

The stone turned to me, letting out an annoyed hiss of breath. Now that I could see the hulking mass better, it was more green than gray, and smoother than the stones we'd passed in the woods. "That son of a serpent *would* drag me halfway across the continent and the Split Seas... Why *not* bring an ocean into it? More water. As if I needed the reminder of last night."

Ocean. Of course that was the name of the shimmering flat surface beside us. I let my eyes roam over the beach, the water, the outlines of ships in the port. If I'd only thought about it for a moment, I would have remembered what it was called.

It was beautiful. I should've been able to remember the names of beautiful things.

I turned to find the stone watching me impatiently. There was enough light now for me to make out the shape of it, and I realized it was not a boulder at all. It was a flesh-and-blood person—not a *human* person, either, although it had the rough proportions of a man. Its limbs were long and thickset, and its shoulders were hunched. Its enormous hands boasted thick knuckles and prominent tendons; it looked as if it could crush my head between its fingers without a second thought. A bulbous nose dominated its face. Most of its body was obscured by a heavy cloak.

The eyes, though. The eyes were utterly human.

Two vastly disparate emotions tugged at me as I took in the appearance of what I had thought to be a lumbering stone. I felt that I loathed the thing, that it was utterly repellent, and that the best thing I could do for it would be to cast it into the sea where I would never have to look at it again. I could not quite make sense of this feeling, and although my repulsion seemed to stem from the very core of my being, it did not feel as though it belonged to me. It was as if someone had *told* me to revile the creature, but my secondary instinct was of pure affection. Tugged between these two emotions, both loving and hating the creature in equal measure, I made a choice.

I would be kind to it.

No, not *it*. To *him*.

"Emerald," I murmured, pleased by this new realization. The stone was not a stranger at all. We were old friends. I had known no one but him since my birth.

I was proud that I had remembered his name, but Emerald snorted and rolled his eyes. He did not speak to me before he turned away.

Seeing no reason for offense, I trotted after Emerald as he led me toward the source of the light, which I now saw was a seaside tavern. I seemed to be able to think more clearly when I tried not to think at all, so I resolved to do exactly that.

The town was not a large one, although I had nothing to compare it to. By moonslight, it seemed quaint and sleepy, as if everyone had gone to bed already. I reached for the door of the tavern, but Emerald got there first, shooting me a curious glance. He kept his hand in place as he leaned toward me.

[Hurry up, Crimson.] His words came directly into my head though his mouth had not moved. I wanted to ask him what our purpose was, but when I tried to use the same inner voice that he did, nothing happened. When he turned to see what I was doing and found me rooted to the spot, he gestured for me to follow him. I could not help it. I *had* to obey. Something at my core flinched, as if it had been pulled by force.

[No time to waste.] Emerald jerked the door open, and the pair of us stepped inside.

I revised my assessment of the town immediately: if it had been quiet outside, it was only because every inhabitant of the little port was jammed cheek-by-jowl into this single building. Emerald made a noise of displeasure as the light and sound flooded over us.

What's wrong? I thought, but Emerald didn't answer. Perhaps I had not asked loudly enough. The trouble was, although he had spoken his last words straight into my head, I didn't have the faintest idea how to respond.

I squeezed my eyes shut. Remembering the feeling I'd had upon looking at him, I tapped into that complicated mix of emotions and cried out, ***[WHAT'S WRONG!?]***

Emerald jumped, but he did not turn his face toward me. ***[No need to be so nervous. Nobody here knows a damn thing. I'll keep my head down and let Crimson do what he always does.]***

His response implied that there were other days to use as a point of reference, and by my reckoning I was only half an hour old.

[Which is what, precisely?] I asked.

[Outshine everyone in the room. Draw every eye. Be the center of attention.]

I straightened up, pleased with the clarity of my purpose. I still was not quite sure what we were meant to be doing, but Emerald's injunction was a comfort. Moreover, he had finally given me a command that I *wanted* to fulfill.

I couldn't help letting my eyes roam over the crowd, taking in their faces. All manner of people populated the room, ranging vastly in size, shape, demeanor, and speech. Sitting beside a short woman with long black braids and skin the color of the night sea was a tall figure with red scales, a brilliant blue head crest, and slitted golden eyes; behind them, a cluster of whitewooled sheep-men raised their small glasses in a friendly toast. A large party of humans drank with a smaller group of dwarves dressed in mining gear, and a man at the center of the gathering strummed a lute. These were more people than I had ever seen together in my admittedly short life, and I was curious about each and every one. I wanted nothing more than to see and be seen by them. The human woman caught my eye, and her gaze raked over me before she lifted her tankard in approval and took a long draught. When I winked at her, she winked back.

To see, and to be seen. That was what I had been born for, and I was already enjoying it. It had not escaped my notice, however, that among those myriad people, none looked like Emerald.

[It will be best if I speak to the owner of the place before I drop the hammer on that lying bard,] Emerald thought. ***[And if that damnable Coirpre tries to get away this time, I'm going to wring his scrawny neck. I don't want another fiasco like the incident in Ten Keeps. That crystal shop owner lodged a lengthy complaint with the magistrate. I don't know why she got so upset about the damage. I was capturing a thief! Or trying to. What's the loss of a few crystal goblets compared to justice? Better let the barkeep here know there's going to be a row, or I'll end up arrested again just for trying to do my job.]***

[Which bard are we after?] I asked, interrupting his self-righteous rant. ***[It wouldn't happen to be that handsome fellow in the green capelet, would it?]***

Emerald stopped short, then looked around the room, keeping his eyes cast low. The lute, whose siren song had tugged at me all the way from the woods, rested in the hands of a golden-haired man in a fine green suit. He struck me as more of an adventurer than anyone else in the room. In fact, he looked like the sort of fellow to whom exciting and notable things happened as a matter of course.

[Handsome?] Even though his voice arrived unbidden in my head, I was aware of a sullen note in Emerald's tone. ***[Coirpre? Ha! That's what they all think.]***

[Are you jealous?]

Emerald's lip curled in undisguised disgust. *[Me? Of a lying trickster dandy like Coirpre, just because people fawn over him like he's some sort of brilliant hero? Hardly.]*

It was the first outright lie that anyone had ever told me, and I wished I had more time to consider the implications of it. Before I could argue, Emerald turned away and moved toward the bar.

[What's wrong with me today?] Emerald chastised himself. *[My thoughts are all over the place. Well, they would be, wouldn't they? Need to focus. The bard's a slippery customer.]*

A young woman in a stained apron sidled past him, and Emerald tried to get her attention. She turned toward him with a smile, but the second she laid eyes on his face, her expression turned ugly. With an air of utter disgust, she pointed him toward the bar and stomped away.

She must have felt the same thing I did at first... but only the unkind half. I didn't know Emerald well enough to sense how he ought to be treated. For all I knew, he was a villain of some kind, and she recognized his wickedness on sight. Judging by the sudden tension in Emerald's jaw, however, I did not truly believe that she had been anything other than rude for its own sake.

As he moved toward the bar, I felt compelled to follow him, but I dug my heels in. Emerald was blatantly ignoring me, and I was finding that I didn't *like* being ignored. Besides, it wouldn't take both of us to talk to the barkeep; my grouchy associate could do so just fine on his own. Surely it was better to divide and conquer. Gingerly, I made my way across the room, weaving between the other guests.

In my attempt to keep my eyes on my feet, I looked down at myself for the first time in my life. Scarlet hair fell into my eyes as I did so, and I pushed it aside with nimble human hands. I experienced a momentary stutter of cognitive dissonance—had these *always* been my hands?—before becoming distracted again by my fine clothes. Emerald had called Coirpre a *dandy*, presumably because of his finery, but my garments were even more ornate and eye-catching. Coirpre's green capelet was embroidered with a handsome floral pattern, but mine was stitched in gold, held in place by three leather buckles that crossed my chest and clasped over my heart with gold buttons molded to look like little flowers. Asters, I realized. A black brocaded tunic covered black breeks, the cuffs of which were tucked into the tops of my tall leather boots. Turning my head, I caught a blurry reflection of myself in the darkened window. My red hair fell almost to my shoulders, and a faint red stubble covered my square jaw. I knew it as my reflection only by the expression of utter perplexity upon my features. Again I wondered: had this *always* been my face?

This raised another question. Why, by every Heaven, would an obviously handsome gentleman such as myself spend my days in the company of a creature whose presence was so distasteful to the general public?

Because he is my only friend.

Emerald had made his way over to the bar and was already engrossed in conversation with the innkeeper, who seemed to view him with pointed skepticism. I was being remiss in my duties. Perhaps, instead of puzzling over riddles I had no hope of solving, I would be better served by assuming that life was inherently confusing. I would pester Emerald with questions later. In the meantime, we had a liar to catch.

The closer I drew to Coirpre, the more of his words I could make out. The tune had the air of a lively ballad, and by the time I reached the outskirts of the group surrounding the table where he held court, I began to understand his lyrics.

"... strong as the west wind, fleet as a cloud,
From the mainland, ill trade-winds brought her,
"Striking with teeth and with talon and sound,
she never a regret bethought her.
"She preyed upon merchants outside Lower Bound
And their lifeblood flowed black in the water
"Until brave Coirpre of Kessingtown

led her like a lamb to the slaughter!"

One of the lambkins who had come over to listen to the song shifted uncomfortably at the last line, but the rest of the entourage applauded wildly.

"Brilliant!" cried one of them, getting to his feet and slapping the smiling bard upon the back. "Another round for the brave Coirpre, the man who saved us all!"

The bard bowed, waving his hands modestly, but his smile was anything but bashful.

[His slant-rhyming is atrocious,] I told Emerald. *[Any old Mumblecrust could do better.]*

A loud snort-laugh echoed through the room, and I smiled to myself, pleased to have amused Emerald. I suspected it was a rather difficult task, and resolved to attempt it more frequently in the future.

[Crimson? Crimson! What in Aster's name are you doing all the way over there?] Emerald's thoughts were a tangle of confusion, amusement, and concern. *[When did you wander off? I wasn't paying attention. Seems to be the theme of the evening. All right, keep an eye on him, and we'll see how he plays it.]*

The bard was already talking again. "Now that you've heard the tale of our harrowing journey along the coast, who can guess what attacked us?" Coirpre pointed around to the assembled onlookers. "I'll buy a drink for the person who guesses rightly. And no cheating, eh, Everett?" He winked at one of the men. "This is only for the ones who weren't there. What about you, lambkin?"

"A siren?" bleated the lambkin shyly.

"No!" cried Coirpre. "But an excellent guess, my friend. Any other takers?"

"A lost spirit?" asked someone else.

The man's companion shoved his shoulder with her own. "Whoever heard of a ghost with teeth?" she demanded.

"I heard a tale, once, in Boulder Falls..." the man began.

Perhaps sensing that the audience's attention was about to

drift away from him, Coirpre cut in. "Not a wandering spirit, I'm afraid. Anyone else?"

One of the dwarves spoke up. "Tooth, talon, and voice? Sounds like a harpy to me."

Coirpre banged his fist triumphantly against the table. "Someone get this fellow an ale! Indeed, it was a harpy."

"Tell the story again!" the closest lambkin said. "I missed the beginning the first time."

Coirpre's friend returned from the bar and thrust a tankard into the man's hand. I watched with some amusement as the bard took a deep swig before standing up in his chair. He placed one boot against the seat and lifted the other onto the tabletop, setting the tankard down next to his foot before strumming a chord on his lute.

"There we were: a dozen merchants, a sailing vessel, and only myself to stand guard against anything that came at us from across the water. All day, we had watched the skies, intent on reaching Lower Bound in one piece. As we sailed north along the Eastern shore of Kovin Isle, bearing much-needed supplies up from Hardwick Home, we could only pray to the gods of the sea and sky that we would be kept safe. And then..."

He leapt forward into a crouch right in front of the lambkin, who bleated in surprise.

"*Down from the sky she came!*" Coirpre's voice took on a theatrical quality, stopping just shy of song.

I decided then and there that Emerald was wrong. He had undersold the extent to which this man was an insufferable headache.

"Her dappled wings," the bard continued, "spanned nearly fifteen feet and blotted out the sun!" He lifted one arm about his head to indicate the size of the creature.

The assembled men gasped, except for those who had traveled with Coirpre on his fateful voyage. They nodded grimly, looking up at the bard with haggard expressions, as if reliving the terror of the encounter.

Coirpre began to pick out a frantic tune on the lute,

increasing the pace as his story reached its crescendo. "Her treacherous claws stretched down from banded yellow legs, her hair was a nest of curls and tangles, and her eyes fixed upon us with a terrible hunger, marking us as her next meal. She swept down upon the vessel, and then...!" His hands fell abruptly still, and his voice dropped to a stage whisper. The whole tavern seemed to be holding its breath. "She began to *sing*."

[Say what you will about the man, he knows how to sell a crock of shite,] I thought. Emerald's answering snort of amusement echoed through the quiet room.

Coirpre continued. "Her voice stirred the formerly calm seas into a frenzy and called rain down from the heavens. The sky darkened. And at that moment, when all hope seemed lost, I began to play. Ladies and gentlemen, you hear me correctly: I outsang the harbinger of storms herself! Locked in lyrical battle, armed with nothing but my lute and my wits, I matched her note for note until her resolve broke, and she flew off into the sky in the direction of Whale Bone Island. She did not make it far before she sank so low that her talons trailed in the water. Even as we watched, the waves swallowed her whole, and we were left to complete our journey in safety!"

Coirpre lifted his arms in triumph, standing up at his full height upon the tavern table, while his rapt audience applauded this victory. The merchants who had sailed with him clapped the loudest of all, thumping their fists on the hardwood and whistling as Coirpre took a bow.

"I've never seen anything like it!" one of the merchants exclaimed. "I thought the captain must be mad, to hire a man who claimed that he could protect our ship with *music*, but I'll be damned if he didn't save us all."

I was unmoved by these words. The bard's act struck me as false and boastful, although I could not say why. If the men who traveled with him could attest to the fact that they had indeed been in danger, and yet had managed to reach the tavern unscathed, Coirpre could not be *entirely* unjustified in his pride.

Unless, of course, the harpy had been just another part of the show.

Coirpre's eyes met mine, and his smile faded. "You there, good sir—I take it that you don't appreciate hearing of my exploits."

[All right,] Emerald thought, *[he's spotted Crimson. Let the real show begin.]*

A few of the onlookers shot me reproachful looks, but I ignored them. My attention was fixed on Coirpre alone. "You mistake me, sir," I said, bowing forward slightly. "You are a master storyteller, and a passable lutist, but I don't believe a single word that has left your lips since I entered this fine establishment."

The crowd had held its breath in anticipation of his story, but the silence that followed my pronouncement was even deeper. Coirpre glared at me and slung his lute over his back, matching my stance. "Is that so?"

I held up one finger. "Allow me to correct myself: I misspoke. I *do* believe one element of your tale, which is that you were on that ship with these upstanding gentlemen." I gestured to encompass the small group of finely dressed merchants, who were glaring daggers at me. "As to whether their money was well spent on your employ, we can agree to disagree."

Coirpre's lip curled. In an instant, he went from looking like a fresh-faced young adventurer in his mid-twenties to a bitter man of twice that age. "Are you calling all of these upstanding citizens liars as well?" A few of the merchants rose to their feet.

"Hardly," I said. "I do believe, however, that you have taken advantage of them."

[Good,] Emerald thought. *[Don't antagonize the merchants. Before a fight breaks out, explain why his story is impossible.]* These instructions were accompanied by a flood of pertinent information.

"A harpy has four sets of vocal cords," I continued aloud, plucking relevant facts from the details Emerald had mentally provided, "and an auditory system that filters out any counter-songs. It's impossible to outsing a harpy. You can outplay one, and maybe hope to drown it out with the proper musical instruments—a Horn of Apocryphal Silence, for example, or a Shrill Flute of Infinite Notes. But to counter-sing it, with only human anatomy? Impossible."

"Miracles happen," said Coirpre firmly. "And I have extensive and highly advanced training in the art of, erm, musical warfare."

I felt Emerald's mental nudge again, with no words this time. A flood of information, previously held at bay, spilled over into my mind, proving all of my earlier intuition about Coirpre correct. I smiled to myself. All of the merchants who had been applauding him were turning to *me* for answers.

See, and be seen. My first opportunity to fulfill my purpose had presented itself, and I was determined to rise to the challenge.

"Before you take your anger out on me, good people," I said, "perhaps you will allow me to tell a story." I took a step forward, and the crowd parted to make way for me. I strode through the gap, up to the table where Coirpre stood, and turned my back to him, facing the now-hostile eyes of the audience.

[A little showmanship might put that rat bastard in his place.] At the bar, Emerald sipped an amber liquid from a crystal goblet, staring at the scene over the rim of the glass with a smug smile on his lips. ***[Now tell them about Hunter's Hope.]*** Again, he shoved a swirl of information at me.

I raised my voice, as Coirpre had done when he addressed the crowd. "Several weeks ago, in the mainland town of Hunter's Hope, three merchants loaded up their cart and prepared to ride out along the roads. I don't know how many of you have traveled there, so let me explain: these roads are ripe with dangers of all sorts. These merchants decided to hire a little protection. Who should offer his services but a charismatic bard who claimed that he could subdue any enemy they encountered with *nothing* besides his music and the power of his voice?"

Three of the merchants, including the one who had bought Coirpre's last drink, were still glaring at me, but I was warming to my subject. I walked around the table, lifting my hand toward

Coirpre as if presenting damning evidence before a local court—which, to some degree, I was. "The bard informed the merchants that they wouldn't even have to pay him in advance. In fact, they would only have to pay him if he should have to vanquish an enemy or defeat a hazard they encountered on the way. They found this *quite* the bargain. And what do you know? Halfway into their voyage, a griffin swooped out of the trees and tried to grab their horse, but the bard played the danger away, much to their relief."

"Hang on," Coirpre said nervously. "What are you insinuating?"

I spoke over him, drowning out his arguments. "Not long after, two armed robbers leapt out of the woods. Two men, armed with only swords! The merchants told themselves that this should be nothing. After all, if the bard could fend off a griffin, two measly human attackers should prove no trouble at all. To their great shock, however, the bard fled, never to be seen again, and the merchants were forced to fight on their own. They were able to defeat the bandits, but they were obliged to travel all the way back to Hunter's Hope and secure a more reliable escort."

"That's s-shameful," Coirpre stuttered. "Men like that give my line of work a bad name..."

I whirled to face him, realizing just in time that I was about to collide with the lambkin standing at the corner of the table. Instinctively, I stepped away, giving the small sheep-man room. "Are you not, then, the same Coirpre who claimed to defeat a siren in a singing contest in Sailor's Reprieve? The same man who claimed to defeat a granite shark that was digging tunnels beneath the streets of Port Haven, despite the fact that granite sharks are *deaf?*" I pointed an accusing finger at Coirpre's face.

The bard frowned down at me from his spot on the table. "Wait, *are* they deaf?"

[Are they?] I asked Emerald.

[No,] Emerald replied carelessly. ***[But he'd know that, wouldn't he, if he really had confronted one. Stop doubting***

yourself.] My companion shook his head and stared at the drink in his hand, as if he had imbibed too much, despite barely having half a glass.

I narrowed my eyes at Coirpre. "You should know whether they are deaf, given you claim to have defeated one with the sound of your own voice!"

Coirpre's expression turned stormy. "If you insist on calling me a liar, explain what these men saw!"

"Yes, young man," said the lead merchant coldly. His eyes darted from me to the bard and back. "I think we would *all* appreciate an explanation."

[Lightweaving,] piped up Emerald, who sounded decidedly bored. *[He's singing up an illusion and making it look like he's also frightening the monster away.]*

"He's singing an illusion!" I repeated. "He plucks out his miserable melodies and causes the victims of his fraud to believe they are staring into the face of unspeakable terrors, when in fact the only real threat to their livelihoods is *him!*" I brandished a shaking finger at the bard.

[Tone it down,] Emerald thought. *[No need to be so grandiose.]*

I ignored him, turning back to the merchants, who stared at me wide-eyed. *They* didn't mind my showmanship. "Stories of his treachery abound. He claims to have faced off against a hill ogre and subdued a whiptail wyvern in the height of mating season when everyone knows they are at their most vicious. And yet when he was faced with two barely armed and wickedly drunk bandits, he abandoned the men who counted on him. That is the real crime, and he must be brought to task for his transgressions!"

[What the hells, Crimson? This is getting a little out of hand...]

The nearest merchant took a step toward Coirpre, and I fell back a pace. "Is that true?"

"Well, now, gentlemen, let's not be too hasty..." The bard stepped back toward the edge of the table.

"Why not?" asked another of the men. "You were hasty enough to spend our money, insisting we stay in the best tavern in town, drinking the finest meads and eating whatever you liked. That's my money you've spent, sir, and I demand honesty. Is there any truth to what this fellow says?"

Coirpre looked from the merchant to me and back again, his mouth open as he searched for some other argument. His silence was his undoing, and within moments, a cluster of angry men rushed toward him.

I beat a hasty retreat toward Emerald, careful to slip between the members of the crowd, who had been whipped into a frenzy by my speech. Emerald leaned over the bar, speaking in low tones to the man who poured the drinks. "This could get ugly," he said. "I think I saw a Conjury title listed in your registry. Is there any chance he could intervene before these men tear that idiot apart?"

The innkeeper backed toward the stairs. "Yes, sir, a Conjury scout checked in earlier. He's been in his room ever since."

"Better go and get him," Emerald said as he stood back to full height, easily a foot taller than any other person in the tavern besides the blue dragon-woman.

The innkeeper ran toward the stairs just as a flash of brilliant light erupted in the center of the dining room. Several patrons screamed, backing away from the fire that now covered the table where the bard had so recently performed.

"Oh, for Aster's sake," Emerald grumbled. He swung his bulky, muscular arms in a surprisingly graceful manner, first upward as though lifting something between his broad palms, then sharply down. In a split second, the fire went out, leaving the table undamaged.

"Light-weaver! Illusionist!" howled one of the merchants. "Where did he go?"

Emerald turned his head, then pointed toward the corner of the room. "*There*. In the green."

Sure enough, a green-clad figure was skirting the walls of the room, clearly headed for the door. The tall, scaly woman that had drawn my eye earlier made a grab for him, but the bard ducked away. He strummed a few notes, and the light in the whole room shifted from oil-lamp yellow to a smothering green. Presumably this was meant to make him more difficult to spot, but it was too late. Everyone in the tavern was up in arms, and within seconds it had descended into a free-for-all.

Several of the other patrons began tossing chairs out of the way. One of them sailed directly toward me, and I closed my eyes, lifting my arms up to block my head before the blow could land. To my surprise, I heard the chair splinter against the stone wall behind me, although I had been sure that I stood dead in its path.

I scuttled around to crouch behind the bar, peeping my eyes up over the edge just far enough to see. Emerald was holding two merchants back by their collars while the rest grappled with a struggling Coirpre. Lambkins held on to his legs, one each, and another merchant snatched the lute from Coirpre's hands and brought it down hard against the cobbled floor. The green light immediately went out, and the watery lamplight revealed just how pale the bard had gone.

"Your nose is next, you charlatan!" the merchant cried. "And if you're lucky, I'll stop there."

"The Conjury should arrest him," Emerald said.

"The Conjury can have what's left of him!" the merchant retorted.

Coirpre trembled, and I felt almost sorry for him. He was a mountebank, a sham, an imposter. But he was also a man who, at that particular moment, was in real fear for his life.

[Don't let them kill him,] I thought toward Emerald.

Footsteps echoed down the stairs, and my companion breathed a sigh of relief that seemed to echo through me from across the room. *[The Conjury scout will sort it out.]*

The innkeeper appeared at the top of the stairs, his thin brown hair rumpled, his forehead gleaming with a sheen of nervous sweat, and his jowls wobbling. "Help!" he cried. "Help! The Conjury scout is dead in his room!"

The moment the assembled crowd heard this, I learned the true meaning of the word chaos. The revelation of the bard's treachery might have been enough to inspire rage in the men he'd duped, but news of a death awoke their primal fear. The lambkins ran pell-mell for the door, bleating in terror, and the merchants let go of Coirpre. Seconds ago, they had been prepared to beat him into submission, but now they fled side by side with him into the night.

[Hmm, did someone kill a Conjury member?] Emerald thought blankly. He reached up to scratch the thick mossy hair on top of his head.

I watched as the last of the lambkins disappeared from view. *[Should we leave?]* After all, the audience had departed, which meant I had no role left to fulfill. I did not fully understand the concept of *death*. Certainly, our scattered audience found it cause for extreme dismay, but in Emerald's mind the idea of death was... complicated.

At the very least, I could not perform for a dead man, and my first great show had ended in failure. My prize was getting away.

[Leave?] His heavy brow wrinkled in puzzlement, as if this question served as further evidence of my odd behavior rather than a logical conclusion. *[Why would I leave? This kind of thing is the reason I'm here.]*

Chapter Two

❧

Within moments of the innkeeper's announcement, the inn all but cleared out. Only a few other souls stood their ground alongside Emerald, but most of them looked as lost as I felt. I took a few shuffling steps out from behind the bar and approached my companion.

[Surely one of these fine gentlemen could be of more assistance than us? That bard is getting away.] I tipped my chin toward the door and mustered a small, encouraging smile. *[Don't you think we ought to finish up one show before we begin another? Unless you suspect Coirpre is involved in this death somehow. Either way, shouldn't we make him our priority?]*

[Oh, curses, Coirpre must have done something to Crimson.] Emerald's eyes narrowed. *[That's why he wandered away earlier and got all verbose and dramatic during the reveal. Well, I can't do anything about it now. I'll just have to—]*

[Don't think about me like I'm not here!] I shot back, balling my hands into fists. He'd given me all sorts of instructions while I was talking to the bard, but other than that, he'd

paid me almost no mind at all. *[You'd treat a babblebird better than you're treating me!]*

Emerald's eyeballs bulged. *[That's enough! I'll sort you out later. For now, go upstairs.]*

I turned toward the steps, but I was none too keen to give up my starring role so easily, even if Emerald asked me to. *[But Coirpre—]*

A rush of furious emotion passed through me, and against my will I stumbled forward, as if Emerald had given me a terrific shove without so much as laying a hand on me. My feet seemed to drag me toward the steps. When Emerald had first ordered me into the tavern, I'd felt the same compulsion, but it was urgent this time and could not be denied. There was something violent about the way I was driven toward the bottom step, and no matter how hard I tried, I could not master myself.

Emerald was doing this somehow, I was certain, but knowing that bought me no control. I had to go. I could not help it.

By the time I mounted the first step, I gave up fighting. Instead, I climbed the stairs toward the frantic innkeeper under my own power. The moment I obeyed, the feeling of being controlled faded, and the anger at the back of my mind dissipated along with it. So long as I was behaving, it seemed, I would not be driven forward like a horse with a spur in its side.

I wasn't certain what my struggle looked like to the people around me, but I tried to add a bit of a confident swagger to my stride. In my hour-long life, I'd had very few role models, so I found myself imitating Coirpre. After all, the man had managed to win over a whole tavernful of strangers based on his confidence alone. Well, the gods knew it hadn't been his *talent* that did it. If I was going to convince anyone that I belonged here, I would have to do the same.

Aster knows Emerald won't, I thought, turning my head slightly to glare at my companion. *Coirpre is all tact and no brains, while Emerald is precisely the reverse.* I waited for a response—a threat or a reprimand for my errant thoughts. None came. It gave me a wicked thrill of pleasure to know that even though my companion could control my actions, my private thoughts were beyond his reach.

"My good sir," I said gently, approaching the innkeeper. "Are you quite sure the poor fellow is dead?"

The man's scruffy face was white as plaster. He leaned against the wall at the top of the landing, with his hand over his heart and a haunted expression in his eyes. "Gods, yes," he groaned. "Oh, my aching head. A Conjury man, kicking it in my inn? They'll have my head."

"May I see him?" This question was Emerald's, though it came from my mouth.

Feeding me lines was one thing, but forcing me to talk was another. *If he'd only be a bit more patient with me, we could find some sort of equilibrium.*

The barkeep's mustache trembled. "What for?"

What for, indeed? Emerald had only told me that getting involved in this matter was *his* purpose, and I could offer no better explanation. I glanced back at Emerald for confirmation.

He put my next words in my head, making sure I had no room for creative interpretation. **[My associate and I are licensed by the Conjury to…]**

"…delve into crimes committed via breach of Conjury law." I offered the poor innkeeper my most charming smile. "If the circumstances of the man's death warrant further investigation, we're your, ah, people." I repeated what Emerald fed into my head with a single embellishment: he had wanted me to say *we're your men*, but the word felt incorrect. No reprimand came for me changing Emerald's instructions, but I did find myself resenting my role as a puppet in the conversation. This particular betrayal was a bitter one, since Emerald had been with me since my birth. I had tried to do what was expected of me. Why wouldn't he give me the benefit of the doubt? Weren't lifelong friends meant to look out for one another?

Perhaps not. Emerald's store of knowledge revealed little on such topics.

"Might I have your names, sir?" The innkeeper dipped his

head apologetically. "My sincerest apologies, but in the case of an untimely death…"

"You want only the best help available, of course," I said. Two names swam into my mind, and I smiled at their comfortable familiarity. "I'm called Simon, and my surly associate is Emerald. But perhaps you will know us better by our titles: Crimson Smoke and the Emerald Flame."

The innkeeper pulled a grubby cloth from the pocket of his leather apron and dabbed frantically at his forehead. It seemed to me that the poor fellow might break down in tears at any moment. "Gods be praised—is it true? Your help would be a blessing, to be sure. I've heard the stories. Although some said you were a woman…" His cheeks flushed. "Never mind, sir, never mind. Rumors get things wrong more often than not."

Emerald's voice had fallen silent in my mind, but anyone could see that the man before me required further consolation. Without prompting, I reached out to pat him on the shoulder.

[Don't touch him!] The force of Emerald's voice was startling, and once again, I lost control of my own limbs.

I stood frozen for a moment before turning my movement into a gesture toward the innkeeper. When I was not directly disobeying whatever command Emerald held over me, I was able to move unimpeded.

"And you, sir?" I asked. "What is your name?"

"McLachlan," he said at once. "Of Lower Bound, born and bred. This was my father's inn. Oh, I reckon he'd turn in his grave if he knew a man had gone to the gods in one of our own beds! And a Conjury scout, no less."

[I see that histrionics are popular this evening,] Emerald mused. He stood on the step below us, which brought him roughly eye level with McLachlan.

[His father is dead, too?] I wondered. *[Do you think there might be some connection?]*

[Between his father and the scout?] Emerald asked.

[I don't know anyone else who's dead.]

Emerald's eye twitched. *[Stop being thick and tell him we*

want to see the crime scene.] This thought was accompanied by another rush of knowledge. According to Emerald, death was usually permanent and almost inevitable, and he made sure to add that everyone with common sense already knew as much.

"Perhaps we might view the room for ourselves and see what we can find?" I asked, wishing Emerald wouldn't go so far out of his way to make me feel stupid.

"I don't mean to doubt you, but do you carry an official license?" The man stopped his frantic dabbing and narrowed his eyes at my companion. "We've had enough illusions in the tavern tonight, you understand, and I've never seen your faces before. Begging your pardon, sir."

Emerald grunted before digging a large hand into one of the pouches hanging around his waist. A moment later, he produced a rolled-up slip of parchment, which he held out before him. I could not read whatever it said from my angle, but McLachlan's round face went paler, if such a thing were possible.

"Of course, sir. Right this way, sir. Don't want no trouble with the Magistrate—just wanted to be certain, what with a dead man in *my* inn and all." He seemed to realize what he was saying and abruptly snapped his mouth shut before hustling along toward a door at the end of the hall.

By now, a group of curious, morbidly brave onlookers had gathered at the bottom of the stairs in the otherwise empty tavern. They tracked our movements with wary eyes; a fair number of them hung back with hunched shoulders and petrified expressions, but there were others whose attention remained fixed on Emerald in particular with hateful mistrust.

Because of his association with the Magistrate? Or because of his appearance? I suspected the latter, since whatever animosity they felt toward him did not seem to extend in my direction.

The tavern itself had taken on a grotesque air now that the majority of its patrons had fled the scene. What had struck me before as a lively and inviting place seemed suddenly grubby and hostile, its floorboards stained with more than spilled ale. What sort of a town was Lower Bound, where the citizens would laud a charlatan one moment and turn on him the next? The merchants had been quick to decry Coirpre for abandoning them in their moment of need, to the point of threatening his life for doing so. Yet when a man turned up dead, they fled the scene with the same anxious haste that the bard had employed when abandoning his previous charges.

Less than an hour conscious in the world, and already I discovered myself jaded by the fluctuating morals of its other inhabitants.

Emerald grunted again, and once more I found myself driven along in a direction I had not chosen. This time I dogged the steps of the innkeeper, who was twisting an iron key in the bolt securing the room. He began to take a step inside.

"Wait!" I cried.

McLachlan stopped and turned to face me, frowning slightly. "What now?"

I was not sure if I had called out on my own, or if Emerald had driven me to do it. The next words out of my mouth, however, were not my own. "Was the room locked when you first came up?"

"Yes, sir. Locked it again when I came out." He averted his eyes. "Didn't want him following me, you know. If you live long enough on Kovin Isle, you'll learn that the dead don't always stay quiet. Besides, Mr. Smoke, sir, I didn't want anyone tampering with the evidence."

Emerald made a small sound in the back of his throat.

I took another step forward. Emerald followed closely, although he had to keep his shoulders hunched to pass below the lantern burning above us. It threw long, uncanny shadows against the wall, lending the whole place a rather lurid and unwholesome atmosphere.

Our guide pushed the open door even farther, then fell back with a shudder. Something seemed to pass through the hall, stirring the tapestries and causing the sconce flames to gutter, as if the last breath of the room's former occupant were being released from within.

There was a corpse in the bed, which had been a man until lately. He lay on the down-filled mattress with his countenance frozen in a rictus of terror, his unblinking eyes staring forever toward the heavens. Seeing the dead man helped explain the panic of the other patrons. If this was death, I could understand their desire to distance themselves from the knowledge that they might one day meet a similar fate.

While I pitied the man unutterably, his condition did not frighten me. Emerald, too, seemed inured to the wretched sight. He didn't so much as blink as he stared down at the mortal remains.

Not so McLachlan or the men who were beginning to cluster behind him. Our host had not stopped blotting his forehead and balding head with his grubby kerchief, his eyes fixed on the sorry *memento mori* even as it stiffened amid the rumpled sheets.

"What happened to him?" McLachlan whispered. "Gods, look at him. He died screaming, but I didn't hear a sound."

I bent closer, examining the scene with more curiosity than repulsion. The immediate cause of the man's death was obvious. His sheet was wound about his throat, and his face was a violent purple; the tongue within his open mouth was very nearly black.

"He was strangled." I considered the scene for another moment before continuing. "But sheets don't simply come alive and strangle their sleeping occupants, and judging by the scratches on his throat, he was attempting to escape. Which suggests," I added with some reluctance, drawing on Emerald's powers of deduction, "that some other hand held him in place until his spirit and his body were well and truly separated."

This pronouncement was met with utter silence. I looked up to find that McLachlan had collapsed against the doorframe, his face as white as the sheets around the dead man's throat—whiter, in fact. An assortment of stains had set in the bedding, alongside the fresh addition of the dead man's blood from where he'd clawed at the bindings in a fruitless attempt to free himself.

What an awful way to die.

The innkeeper gasped. "M-m-murder? Of a Conjury representative? Under my own roof?"

"Isn't it obvious?" I gestured to the unhappy victim. "Did you really think that the poor man somehow strangled *himself?*"

"It might be an accident," the proprietor blubbered. "Maybe he had a bad dream, thrashed about a bit, and throttled himself in the sheets before he could get free."

A squat, bearded man—a merchant, I guessed, from the look of him—watching from the hall spoke up. "Aye, it could have been an accident. I once knew a man who choked to death on a sweetfruit. When your god or goddess wishes to reclaim you, their hand cannot be stayed." He bowed his head somberly.

I stared at the merchant and the innkeeper in turn. I had limited enough experience in the world, but even I could see an abundance of flaws with this theory. Perhaps these men had never encountered a murder before. Then again, neither had I, and even *I* hadn't leapt to such a simpleminded conclusion.

"Look at him," I said slowly. "The man is still fully dressed. His mud-speckled boots are on his feet. Do you truly believe he crawled into bed like this and fell into such a deep slumber that even an inanimate bit of linen was able to overpower him?"

McLachlan dabbed at his brow again and said nothing. The man in the hall made no reply, but he continued to scowl at me as if I'd personally offended him and his ill-fated, fruit-slain associate.

"It can't be murder," McLachlan said at last. "Imagine the consequences if—no, I'm sorry, Mr. Smoke. I cannot entertain such an, ah, *unprofitable* notion."

I pointed to the man on the bed, trying to smother my rising annoyance. I could only make my performance so compelling. At some point, common sense would have to serve as sufficient evidence.

[You'll never convince him in this manner,] Emerald interrupted. *[To admit that a man was murdered under his roof could make him culpable with the Conjury, the local law enforcement, and his other patrons. The paperwork*

alone could be his undoing, and if he managed to keep his head above water, he might still lose his business. Nobody would rest easy in an inn with such a grim reputation.]

His point was sound, as far as I could tell. None of that seemed fair to the dead man, however. My eyes drifted from the corpse to McLachlan to the men gathered in the doorway.

[A man is **dead.***]*

Emerald gestured one hand vaguely to the corpse. *[They're not worried about him now. We're here to find trouble, and everyone here wants to avoid it. McLachlan has his own reasons for denying the obvious. No doubt the others do as well.]*

I had assumed that Emerald's job was to find the facts, at which point it would fall upon me to reveal them. To that end, I had done my best to fulfill my purpose. It had never occurred to me that anyone else's purpose would be to obscure the truth, unless they were culpable.

Evidently, I still had a great deal to learn about the world.

Emerald nudged me into speech again. *[Did you bring him dinner in his room...]*

"...before he expired? Did he have anything to drink?" I asked. If my line fell a little flat, it was only because I was beginning to doubt my role.

"No, sir." That question, at least, McLachlan could answer. "He arrived around the same time as that lying bard and his crew. I set him up in the room and told him we serve dinner until ten. That was the last I saw of him. Once that bard and his friends showed up, I rather lost track of things."

[So he was sober, hungry, and yet somehow...]

"...managed to pass out and suffocate himself in his sleep?" I narrowed my eyes at the tavern owner.

"Believe me, sir, your guess is as good as mine. Better!" McLachlan waved his arms frantically to encompass the entire scene. "The door was locked from the inside. There are only two copies of the key. I carry one, and *he* carried the other." He gestured to the corpse but kept his eyes averted.

"Strange run of bad luck," one of the merchants grumbled. "Ain't that the third Conjury scout to bite it in a year?"

I whirled to face the speaker. "Is that so?"

"Come, now." The short, squat merchant who had spoken about sweetberries clicked his tongue derisively. "You're seeing a pattern where none exists. The old scout kept the same route for nearly forty years. Accidents happen. That first fellow couldn't swim, and the woman who replaced him didn't know her head from her ass."

"Best not to speak ill of the dead," McLachlan said, glancing at the corpse once again. "That poor girl simply didn't know the area."

"What became of her?" I asked, before Emerald could think to prompt me.

McLachlan shook his head sadly. "Fell to her death, I'm afraid, from the cliff of one of the high passes over the mountains. Nasty business. Poor thing didn't even make it back from her first route."

"There are ghosts in the hills," one of the men murmured. "Unquiet spirits."

"Strange doings," another agreed. "There are some folks who've been saying that the whole island is cursed of late, what with all the deaths of the mainlanders."

"I blame Dyrne."

I was not certain who first voiced that concern, but the mutterings were immediately taken up by the group at large.

"Who or what is Dyrne?" I asked.

"The next-to-last town on the route the scouts take around the island." McLachlan jerked his chin at the dead man. "A grim, displeasing place, make no mistake. We avoid it at all costs."

The short merchant scoffed. "Not all of us. It's a town like any other. The folk there might be a bit shy and pious, but their money spends as good as anyone else's."

[Well,] thought Emerald.

"Well," I said aloud.

The merchant glared at me and did not speak again.

"I don't know what happened out there, but I don't think he would have been with us long anyway." McLachlan's fear had faded, and a sort of low melancholia had set in.

"Do you think he was marked for death in some way?" I wasn't sure how anyone would be able to tell, but I supposed it was possible.

Emerald grunted. *[Don't feed into their superstitions. They're backwards enough out here without your encouragement.]*

"I didn't mean long for this world. I meant in town." The innkeeper tucked his sweat-soaked kerchief back into the pocket of his stained leather apron, where I deduced it would stay rather than be subjected to the laundry tub. "The gentleman had mentioned an interest in booking passage across the sea. The scouts don't live here, you know, although some of them choose to stay. Whether he had something to report back to the Conjury or if his route was changed with the new assignment, I can't guess with any certainty."

I turned to meet Emerald's eyes. "Interesting."

Throughout the course of the night, my companion had insulted me, compelled me, and controlled me as he saw fit. From our silent connection, Emerald could wield a turn of phrase as artfully as a blade. Now, as I stared significantly into his eyes while McLachlan and a cluster of curious gadabouts looked on, his only response was, "Mmph."

[Mmph? What in the name of Aster's Holy Garden does "mmph" mean!?]

Emerald's frown deepened almost imperceptibly, and his eyes flicked toward our host. *[He's told us all he can. I need to examine the room. In private.]*

I waited for him to tell everyone else to get out, but when he simply stood there, dull and uninspiring as a lump of old driftwood, I returned my attention to our audience.

"Gentlemen, I think we can agree that the events of this evening are most unfortunate. While my colleague and I are primarily interested in the gross misuse of magic, I believe that gross misuse of *bedding* also falls within our purview." I smiled the way I believed Coirpre might have, if he wanted to win over a particularly uninspired audience. "To this end, I must beg your indulgence and politely ask you to..." I lost control of my speech patterns as Emerald pressed his own desires upon me. "...get the Hells out."

The audience grumbled, but McLachlan leapt at the chance to dismiss the onlookers. He retreated at once, shutting the door behind him and cutting off anyone else who might have wished to bear witness to our investigation.

I smiled charmingly until the latch clicked. The moment we were left alone with the corpse, I scowled at my erstwhile companion.

"What was that for?" I demanded.

Emerald stared at me as if I had spontaneously sprouted a second head. He didn't bother to answer me, either aloud or through what I considered to be our private connection.

"I was..." I sucked in a deep breath and lowered my voice so that the people outside would be less likely to hear. Perhaps approaching him though our mental link would have been easier, but I was vexed, and scolding him silently wouldn't have been satisfying. "I was trying to do what you wanted, but you didn't back me up!"

[I'll fix Crimson later,] Emerald thought. *[For now, I need to examine the room.]*

"Oh, that's rich," I sneered. "Talk about me as if I'm not here."

[Stupid bard and his stupid sleight of hand. I bet Crimson's going to act like this all night. How come that handsome bastard always manages to make a hasty getaway no matter the circumstances?]

I perked up at this perceived compliment. "Who's a handsome bastard? Me, or Coirpre?"

The look Emerald shot me could have curdled fresh milk. *[Neither.]*

My sullen mood returned, and I watched in silence as Emerald prodded the dead man, examining the remains intently.

[Hm. Still warm—which means it just happened. But McLachlan said the door was locked when he came in, so if he was strangled, how did the killer get in, much less escape?]

"Is the window unlatched?" I asked. I was rather enjoying my sulk, but to do so at the expense of a dead man seemed unnecessarily cruel. Now that we were the only three people in the room, I did a small examination of my own. His face was difficult to look upon, in part because the idea of a person treating *another* person in this manner was much too sad. This was not the work of an angry moment. Whoever had killed the scout must have held the blanket tight around him for a long time.

How badly must one man despise his fellow to cause him such suffering and end his life? Not a person at all, surely, but a monster.

As for his clothing, it was fairly well-kept. The materials were more homespun than the ones I wore, but I thought his dress somewhat finer than the rough wool outfits favored by the locals. I could divine nothing more personal about him from his appearance. How terrible it seemed to me, to be erased in every way that mattered.

Emerald scowled at me again, then turned to examine the sash. *[Window's closed from the inside. No broken glass. I suppose whoever did it could've manipulated the interior of the room from outside. But we're on the second floor, and without a line of sight, that should be impossible.]*

"Perhaps someone teleported into the room and left once the deed was done?" I suggested.

[As for transportation, it would take extraordinarily powerful magic to accomplish such a feat, and anyone in the neighboring rooms would likely have had their eardrums blown out with the change in pressure associated with translocation…]

"What about shadow magic?" The phrase had passed through Emerald's mind earlier.

[There have been reports of a wizard who was able to compel his own shadow to manipulate his surroundings by

using the shadows of objects in a room to influence the material objects themselves. Now, what was the catch there? Ah, yes, the static.] Emerald plucked a black hair from his head and approached the door, waving it about apparently at random. *[Of course not—I would've noticed it right away. Don't know what I was thinking. Stupid theory.]*

"Perhaps an invisible man snuck into the room and disappeared once the door was opened!" I exclaimed, throwing my hands in the air at the absurdity of this largely one-sided conversation.

[Also unlikely. The only man in the Conjury's file capable of turning himself invisible did indeed retire to Kovin Isle, but according to the records, he died more than three centuries ago.]

"What about ghosts? Spirits? Things of that nature? Perhaps some wandering shade might be held accountable?"

[Aster's sake, you're really grasping at straws now. What self-respecting ghost would stoop to murder?]

"A cabal, then?" I lifted my hands in outraged frustration. "Or maybe Kovin Isle really is cursed!"

[What an oddly unspecific curse.] Emerald didn't bother to elaborate.

"*Emerald!*" I bellowed. "If you keep ignoring me and talking over me and taking credit for my *perfectly sound ideas,* I am going to go mad. And then I'm going to kick you right in your ample shins." My outburst might have been disrespectful to the dead man's memory, but surely he would understand that I was only yelling to aid his cause.

Emerald turned to scrutinize me. *["Ample shins?" Is that supposed to be an insult? That bard really is off his nut.]*

I crossed my arms over my chest. "You've got some nerve…"

Emerald swung toward me and swept his eyes up and down my person. I had been privy to his thoughts for the duration of the night, but his spoken words had consisted of little more than inarticulate *hems* and *haws.* Now, though, he addressed me directly for the first time.

"I don't know what the problem is," he murmured. "But I need you to cooperate, at least for tonight. Whatever Coirpre did to you, it will be fixed tomorrow." His voice was low and powerful, like two great boulders striking together. It was a truly remarkable voice. Why didn't he use it more?

I opened my mouth to argue, but Emerald had already turned back to the bed and the limp, cooling figure at its center. *[It's one thing after another, isn't it? I thought I finally had him, and once again, he slips away. I don't suppose Coirpre could be responsible? No, that's unlikely. And look at this sorry wretch. How many ordinary men sell their bodies to the Conjury for a few coins a month, only to lose their lives in the field? All while those high-handed bastards rule from a distance and never pay the price.]*

It was the first time I had ever heard my companion be kind or sympathetic toward anyone, and it softened me. Instead of arguing, I folded my hands contritely before me.

"What can I do to help?"

Emerald kept his eyes fixed on the dead man. *[His boots are muddy but not badly scuffed, and those breeks are worn at the thighs. He did not make his rounds of the mountains on foot. I'd wager he was riding.]*

I headed toward the door, and Emerald moved to open it for me, which I found most considerate indeed. With one parting glance at the sorry fellow left in our wake, I stepped out into the hall.

We'll do what we can to give your spirit peace, I thought. But the former Conjury man only leered back at me with his ghastly, contorted visage, and even with all the naivete of my relative youth, I was not sure that I would be able to keep my silent promise.

Chapter Three

Down in the common room, McLachlan was tidying up the wreckage of his bar. The barmaid who'd scowled so unpleasantly at Emerald had fled with the others, leaving the man on his own to right the toppled chairs, mop up the spilled drinks, and wipe down the filthy tables.

"Gods above and below," I murmured as we stepped into the room.

"What a mess."

The innkeeper looked up at me. "This? It's no worse than any other night, sir. That's why I invest in solid oak furniture." His tone was more measured than before, but he kept glancing up at the ceiling in the direction of the dead man's room. "Have you learned anything from your inspection?"

I nodded. "I believe we found everything there is to find. I have two further questions that I hope you might help me answer."

Emerald glared sharply at me, since *he* only had one question, but I had another query of my own.

"I'll help you in any way I can, of course." McLachlan leaned on his seeping mop, and a sickly rivulet of brown liquid trickled across the floor.

I clasped my hands in front of me. "You said that you keep a book of your guests?"

"I only collect the names of those who spend the night," McLachlan said. "That's city ordinance. I'm not required to keep track of *all* of 'em."

I held up a hand. "Rest assured, I am not concerned about the regulatory compliance of your fine establishment." *Although, if I were, I might question its cleanliness first and foremost.* I tried not to let my gaze wander to the runny mop. "I'm more concerned with the name of the scout upstairs and the names—if you have them—of his predecessors."

"Oh." The man's expression cleared. "That's easy. I can fetch you the book at once, and you can see the records of their comings and goings for yourself." He leaned the mop against a table and trotted off in search of the ledger, leaving Emerald and myself standing in the empty room.

In his absence, I examined the tavern again. It was certainly shabby, but it did not seem to have begun that way. More than anything, it felt weathered and careworn and gave the impression of having seen better days—rather like Emerald, although I doubted that my accomplice would appreciate the comparison. A strange assortment of art hung from the walls, some of which was surprisingly magnificent. There were portraits of minor gods and famous figures, and one large canvas depicting a cluster of deeply unhappy people. Below the latter, a label on the bottom arm of the frame read, *The Conjury.*

[Gods,] I observed as I peered at the dour likenesses, *[what a sorry lot.]*

[They aren't generally known for their good humor,] Emerald noted.

[What are they known for?]

[Sticking their noses where they aren't wanted and sending scouts around to make sure that everyone's following their rules and keeping up with their taxes.]

[And we work for them? Why?] So far, I had heard very little to recommend the Conjury to me.

[I do, because they pay me to do one of the few jobs that results in something akin to justice. And you do, too, because I tell you to.] Emerald leaned back in his chair until it balanced on two legs. ***[When you aren't malfunctioning, it's a perfectly cordial arrangement.]***

A number of retorts came to mind, but I decided to be the bigger person—if not in stature, then at least in spirit—and let the matter go.

On the wall behind the bar stood a tall wooden carving inlaid with colorful enamel. It looked to me like one great shapeless mass stippled with tiny trees until I read the words at the bottom: *Kovin Isle.*

"Ah! A map!" I hurried forward to examine it, while Emerald hung back. "Excellent. This will be *immensely* useful." I meant this as a hint for him to join me, but once again, I went alone.

Kovin Isle, according to the mapmaker, sat at the middle of the Split Seas. The map itself was nearly meaningless to me, however, since I had only ever visited one building and was still standing within its walls.

"If you plan to grab a bottle from behind the bar, sir, I must insist that you pay, Conjury license or not." McLachlan trundled back into the room bearing his heavy book.

"I was only looking at the map," I informed him. "But now that you mention it, what would stop a guest from helping themselves to a bottle after hours?"

"The staying guests usually come and go by the back entrance. They only use the bar entrance when they first sign, asking for their keys and whatnot. When the bar's closed, I can lock up without having to enforce a curfew."

"There are two entrances?" I asked. ***[And thereby two exits.]***

[What a novel deduction,] Emerald deadpanned. ***[Doors work both ways.]***

McLachlan carried on, blissfully ignorant of our ongoing tiff. "Yes, sir. One for those who intend to stay the night and the other for those who're only here for the bar. We lock the tavern up at night, but on the off chance that someone wishes to come and go after hours, we keep the back door unlocked."

This struck me as a strange and rather ineffectual system, since leaving one door unlocked was as good as leaving the whole place open, but before I could mention it, McLachlan dropped the book onto one of the nearby tables. He turned to look at me as Emerald opened the cover and began to skim through the pages.

[Ask him who I'm looking for,] Emerald told me.

I examined my nails. *[Ask him yourself.]*

Emerald glared at me. He could, of course, make me do whatever he liked, but for once he piped up on his own. "The scouts. What were their names?"

"You'll find Maximilien of Leviathan Loch on the last page. That's him." McLachlan pointed toward the ceiling and shuddered. "Cassandra of Wishwind was his Conjury scout predecessor, poor girl... The man before her drowned. Gods forgive me, I forget his name. Hoofer? Cloven? Something along those lines. And for forty years prior, as I said, the position was held by the same man: Dawyd of Sailor's Reprieve."

"Sailor's Reprieve," I repeated. Those selfsame words were etched on the western edge of the island's map. "So Dawyd hailed from Kovin Isle?"

"Yes, sir." McLachlan nodded. "Sailor's Reprieve is our sister city along the westward coast."

"And the city we're in...?" I asked.

"Lower Bound, sir." McLachlan nodded and gave me a funny look.

"Of course," I said hastily. "Forgive me, it's been a *very* trying day."

[Has it, now?] Emerald taunted, but I ignored him.

I scanned the map until I found Lower Bound on the easternmost protrusion of the island, down the river from Upper Bound, on the bank of a river labeled, *The Bounder.* The Bounder sat directly across but the whole width of the island away from

Dawyd's hometown. This provided me only a little context, until I noticed the nearest town marked on the map.

Dyrne.

That name was already familiar to me, but other than the fact that the merchants had whispered it in hushed tones, I did not associate it with anything in particular.

"Here's your ledger. And, listen, sir, I've no intention of hurrying your investigation, but there's a dead man lying in one of my rooms. When might I begin to make arrangements?"

[Tell him that he can go at once,] Emerald thought. ***[We're done here.]***

"You may do so at your convenience," I said sweetly. "And thank you *so* much for your consideration."

McLachlan smiled thinly and reached for his keys. "It's getting late, so I'd best go now, or the man will be waiting until morning without anyone to see to him." McLachlan headed toward the door.

Just before his hand fell upon the latch, another notion struck me. ***[Where are we sleeping tonight?]***

Emerald turned another page. ***[Silly question: in the woods, as always.]***

"My good man?" I asked. "One last thing—have you any free rooms tonight?"

"Of course." McLachlan grimaced. "Even a few of my paying customers left, after... what happened, n'all. If you and your man are in want of a room, you may have one at my expense. I'll arrange it upon my return."

"Marvelous," I gushed. "How thoughtful of you. You run a fine establishment, sir, a very fine one, and we'll be sure to recommend you—won't we, Emerald?"

[Laying it on a bit thick,] Emerald thought distractedly.

"People like to be thanked for their time, Emerald," I said, addressing my companion in a slow, patient voice. "Perhaps we *both* ought to thank him for his abundant assistance?"

Emerald shot me a poisonous glare. "Thank you," he muttered, not even looking at our host.

I despaired then and there of my companion's manners and left McLachlan to his own devices. I looked over the map again, but finding nothing new to interest me, I wandered back to where Emerald sat and looked over his shoulder. As he skimmed, I saw a few of the names repeated, including Dawyd of Sailor's Reprieve, Binderwick Sludgeon, Cantrip of Oakwood, Shale of Dyrne...

Dyrne. There it was again, the name of that little village. Every time I saw it spelled out before me, I felt a little more drawn to it. I was quite certain we would find ourselves there one of these days.

[Dawyd passed through every six months or so,] Emerald thought. ***[He must have made his rounds for the Conjury twice a year.]***

"So Cassandra died on her first tour of the island, after her predecessor drowned," I mused. "And this fellow passed on his first tour as well."

Emerald glanced peevishly over his shoulder. ***[Obviously.]***

"There's no need to be rude about it," I grumbled. "Would you please turn back to the most recent page?"

Emerald ignored me and flipped backward at a steady rate, until I leaned in and attempted to snatch the book from his hands. Before I could touch it, he clicked his tongue and returned to the current entries.

"That wasn't so hard, was it?" I asked in my honeysweet voice. "And look." I pointed over his shoulder to an entry on the page. "Shale of Dyrne. Whoever that is, they were here tonight."

[And?] Emerald thought.

It annoyed me to no end that he couldn't be bothered to use his words with me, but there were more pressing matters at hand. "*And* I saw his name throughout the book. *And* the men upstairs mentioned that Dyrne was a bit, you know, *spooky.*"

[Spooky.] Emerald didn't seem impressed with my deductions.

"You know, cursed by the gods and whatnot. Did you find the page from Cassandra's visit? Ooh, and the one from Maximilien's first stay? They must have both stayed here at least once, if Lower Bound is the start of their route. McLachlan wouldn't have known both of their names otherwise."

With a growl, Emerald flicked back through the pages, evidently seeking the information I had requested.

The time between their routes was, it seemed, calculated almost to the day. Maximilien had come through Lower Bound once before at the start of spring, and it was nearly a month between that date and the current one. His route must have taken him the entirety of the way across the island in that time. Cassandra had visited at the start of the previous fall and had not returned—she had died before her circuit was complete. The name *Trotter of Shantytown* was noted exactly six months before Cassandra's. Dawyd's arrivals fell at similar intervals: once at the spring equinox and once in the fall. That made sense. If he was based on the far side of the island, he would only come through Lower Bound once.

"Strange," I murmured.

I did not elaborate, and after a moment, Emerald turned to me, as if waiting for me to continue.

Ha ha! I nearly cried. *So you* do *care to hear my opinion!* But rather than mock him and thereby ruin the moment, I elected instead to gesture toward the map behind the counter.

"Dawyd came and went for nearly forty years without any apparent issue. He obviously knew the island well. The other deaths might well have been tragic accidents, but consider this: all three of the scouts passed through Dyrne before succumbing to an untimely demise."

Emerald eyed the map. **[Could be a coincidence...]**

"Oh, not you, too!" I sailed away from him, following a well-worn track against the grain of the hardwood floor. "That man's death was no accident, and the timing is too convenient. Surely there is a definite connection between the two!"

[This could be a case of overlinkage.] Emerald closed the leather-bound guest book with a thump. **[We *must* never leap to conclusions.]**

"Fine, then what do you reckon? Should we check the back door and see if there are signs of tampering? Or perhaps we ought to save our investigation for the morning, when it isn't so dark."

[I like the dark. Easier to hide in. Harder for people to see...]

Emerald's thought trailed off, but as he got to his feet, I couldn't stop myself from attempting to fill in the blanks. My associate was tall and broad-shouldered, built more like a mountain than a man, and his blunt features and gray-green skin did not strike me as attributes that allowed him to come and go quietly. So far, his mind struck me as the only thing nimble about him. He was not, I deemed it safe to say, gifted in the thieves' arts. Why, then, would he wish to pass undetected?

Not out of necessity, I suspected. More likely, he simply wished not to be noticed. In that moment, I again experienced that odd, ambivalent sensation of being pulled two ways: of both adoring him and reviling him. The first time, I'd been too young to understand what the feeling meant, but I'd grown wiser in the last few hours.

The adoration was my own thought, and the revulsion was intrusive, thrust into my mind the way the rest of Emerald's thoughts arrived.

Not every thought he put into my head was intentional. Sometimes, I knew what he was thinking, even when he didn't want me to.

"Emerald," I said, with all the empathy I possessed, "you don't have to hide."

"Oh, for Aster's sake!" Emerald launched to his feet with such force that he overturned the chair on which he sat. "Crimson, I don't know what's wrong with you, but I desperately need you to *shut up.*" He towered over me, his great hands curled into fists. I stared up at him in bewilderment. Every gesture, every aspect of his body language screamed *anger*, but I had a direct line to him, and all I could feel from him was a roiling mass of shame and self-loathing.

Until that moment, I did not know that it was possible to hate anything as much as Emerald hated himself.

"Let's get one thing very clear." Emerald jabbed a finger at my face. "You have one purpose, Crimson, and that's the purpose I *gave* you. Not a single thought enters your head that I don't put there. You aren't smarter than me, you don't know better than I do, and you certainly aren't qualified to give me personal advice. You're *nothing*. You're air and vapor and refracted light. So do us both a favor and *shut up*."

Emerald was breathing hard by the end of this rant, but I hadn't budged an inch.

"If that's so," I asked in an admirably patient voice, "then why do I know things you wish I didn't? Why"—I reached up to jab one finger at his chest—"do I know that you think that Coirpre fellow is more handsome than you are, even though we both know he's got the same inner charm as a louse's ass? Why do *I* know that you think you're repellant, even when *I* don't believe it?"

Two things happened at once. First, my finger reached the ragged leather of Emerald's vest and sunk clean through not only the tatty hide of the jacket but straight through Emerald's flesh itself. The second began as a wall of sound that hit me with such force I forgot everything else. It came in the form of a terrible cry, an all-encompassing sob of anguish laced through with other, softer voices:

Beasts like you don't deserve to live.
What you desire is an abomination.
You are tainted.
...unlovable...
...pathetic...
...unnatural...
Monsters like you should be killed at birth.

I reeled back, and the sound stopped at once. In my haste to get away from him, I stumbled into a table—but instead of catching myself on it, or even knocking it over, I passed through the wooden surface entirely.

"What?" I cried, lacking words to express the scope of my question. I held up my hands in front of me, then looked down at my torso, which now stood above the table, while my lower half was hidden on the bottom side. I was not transparent, nor even translucent, but there was nothing to me.

"What...?" I repeated. I looked up helplessly at Emerald, not sure what question to ask first. *What were those voices? What just happened to me?*

What am I?

Emerald shook his head and rolled his eyes. He didn't seem to have heard the sounds that had pulsed through my mind, but he was clearly annoyed at my current predicament. **[Gotta move him before someone comes in and starts asking questions.]**

Once again, I was compelled forward, and this time I didn't fight at all. I allowed myself to be dragged back out into the regular walkway. It was a good thing, too, because a moment later the tavern door opened, and McLachlan stepped through with two uniformed men and three black-clad women in tow. The men followed the innkeeper directly to the stairs, but the women paused to look around the room.

"There is an unfamiliar power in this place," one of them observed.

McLachlan hustled them along. "This way, Sisters. The body is upstairs. Come along, I'll show you where he lies."

Despite being in the midst of a personal crisis, I found the appearance of these three Sisters to be entirely compelling. They were dressed in loose black garments that completely obscured their figures. I could not tell what species they were, let alone what they looked like beneath their veils. One was small enough to be lambkin, and when I peered closer, I saw telltale cloven hooves beneath the hem of her robe. One was of middling human height, with a generous figure that made her presence the most solid of the three. My eye, however, was drawn to the third one: this Sister was tall, with broad shoulders and a narrow waist, and a strange enamel brooch that held her black cloak in place, the only pop of color on her otherwise somber garb. When her eyes flashed toward me, I turned away. She could see too deeply, and I was still not sure what to think of myself.

"Who are they?" asked one of the uniformed men, tipping his chin toward Emerald and me.

"I mentioned them before, Officer Bream." McLachlan's voice shook—his nerves were clearly unraveling. "Those are the fellows with the Conjury."

Both officers nodded to us, and even in the midst of my own confusion, I recognized how much sway the title held over every person we'd met.

McLachlan took another step up toward the dead man's room. "Let me show the officers and the Sisters where the dead man awaits, and I'll return for you at once, good sirs." McLachlan nodded to us, then mounted the stairs with the three Sisters in tow.

Once more, I was left alone with Emerald, questioning everything I thought I knew. I was so shaken by this most recent encounter that I had nearly forgotten our purpose. An explanation of my predicament would be most helpful, but I doubted that I would get one tonight. Emerald had turned his back on me, and I was neither brave enough nor confident enough to broach the topic again.

"What rites will they give him?" I asked in a small voice, speaking of Maximilien. "How will they know which god he follows?"

"Doesn't matter," Emerald grunted. "The Sisters' rites will be the same regardless." The rest of his words were silent, and I wasn't sure if they were meant for him or me. *[Kovin Isle is far from the mainland, and they follow the old ways more closely than the rest of the world. They're more pious out here. There will be some investigation, and the body will be prepared for burial. When they're finished with their rites, the Sisters will send him back to Leviathan Loch, and his family will do as they see fit with his remains.]*

That struck me as fitting, at least. Better to send the man

back where he belonged than to inter him on an island he had never visited until it claimed his life.

By and by, McLachlan returned, and he bustled about as he signed us in, and then led us to our room at the top of the stairs. To my relief, the quarters he showed us were at the other end of the hall from where the three Sisters completed whatever rituals they deemed appropriate.

Emerald accepted the key, then locked the door behind us, all without looking at me.

"I'm sorry about what happened down there," I murmured. "I didn't mean to—"

Emerald held up a hand. "Enough, Crimson. We're done for the night."

"But what am I?"

"*Enough.*" He kicked his boots off and lay down in the bed closest to the window. ***[Tomorrow, I'll check the back door and see his horse, and I'll proceed from there. Too many strands, too many variables. There must be answers. Plenty of reasons to hate Conjury scouts, but killing them is a messy solution. Whoever did it must be afraid. In fact, they'd have to be terrified, wouldn't they, to risk attracting that sort of attention?]***

And then, quite suddenly and without any warning whatsoever, I ceased to exist.

Chapter Four

My next conscious thought was one of alarm. I did not know where I had been, but I was certain that I had been *somewhere,* and that it had been a restful, quiet place.

It was light outside, although there was no real sunlight in evidence, only an overcast sky. The room where I found myself was the same one where we had stayed the night, but Emerald was already moving about the cramped space. I watched in puzzlement as he intentionally mussed the sheets of the nearest bed, the one which should have been mine.

"What are you doing that for?" I wondered aloud.

Emerald groaned, and his shoulders slumped in defeat. "You're still broken, I take it?"

I would have taken umbrage with his tone, except for the fact that I still felt guilty about our ill-fated conversation the previous night. I was certain that I had looked directly into Emerald's thoughts, and although I had not done so intentionally, it was still an unforgivable invasion of privacy.

"If being broken consists of having an opinion and wanting to be treated with decency, then yes, I suppose I am." I crossed my arms and turned my nose up at him, and only then did I catch a glimpse of my new garb.

"Ooh!" I spun toward the mirror, my sullen attitude forgotten. "Oh, *Emerald*, look at this! I feel positively *rakish*." I ran my hands over my torso, admiring the tight fit of the black leather riding gear that I now wore in place of my silks from the night before. Red-lacquered plate armor covered my shoulders and forearms. It was reassuring to note that I couldn't accidentally put my hand through myself the way I had done with Emerald. Whatever I was, I was real to myself.

"Stop preening and focus," Emerald sighed as I tossed my red hair over my shoulder.

Just to annoy him, I made kissy-lips in the mirror. "How can I tear my eyes away? I'm *scrumptious*."

"For Aster's sake..." Emerald scrubbed his hands over his face and didn't bother to finish his oath. "That's the point. People are supposed to look at you, Crimson."

"I'm well aware. According to what you told me last night, it's my *job*." I turned my back on the mirror at last and faced Emerald. "You might think I'm broken, whatever that means, but if we're going to work together, I'm going to need a *bit* more explanation than that."

It was obvious that Emerald would have liked to argue, and equally obvious that he could think of no good reason to deny my request.

"You," he said at last, "are an illusion. A lightweaving. A conjuring of *aidea*. You do not exist. I summon you when I'm on a case so that people will talk to you. You're handsome, you're charming, and you're..." He held one hand out to me and frowned. "Well, people *like* you, for whatever reason. You fit in."

The rest of his thought went unsaid. *And I don't.* All of the ugly words that I'd heard crashing about in his mind last night were proof of that. I didn't believe them, but Emerald did.

As for his assertion that I was an illusion? That was a bitter pill to swallow, but it made a certain amount of sense. Every time that I'd tried to open a door or touch a person, Emerald had swooped in to stop me. He could compel me, and think orders straight into my head. Moreover, it *felt* true, possibly because we were still connected in spite of my newfound identity, and Emerald's words and his thoughts were in sync on this topic.

I looked down at my outfit again. I believed whole-heartedly that I cut quite a dashing figure, but it occurred to me that I wasn't just handsome. I was, more specifically, Emerald's idea of what a handsome man ought to be. In many ways, I was his opposite: slim, muscular, with delicate hands more suited to an instrument than hard labor. I looked rather more like Coirpre than Emerald, but even more dashing, more eye-catching. More everything.

"You've summoned me before last night?" I asked warily.

"Hundreds of times. I've lost count. But last night, Coirpre must have realized what you were and done something to make you act all... erratic." Emerald's nose wrinkled in distaste. "Who knows when it will wear off, but until it does, we need to set some ground rules."

He'd moved on so quickly that I didn't have time to argue that whatever it was that had happened to me, it had begun before we crossed paths with Coirpre. If he'd summoned me as many times as he'd said, there must be some reason that last night had been different.

Emerald held up one thick finger. "First: don't touch anything. For one thing, you can't, but if you try it's going to look strange. Just act all fancy and haughty and get your manservant to do the work. You shouldn't find that difficult."

"My manservant?" I gave him a shrewd look. "Presumably, you mean yourself? So I'm going to do all the talking, and you're going to go around grunting and picking things up for me so that I don't tarnish my delicate fingers?" I wiggled said fingers in his direction.

"Exactly." Emerald nodded, oblivious to my sarcasm. "You just do as I say, put on a show, and distract people from what I'm doing: the actual investigation."

"What's my motivation?" I asked.

Emerald's brows drew together. "In terms of...?"

"I'm a dashing individual traveling through the countryside, solving murders and righting wrongs for the common folk in search of reknown? Glory?" I pursed my lips and stared up at the ceiling. "No, for their own sake. I'm an instrument of the people."

Emerald groaned and stood up. "Stop being dramatic. That's how I know Coirpre's responsible for whatever happened to you. And to answer your question, we're on the Conjury's payroll."

"And we *like* the Conjury?" I asked. So far, nothing I had heard made me think well of the people who made everyone else so uncomfortable.

"We like the money," Emerald said flatly.

"Hm." I tapped my fingers against my lips. "I'd been hoping for a more noble motive, but I'll settle for a practical one. For now, at least. Very well, Emerald, I agree to your terms, but only if you agree to mine. First and foremost, don't just grunt like some wild swine who's wandered in from the woods in search of better fodder. Speak. *Aloud,* both to me and to the people we encounter."

I could tell that this didn't sit well with him. "It's better if people see what they want to see," he muttered.

This sentiment could be unpacked at another time, so rather than argue with him, I decided on a theatrical line of reasoning rather than an emotional one. "A fine, well-bred, *cultured* gentleman such as myself would never consent to travel with a boor." I smiled in triumph at my own wordplay, although Emerald didn't seem to appreciate it. "I'm not asking you to speak in rhyming pentameter. Just be a bit more..." I curled a lock of my red hair around my finger as I considered my word choice. "Unexpected."

Emerald's smile revealed his canines. The tusks had been ground to stumps that protruded slightly, even after being whittled to mere nubs. "Not as dumb as I look, you mean?"

I didn't take the bait. "Between the two of us, I expect that we can talk circles around anyone we meet. Even that scabrous bard from last night is no match for our combined wit. Let us put it to good use, shall we? Now, if my terms suit you, then perhaps we can stop babbling and get to work solving this murder."

"Fair enough." Unless I was very much mistaken, a small smile was tugging at Emerald's lips. He didn't seem to know what to do with it.

He does not have much experience with smiling.

It was a sad thought, but perhaps we could remedy that shortcoming in the future. In the meantime, Emerald opened the door, bowed like a proper but not entirely subordinate manservant, and ushered me out into the hall.

We said our farewells to McLachlan, returned our key, and headed out via the back door. The rear entrance was unlocked and undamaged, much to my chagrin.

"No reason to kick in a door that isn't locked," Emerald pointed out. "Perhaps we'll learn more from the man's horse."

"If you say so." I scowled at the lock to let it know that it had personally disappointed me before following Emerald around to the stables.

A young woman in canvas breeches and a shapeless tunic was mucking out the horse stalls when we arrived. She stopped shoveling as we approached and wiped the back of her palm across her sweating forehead, frowning at Emerald as she did so.

"You might want to stay back from the horses," she warned my companion. "They're skittish."

I winced at the implication that Emerald's very demeanor might be too much for the animals, and was about to tell her off when my companion spoke up for himself.

"No need. Animals like me." As he said this, he reached out to pat the nearest beast, a wild-eyed, velvet-black stallion that put its ears back as he lifted his arm. The moment Emerald's hand landed on the horse's neck, however, I saw the tension drain from its taught muscles. Within seconds, it was snuffling at his pockets in search of a treat.

"Huh. Well how about that." The woman put aside her shovel and looked Emerald over again.

He didn't turn his head, but he smiled again, ever-so-slightly. *[Be a bit more unexpected, eh? Is this what you meant?]*

"He likes you," I said aloud. "And people always say that animals are a good judge of character. They, er, do say that, don't they?" I was relatively certain this was true, according to Emerald's secondhand knowledge, but I had never heard it spoken aloud.

"That they do." The woman approached and leaned against the stall door, her eyes fixed critically on Emerald. Her mistrust had been replaced with obvious curiosity. "Animals are like people, you know, but with better instincts. We both like a steady hand and a soft touch."

I stared at her, trying to make sense of the change in her posture, and the intent with which she was now staring at my companion. She was driving at something, but I was not sure precisely what.

Emerald patted the horse again. "This wouldn't happen to be the horse that belonged to the dead Conjury outrider?"

"That he would." She batted her eyes at him. "You can tell by his form, can't you? Strong flanks. Sleek mane. He's used to being ridden by a professional."

I had never seen someone flirt before, and I gathered that Emerald wasn't at all used to it, either. Because of this, my companion realized her intent a second before I did; in fact, I would not have understood the reasoning behind her intensity or her confusing posture without a bit of help from Emerald's subconscious. I would have laughed at the realization if it hadn't been accompanied by a sense of deep discomfort. My half-Jotunn companion shied away from her, rather like a skittish horse himself.

"We'll be taking the horse," I said loudly. "As part of our *official investigation.*"

"You're hoping to discover what killed him, then?" she asked, ignoring me altogether. "So you're a lawman? Wouldn't mind seeing your credentials." She winked.

The woman was pretty despite her grubby clothes, and I respected that she was comfortable making her desires known, but Emerald was so alarmed by her behavior that his mind seemed to have stopped functioning altogether. Even though our connection, I couldn't hear a single clear thought.

If I was still nothing more than a simple illusion, would I stand here mutely while Emerald tried to think of what to say? The idea of being so alone that you had to summon an imaginary friend was a rather sad one, especially when that friend could only help you inasmuch as you could help yourself.

The woman reached for him, and the thought of her touching him when he was so clearly uncomfortable enraged me. She might not be able to read his mind as I did, but there was something about her words and her gestures that made me realize that she saw him as a sort of animal, too—one that she might use as she pleased. In her mind, they were not equals.

People thought this all the time, I realized: that Emerald was a means to an end, a cipher for their own desires and insecurities.

"We don't have all day," I snapped. "Bring the horse, and let's go."

My words startled Emerald into action, and he hastily unlatched the stall door and led the horse out by its tether. The young woman winked at me and made a big show of watching Emerald's *flanks* as he withdrew. There were, I supposed, plenty of men and women who wouldn't have minded a tumble with her in a clean pile of straw away from prying eyes, but all the same I disliked her for her indifference to Emerald's obvious discomfort. Whether or not people appreciated what they saw when they looked at him was besides the point if they failed to treat him with respect.

"Does that happen often?" I asked as we left the stables behind.

Emerald didn't answer. Although I could not currently hear

the tumult in his mind, I was certain that if I put my hand on his shoulder—or through it—I would hear a hundred old insults rattling around in his brain.

Deciding that the best thing I could do was to distract him, I turned my attention to the horse. "What do we intend to do with this fellow? I expect he's rife with evidence. Perhaps we might analyze the splatters of dirt across his belly, or consult the grass between his teeth? Is there a regional species of mite on his eyelashes that will tell us where he's been?"

Emerald visibly relaxed as he shook his head. "There's no need for any of that. We'll ask him directly."

"And how shall we manage that?" I teased. "We don't even know his name."

"Ha ha," said Emerald flatly, but his panic had dissipated almost entirely. "Don't be ridiculous, we're not going to have a conversation with a horse, Crimson. We're going to pay someone else to do it."

I t had not occurred to me to question how the land around us might be divided, although I had some vague sense that the world was split into three parts: wild woodland, sprawling towns, and glassy seas. It had not yet occurred to me that there were in-between places that were no longer town and not yet countryside, but that was where Emerald led me. The houses were spaced farther apart, with trees springing up in between, and the trees and gardens were in bud, aching to burst forth in bloom.

The weather, too, could not make up its mind. As we left the stable, the sunlight was still filtering between the clouds, but not long after it began to drizzle, and then to rain in earnest. Emerald was soon soaked to the skin, and the horse's coat turned dark and sleek, though it didn't seem to mind overmuch.

My companion's boots splattered in the mud. The same mud, I recalled, that had spotted the dead man's boots the night before.

I paused under a tree and held up one hand, watching as the drops fell straight through the branches, and then through me.

"Emerald," I said, "it's raining."

"Didn't take a genius to work that out," he grumbled, not bothering to look over his shoulder at me.

I rolled my eyes at his broad back. "Don't you think you should do something about it?"

That brought him to a stop, and he turned to scowl at me. He scowled a great deal, I had noticed.

He made a sharp gesture upward. "What in Aster's name do you expect me to do about the damned sky?"

"I didn't mean the sky." I pointed to him, encompassing the entirety of his mud-speckled personage. "You look like you've been walking in the rain. *I* look as pristine and handsome as ever."

"And so modest, too." Emerald closed his eyes.

"Just because you're not looking at me doesn't solve the problem."

He bared his teeth and opened one eye. "Two seconds of silence, Crimson. That's all I ask."

The world around me flickered, and for a moment I was somewhere else altogether, but it lasted less than a second. I had been looking at my arm the whole time, and quite suddenly my clothes became visibly sodden.

"Happy now?" he asked.

I looked myself over and found that he'd thought of everything. My red hair now clung to my shoulders, and anyone taking note of my fine boots and breeks would have thought I'd been slogging through the mud for hours.

"Much better." I nodded my approval, for the first time ever enjoying a disheveled appearance.

[Never met anyone so vain. Aside from Coirpre...] Emerald carried on, the horse followed dutifully in tow, and I came last of all.

"You think about him a lot," I noted.

"'Cuz he got away!" Emerald barked. "Which means I won't

get paid for the contract, and he'll be off scamming someone else the second he gets back to the mainland."

Sensing an opportunity to needle my companion, I pretended to think this over. "So, in that sense, we might refer to him as *the one that got away...*"

[Shut. The hells. Up.]

My mouth snapped closed, and try as I might I could not speak again. I pondered the mechanics of that for a moment. I didn't have a tongue, or lips, or teeth. How could he force me into silence if I was little more than a trick of the light?

But of course, he couldn't silence me entirely.

[So, Emerald, how long have you been tracking this particular bard? Surely there are other vagabonds that are worthy of investigation...]

"Oh, look," Emerald said, so loudly that the horse balked in alarm. "We're here."

I had not been entirely certain of our destination, and even now that we had arrived, I was not clear why we had walked this distance only to arrive at a small hut far past the outskirts of town. The home itself was quite modest and bore little resemblance to the wood and stone structures that dominated the harbor. The front wall was made of thick slabs of mud plaster, and the sloping sod roof reached all the way to the ground at either side of the door. An herb garden stood to the left of the squat building, and strange plants climbed a trellis on the right.

"What is this?" I asked, happy to be allowed the use of my voice as I inspected the second bed.

"A poisoner's garden." Emerald placed himself between the horse and the plot in question. "The other ones are healing herbs. The Augurs of the Old Ways don't make a strong distinction between *good* and *bad* in nature."

I stood upright again and returned my attention to my companion. "Do you?"

"Used to. Now I figure people are the real problem." To stay my barrage of questions, Emerald knocked heavily on the door. The wood gave slightly beneath his broad fist. Emerald struck me as someone who was very careful about when and how his strength was applied; most likely, the door was slightly rotten.

For a moment, the only sound from the house was that of raindrops landing on the now-muddy roof. The horse sniffed at the healer's garden, but seemed to decide against investigating further.

"Maybe they aren't here," I suggested.

Emerald snorted. "Maybe you're too impatient."

"Maybe I'm tired of standing in the rain."

[You're not even getting wet.]

"Maybe I'm tired of your condescending—!"

I fell silent as the wooden door groaned open, and a face appeared through the opening.

I had never met an Augur before, not to my knowledge at any rate, but the face that peered out at us could only have belonged to someone who took a particular interest in the natural world. The woman inside was middle-aged, sturdily built, and wore a short-sleeved tunic that revealed strong arms. Her hair was slightly unkempt, and one of her eyes drooped at the corner. The fingers resting on the door were dyed red with some sort of powdered herb.

"Hello," she said warily. When she spoke, I realized that her eye was not her only unusual feature. The entire left side of her face was slack. "How can I help you?"

Usually, Emerald was quick to put words in my mouth, but this time he was the one who bowed. "Greetings. You're Amaya, a Finder of the Glade, aren't you?"

The woman's face half-creased in a wary smile. "I am." Her eyes passed over me with disinterest, but lingered on the horse. She grunted as her brows pinched together in confusion. "Back again, Harpax? What became of your master?"

"Maximilien is dead," I said, as if she had been speaking to me, bowing my head. "He was killed last night."

Amaya pursed her lips. "Can't seem to keep a scout, can we? Falling off cliffs, drowning in ponds... Very careless. How did this one die?"

"Strangled in his sheets, ma'am."

The Augur laughed at me. "Do I *look* like a lady to you?"

"You seem as deserving of the title as anyone *I've* ever met," I replied without artifice.

Amaya smirked. "Flatterer."

"Perhaps we might step inside somewhere? Out of the rain?" I gave her my most charming smile.

With a shrewd half-grin, Amaya cocked her head. "What do you care? The rain doesn't strike you, does it?"

Emerald choked, and I paused, unclear if this discovery was of real concern, or to be expected from someone of Amaya's talents.

Without waiting for my response, the Augur motioned for us to follow. "Come in, then."

"Even the horse?" I asked.

She chuckled. "I trust the horse more than I trust you."

I wasn't entirely sure that horses belonged in houses, but it was her home, not mine. I stepped inside, and Emerald and Harpax came after me.

It didn't take long to see why Amaya was so comfortable hosting a beast. Her home was already full of life. Birds fluttered among the rafters. Mice, voles, minks, and even a gridgen lay curled by the hearth, sleeping contentedly. Plants occupied every available surface, planted in teacups and old wine jars; dried herbs hung from the ceiling. The place was both cluttered and cozy, another commingling. Amaya had brought the outside in.

"If you've got business to do, take it back outside," Amaya told the horse. Her movements were clumsy and uneven, as if one whole side of her body was reluctant to obey her. I watched with interest as she disappeared into another room and returned with a wrinkled apple left over from last autumn. She offered it to the horse, who took it gratefully, snuffling against her palm as he did so.

"You're welcome," she said. That business concluded, she turned to us and crossed her arms. "Now, what have you come for?"

"You know the horse," I said. "Did you speak to Maximilian of Leviathan Loch?"

Amaya ignored me. "There's no need to make your light-weaving speak to me, sir. Don't put words in its mouth. Dismiss it, and speak to me directly."

Emerald cleared his throat, and I lurched forward. "Don't you dare!" I exclaimed. "I don't want to miss anything, and I *know* you won't tell me later."

"I could dismiss him, if you want," Emerald said to the Augur. "But I'm having a bit of trouble making him follow orders lately. He's being obstinate."

"When I start being dull and churlish, then you'll know he's the one in charge." I pointed accusingly at Emerald.

Amaya blinked a few times, evidently revising her opinion of me.

"Please let me stay and listen," I begged. "You'll let a horse into your home, so why not me? I promise to be as quiet as a mouse."

"Mice aren't quiet," she informed me.

Emerald chuckled. "Nor is he."

"I can see that." Amaya shrugged. "Very well, I'll answer your question: I did indeed speak to Maximilien. He wanted to send a babblebird yesterday, off to the mainland, but I didn't want to, not with the storm coming in. He had an urgent message to deliver, though he didn't tell me the details."

"A message?" Emerald frowned up into the rafters, and the birds stared back. "And he didn't say anything about who he intended to contact."

"Oh, he did." Amaya's face was not entirely responsive, but her expression managed to convey her anger nevertheless. "He was a real prick about it. He has—*had*—his job to think about, but I have mine, and I don't like to send one of my flock off over the ocean when the winds are high. I argued with him until he threatened to report me to the Conjury. I sent one of my strongest flyers, sweet Rafela. Thought she might have a chance of making it across the sea."

"I take it she didn't," Emerald said.

"Never got the opportunity. She was shot out of the air with a slingstone before she reached the coast. She didn't deserve that." Amaya shook her head bitterly.

"I'm sorry for your loss." Emerald bowed his head. "But a man is dead, no matter how rude he might have been. Will you help us try to understand what happened?"

"That's why you've brought me his horse, I take it? To help you solve a Conjury matter, after one of their scouts cost the life of one of my darlings? Let the Conjury sort it out on their own."

"Pardon me." I raised one hand. "I know that I said I would be quiet, but one quick thought... doesn't it stand to reason that whoever killed the scout, prick though he may have been, is the same person who killed Rafela?"

Amaya paused. "I suppose."

"Whatever Maximilien knew cost him his life," Emerald added. "It seems to me that it cost the babblebird's as well."

"*Rafela*," I corrected. **[Not "the babblebird."]**

Emerald shot me a quizzical glance. **[Same difference.]**
[Not to her.]

Amaya frowned down at the weathered floorboards. "Mainlanders are often out of touch with nature, and the island can be treacherous. It's not impossible that two outsiders died by accident... but if their deaths are all connected, then someone had thrown the natural order out of alignment, and they are willing to harm true innocents in order to further their cause." She looked up sharply. "And you two seek to rectify this?"

"If we can," Emerald replied.

"But without your help, we're shooting in the dark," I added.

Amaya glanced around at her sleeping housemates, then up at the surviving birds. "Babblebirds are bred to carry messages, but their lives are no less valuable for that. Whoever has done this seeks to assert dominance over both man and nature." She nodded sharply. "Alright, Harpax, my love. Tell us what you know."

She held out her hand, stroking the broad flat plane of the

horse's forehead, and her eyes fluttered closed. I had any number of questions about what was happening, but for once I held my tongue, not out of fear of recrimination but because I was certain that something intimately sacred was occuring, something that I could neither access nor understand.

"Huh." Amaya opened her eyes. "That isn't much to go on."

"What did you see?" Emerald asked.

Amaya rubbed Harpax's nose. "His rider left a village in the mountains and rode him hard all the way here. The terrain in the Mooncrest Highlands is rocky, but Maximilien drove him hard. He was afraid, but Harpax does not know of what, only that he kept looking back over his shoulder the whole way."

"Did something happen that set them off?" Emerald asked.

Amaya shook her head. "Nothing that Harpax understands. He was in the stable when Maximilien arrived, threw his tack on in such a frenzy that the saddle girth pinched Harpax's belly, and rode him nearly to exhaustion."

"Maximilien knew what was coming," Emerald said darkly.

I had to ask a question, although I already knew the answer. "This village, the one they fled, where was it?"

Amaya sighed. "It was the last stop on his route, the last settlement they passed before they returned to Lower Bound."

Emerald met my gaze, and we both remembered the map behind the bar. The name of that town had already taken on grim significance in my mind.

Dyrne.

Chapter Five

❧❦❧

"You don't even have to walk," Emerald scolded. "What's taking so long?"

"I'm not *that* far behind," I retorted. "I'm enjoying the view."

We had left Maximilien's horse with the Augur and set out on foot. The rain had not let up, and Emerald slogged through the thick mud until it formed great clumps on his boots. His small leather pack was dripping; I wished good luck to whatever he kept inside.

He was right that walking took no effort at all. While my companion groaned and grunted as the incline increased and the rocky terrain grew more treacherous, I ambled after him, looking about at anything that caught my fancy.

Within half an hour of leaving Lower Bound, we crossed a bridge that spanned the Bounder itself. I stopped to gaze first out to sea, then up the river to the city. Upper Bound was a lively place, with a citadel that overlooked the waterway.

"I wish we could go there," I sighed. "Imagine all the things we might see. All the *people*."

Emerald, who was never impressed by anything, only grunted. "Come on, Crimson."

I followed him up the hill, which grew steeper with every passing minute. When we crested a ridge, I stopped in wonder to look down at the view of the sea. From up here, Lower Bound was little more than an a distant smudge. Last night, it had felt like the whole world. Now I could see the plains, the farms, low boggy patches, and the outline of the inland town nestled in the valleys between the jagged cliffs, half-obscured by sheets of rain.

"Have you ever seen anything like it?" I asked.

"Loads of times," Emerald said, trudging onward. "It's nothing special, just a few grubby little settlements on a soggy island. Come on, I'll recast you if you don't hurry up."

"There's no need to be rude. I'm right behind you." Even so, I kept pausing to admire the scenery until the path turned and the trees obscured my view.

"So, how long have you been working for the Conjury?" I asked.

Emerald let out a long-suffering groan. "Don't you ever stop talking?"

"If you weren't so reticent, I wouldn't be forced to fill the silence."

"Nothing wrong with silence. In the future, feel free to leave it empty."

"Don't you think we ought to get to know each other better? Since it seems we'll be stuck together for the foreseeable future."

Emerald stopped in his tracks and turned to me. "There's nothing to get to know, Crimson. I made you. I plucked you out of thin air and filled that agonizingly empty head of yours with whatever thoughts were needed at the time. I don't know what's gone wrong with you lately, but we don't need to talk. I know everything about you, and the only things you know are things I put there."

I smiled and batted my eyelashes at him. "So my theory about your interest in Coirpre..."

Up until that point, needling Emerald had been my primary source of entertainment, but his contorted expression at my words was matched with a battery of emotion that overwhelmed me so completely that for a moment, I forgot myself.

Not interested.

Don't like him.

Don't like anyone.

Don't need *anyone.*

Better off alone.

Don't deserve—

And then his thoughts were gone, and not just the immediate ones, either. I was left reeling from the mental assault, from the sheer ferocity of his conviction. For a terrifying moment, I thought that our connection had been completely severed.

"Emerald—" I began.

"Stop pissing around, Simon. We've got miles to go." Emerald turned his back on me and continued, as though we hadn't been talking in the first place.

He hadn't shut me out, I realized. He'd shut the *thoughts* out. He'd shoved them so far out of reach that it was as though they'd never crossed his mind in the first place.

"I'm sorry, Emerald," I whispered, but either he didn't hear me, or he didn't care.

Our silence lasted through the afternoon. When Emerald stopped to dig a pouch of jerky out of his bag, I stood off to one side and examined the lichen growing on the trees. When he stepped off the trail to relieve himself a short while later, I waited patiently for his return. Despite his threat to dispel me, I did not blink out.

At nightfall, he found shelter in the mouth of a small cave and dropped his pack into the dirt. He stepped outside again, and returned a moment later with an armful of wet wood, which he dropped in a heap on the ground. He produced two stones from his belt and struck them over the damp kindling again and again until a spark flared; the moment it landed among the broken branches, they burst into flames, blazing merrily as if they'd been going for hours.

Emerald moved to put the stones away, then stopped. He held them up toward me. "The grey one's flint," he said. "And the green one's Ignius. I bought it back on the mainland. It's enchanted, hence the flame. No self-respecting wood would light under these conditions."

I settled down beside him, accepting his peace offering. "I'm sorry about earlier. I didn't mean to—"

"We weren't talking about earlier, Simon. We're talking about the damn rocks." He dropped them back into the pouch and held his hands out to the flames. "It's cursed cold in these mountains, not that you would know it. Spring comes later at this altitude."

"It's the equinox," I said. "Or it was, recently." When Emerald cocked his head, I shrugged. "When we went through the log book, the scouts passed through Lower Bound at the equinox. Maximilien passed through here yesterday, so I presume it's about that time."

"You're right," Emerald said. "It was two days ago. Maximilien's route took longer than usual, so perhaps he stayed in Dyrne longer than he intended. I think there's another town where he'd usually stop, although it's off the main route. I don't know the island well."

I smiled as I stared into the flames.

"What's with that smug look, now?" Emerald demanded.

"Imagine, you admitting that you don't know something," I teased. "We should make a note of it."

"I know a lot more than you." Emerald reached for his pack.

I couldn't restrain myself. "By your logic, I know *exactly* as much as you."

"Except that I know when to keep my mouth shut."

I pouted in Emerald's general direction, but he ignored me. It was unnerving to travel with someone who believed that he knew me better than I knew myself. It was certainly bold of him to claim so. He might be responsible for my appearance and even my presence, but while our consciousnesses were intertwined, I was certain that we were not the same person. Even Amaya had seen it when we visited her little house beneath the hill. Emerald had all but *admitted* that I was my own person, and yet he still denied it now, even when I presented him with inalienable proof.

"How do I make you believe it?" I murmured, wrapping the illusion of my arms around the illusion of my legs.

"Believe what?" He turned to me in the firelight, and once again, I was struck by two grossly conflicted emotions. At least I could identify them now. The self-loathing was all his. The affection was all mine.

You don't love yourself, but I love you.

There were a hundred reasons I couldn't say those words, or even think them too loudly. For one thing, I was afraid that he would shut me out again. For another, he might mistake my meaning. He might be my progenitor, but I didn't love him as a father. Whatever tangle of emotions he felt toward the bard did not resemble my emotions, either. Yet in some profound way, with the same conviction that I believed in my own independence, I wanted him to be happy.

And he didn't.

I could not make sense of that.

Leaving all of that unsaid for the time being, I followed another track. "How do I convince you that I'm not just some trick of the light? That I'm *real?*"

Emerald stopped chewing and waved one hand in my direction. It passed through my arm, and I yelped in surprise.

"What are you doing? *Rude!*"

"I'm proving that you're not real," Emerald replied, and went back to his sorry excuse for a meal.

I massaged my arm as though he had hurt me. In fact, he had, although not in any physical capacity. "What if you just proved that *you* aren't real?"

"If I'm not real, how come I remember my childhood?"

"If *I'm* not, how come everyone sees me when I walk into a room, and yet ignores you?" I retorted.

Emerald fixed his eyes on the fire. I suspected that he did not want me to read his emotions in his face. "I choose to fade into the background."

"Perhaps I had a terrible childhood and chose to forget that!"

Emerald tucked away the last of his rations. "Impossible. If it worked that way, *neither* of us would remember our past."

Once again, I had walked right into dangerous territory without realizing it. Once again, I lapsed into silence. *Dammit. If I know everything he does, how come I keep hurting him in ways he doesn't expect?*

Then again, he seemed unusually gifted in that regard as well.

"If you can solve this mystery without my help, I'll admit that you're real." He rolled his pack in on itself, lay down, and tucked the sodden leather beneath his head. "But you won't, because you can't, because you aren't."

"And if I do?" I lifted my chin defiantly. I had already proven that I could pay attention and connect the facts.

"Then I'll believe you."

"Then let's make a deal," I suggested. "If you solve this mystery before I do, don't tell me. Don't cheat. I want to figure it out on my own. If I do, will you start treating me like a person, and figure out a way to make me independant?"

Emerald folded his hands over his chest and closed his eyes. "You're not a person, Crimson."

I sat in sullen silence, gazing into the flames. They were precisely as bright as they had been when Emerald first lit the fire, probably a result of the enchantment on the Ignius stone.

"If you can solve it, I'll believe you. Let's start there." Emerald didn't open his eyes, but he didn't seem tired yet, in spite of our long journey through the mountains.

"Excellent." I smiled to myself. Small victories were still victories. "Now, onto another matter. Are you really going to sleep in your damp clothes?"

"I don't have dry ones. What would you have me do, strip

down to my smallclothes and air dry? While you sit there, watching?" He snorted. "Pervert."

"If I'm a pervert, you're a pervert. Apparently."

He opened one eye and smiled crookedly at me. "Who says I'm not?"

"Oh, look, he has a sense of humor."

"Or I'm being brutally honest." Emerald settled back down, once again proving that, when he put his mind to it, he could be as still as a stone. "Goodnight, Crimson."

Even then, he did not banish me. I sat beside the fire, mulling over everything I knew about our case, and this island, and my troubled associate. At some point, I grew bored, and got to my feet. I caught movement in the corner of my eye and whirled, prepared to sound the alarm if some intruder or wild animal beset us.

It was not some predatory figure sneaking through the darkness, however. It was my shadow.

My *shadow*.

I hadn't realized that I cast one.

I approached the wall, and my shadow did the same. It was a misty, incomplete thing, but it puzzled me. My bewilderment only grew as I traced my fingers along the stone. I could not touch it, and when they reached a bump in the stone, my fingers passed through it to the first digit.

So the tangible world did not acknowledge me, but the light did. Whatever I was, I was real enough to affect the world in this small way. The discovery was comforting.

Validating.

I pulled my hand away sharply and turned to the mouth of the cave. The rainstorm was over, and the clouds above us had begun to scatter, revealing silver stars in the firmament. There were four moons in the sky now, in various stages of wax and wane. I stood there for a while, staring up. The stars were made of light, weren't they? Which meant that they, too, acknowledged me, even in some slight way.

I kept my eyes fixed on the velvety darkness, until I

Chapter Six

I awoke amid a grove of tall, narrow evergreens whose branches shifted in the breeze, casting stippled shadows on the bracken and heather around me. We were no longer in the cave. We were not, in fact, in any place I recognized, and the sun was already climbing through the sky, scattering beams of golden light across a nearby lake. Yesterday, Kovin Isle had been dreary but beautiful. Today, seen by mid-morning sunlight, it was positively enchanting.

"Where are we?" I asked.

Emerald stood in the overgrown path. Cart tracks had worn the weeds down at either edge of the road, but apparently not much traffic came this way. He pointed to the lake, which was half-obscured by the trees from where we stood.

"That's where Trotter of Shantytown drowned."

I glared at him accusingly. "You came all this way without me. You've probably passed the point where Cassandra of Wishwind fell to her death! You promised not to cheat! What if I missed something?" My voice sounded different today, but then again, I was furious. Perhaps it was an octave higher as a result of my pique.

"Neither of us have the slightest idea where she fell,"

Emerald said soothingly. "We'll ask in town and come back when we know more."

"*Neither of us*," I repeated, crossing my arms. "Does this mean that you believe me? Or are you just trying to placate me?"

"If I was trying to placate you, wouldn't that also be an indication that I believe you, by virtue of the fact that I believe you have feelings?" Emerald ran a hand through his messy black hair. He was more haggard than the day before, with dark bags below his eyes.

I relented slightly. "You didn't sleep well?"

"No. And on top of that, you're a drain on my mental capabilities."

I bristled at the perceived insult.

"Not like that," he said. After a brief pause he added, "Well, a *little* bit like that. But it takes an effort, you know, keeping you around all the time. I needed a rest, and some time to think. I promise, you didn't miss anything."

This appeared to be the truth, so I bit back my annoyance and turned to the lake. "Let's look while we're here, and then carry on to the village. You haven't been to the *village* without me, have you?"

"That would look suspicious, wouldn't it? I wander into town on my own, then wander back with a beautiful lady in tow..."

I had already begun marching through the heather down a towpath, but at his words I stopped in my tracks. "*Lady?*" I glanced down at myself in alarm. Sure enough, my physique had changed significantly since the night before, and instead of my elegant breeks and jacket, I was now wearing a handsome forest-green walking dress embroidered with tiny white flowers.

Asters.

"Crimson—" Emerald began, but I didn't wait for more. I broke into a run, weaving between trees. The ferns and heather blossoms were unmoved by my skirt and remained untrampled in my wake. I flung myself down at the lakeside and crouched between the boulders along the shoreline to admire my reflection.

"Oh," I breathed, lifting my fingers to my face. I was the same, and yet not the same. My features were clearly feminine, but just as there had been an undeniably effeminate quality to my appearance in Lower Bound, this face, this *body*, had a touch of masculinity about it. The prominent cheekbones, my proud jaw, and even the slight cleft in my chin were still distinctly *mine*, and my figure was more narrow and muscular than curvaceous. While the details of my features had shifted from what I would have called *ruggedly handsome* to *delicate and refined*—part of Emerald's plan to draw eyes away from himself, no doubt—there was still an androgynous note of pure Crimson at their core.

I stared at myself in wonder for a time, until Emerald approached from behind, his steps surprisingly quiet despite his size.

"Didn't mean to startle you," Emerald said, dropping onto a boulder beside me. "You've been Simone before."

"I don't remember."

"But you remember being Simon?"

I tore my gaze away from my reflection. "I remember everything since that night in the woods. And when we spoke to the innkeeper, you had me tell him that my *name* was Simon. As far as I'm concerned, I've always been Crimson, and still am."

Emerald's face turned ashen, and he swallowed so hard that his throat bobbed. "Which night do you remember, exactly?"

"The night we caught up with Coirpre in Lower Bound." I got to my feet, watching him carefully. He was acting very strange, but what could I possibly remember that would alarm him so?

He let out a relieved sigh and crossed his arms over his belly. "Right. I... right. Perfect. Well, sometimes I cast you as Simon, sometimes as Simone. Simon's good when I need a hammer, Simone works better when a lighter touch is called for. You'll open more doors this way. More flies with honey than vinegar, and all that."

I took a step forward. "What are you hiding, Emerald?"

"Nothing." He stood up and turned toward the towpath that

circumnavigated the lake. "We're here to solve three murders, and you want to prove that you're real. So prove me wrong, *Simone*. Let's go."

I risked one last glance at the still water. Simone and Simon were two sides of the same coin, both compelling in their own way while still being fundamentally *me*, and I wondered: now that I had a mind of my own, would Emerald choose how I appeared on any given day? Or would I?

The lake was only a mile or so wide, and we walked around it at a steady pace. For my part, I was watching intently for any hint or sign that could explain how a man had drowned here. The shoreline was shallow, although I had no sense of what the depth might be in the middle. There were no cliffs around the edge, either, for a man to trip over in the dark.

Perhaps something ominous lived in the lake itself, prepared to pull unsuspecting men into the depths? That would explain one death, but not the other two. If Trotter of Shantytown had been drunk, that would go a long way toward explaining things. Drunk, or drugged. If someone in Dyrne had plied the scouts with poisoned herbs, they might have become clumsy as they made their retreat. Amaya had kept a poisoner's garden. Why couldn't one of these villagers do the same? But poison couldn't strangle a man in his sheets, or strike birds down with a deftly-flung stone...

Keep grasping at straws like this, and Emerald will never *believe you.* No matter how hard I looked, though, there was no sign of where the dead man had been.

It was a year ago, almost to the day, that Trotter had drowned in these waters. Something that Emerald had said last night came to me, and I called out to him. "Is it cold again today?"

My companion paused. "Yes, as a matter of fact. It's quite cool."

"Warm enough that you'd consider swimming? It's the same time of year that Trotter drowned. Last night, you said that it was cold, but if it was too cold to swim, then Trotter would have no reason to be bathing in the first place..."

Emerald grinned. "Sorry to dash your theory, but take a look at this water. Can you see anything odd about it?"

I stared out at the lake in consternation. This seemed like a cruel trick. I had never seen a lake before, and at the moment that he asked, Emerald had shut me out of his mind. For all I knew, this was the only lake in the world.

"I don't know," I said sulkily. "But I'm sure you'll tell me."

Emerald held his hands out toward the lake, as he had done to the fire the previous night. "Steam. Look closely and you'll see it coming off the water. This is a natural hot spring. It would be perfectly refreshing this time of year."

So there was another point against me, one that would make it difficult for me to find clues on my own. Emerald had senses I did not, because I had no body with which to experience them.

We carried on until we heard the sound of a bell. This was accompanied by a sharp bleating that reminded me of the lambkins back in Lower Bound. The sound soon revealed itself to be coming from a herd of goats grazing in the brush; one of the nannies wore a hand-beaten copper bell around her neck on a ribbon. She looked up when she saw us, examined us with her canny brown eyes, and then—deciding that we posed no threat—returned to the business of foraging. The rest followed her lead, staying within sight of one another as they searched for the tastiest morsels.

"Are their eyes meant to do that?" I whispered. "The pupils go the wrong way. It's unnerving."

"It's normal," Emerald assured me.

"And is it normal to leave them to fend for themselves?"

"That," he admitted, "is not."

The goats were only moderately interesting. What drew my attention far more was the bundle of colorful cloth slung over a tree branch at the lakeside.

"They weren't always alone," I said, pointing to the clothing.

"No." Emerald moved toward it. He passed directly by the lead nanny as he did so, although the goat didn't bother to look up from her studious investigation of the roughage. I thought again of the woman in the stables who had told Emerald that he would frighten the horses, but so far I hadn't seen a single creature take issue with his presence, aside from people.

The colorful bundle turned out to be an outfit. The cloth was dyed an array of brilliant colors: a deep, jewel-toned blue, offset with patches of vermilion and cheery yellow. Leaning against the trunk alongside these articles was a carved staff, and a slingshot and belt were draped over it for safekeeping.

"I wonder who these belong to?" I peered at the items, wishing that I could run them between my fingers for closer inspection.

Instead, Emerald was the one to shake the clothing out. "It's homespun cotton," he said. "Rough at the hems. They're handily made but inexpensive."

"Something a goatherd might wear?" I asked.

"Maybe." Emerald held up the empty clothes. "But where's the goatherd?"

Emerald looked toward the forest, but my first instinct was to turn to the water. Given everything that we had heard about this place, I was afraid that I would be met with a grisly sight: a bloated corpse floating just beneath the surface, or some half-human creature watching us with bloodshot eyes and the goatherd's remains staining its needle teeth.

But there was nothing. Only a flat, calm expanse of water, unthreatening and glassy. A few sets of footprints, both human and animal, marked the lakeshore, but yesterday's rain left it swollen almost to the high water mark among the stones. Barely a ripple marred its surface, except when a breeze blew and stirred the reeds.

Trotter had died here. No, he had been *murdered* here. As placid and picturesque as this place seemed, a malignant presence lingered in the wake of his violent death.

I turned back to Emerald, who was watching the woods intently.

"What's the matter?" I asked. From where I stood, I saw no clues.

"There's something in the woods," Emerald said, clutching

the clothing even tighter. "Watching us. I can feel it."

Once again, a *feeling*. Perhaps in this case it would be more apt to call it a premonition. When I mentally reached out to Emerald, I could feel it too. A prickle along the back of his neck, a twist in the gut... sensation that I could never experience on my own.

More proof that I was still bound to him, despite my growing independence.

"Should we go look?" I whispered. At this juncture, it was probably foolish to attempt to hide. We had made no secret of our presence until now, and if Emerald was right about something watching us from the bracken, it was far too late to hide.

"No." Emerald slowly returned the clothes to their original position. "The goats aren't alarmed. Perhaps someone left these clothes along the lakeshore so that they could find their way back. They're bright enough to be visible from a distance. Let's continue to the village."

"You've already worked something out, haven't you?" I demanded.

"We haven't even been to the village yet. What's the sense of stomping around through the woods when we don't know the area at all?" Emerald quirked a dark eyebrow at me. "If I'm attacked, do you plan to defend me?"

I clamped my mouth shut and crossed my arms, but he had me there. If anything harmed my associate, we might both be in danger. I would be of no use if we encountered trouble.

We carried on, leaving the goats to their own devices, although I looked back more than once to see if anything emerged from the undergrowth. Nothing did.

We completed our circuit of the lake and returned to the road without further incident.

"There was a slingshot there," I remarked. "Perhaps whoever left it was the one to bring down the babblebird back in Lower Bound?"

"It's possible, but that would be a trick. Kill a man, leave town, and return in time to herd the goats?"

"It's possible," I said. "If they were on horseback. Maximilian was able to make the ride in one stretch."

Emerald stopped in the middle of the road and turned to me. "I can't believe I'm saying this, but let me give you some advice. Don't make your mind up before you have the evidence. If you do, you will twist everything you encounter to suit your theory and miss where the clues point. You will ignore key information if it does not match your expectations. Do you understand?"

"I suppose..."

"The innkeeper did not want to believe he had a murder under his roof. He was able to look at the same scene we did, and yet he refused to believe the obvious. Don't come to any conclusions until you've analyzed everything. Otherwise, you'll look just as foolish as he did. And we can't have that, can we?" Emerald swept an ironic bow in my direction. "The inimitable Crimson Smoke has a reputation to maintain."

"And so do you, presumably." I dipped into a slight curtsy. "I will endeavor to take your advice, o great Emerald Flame."

We walked on, and I kept close watch on the woods around us in hopes of spotting some new clue. So far, it was easy to do as Emerald suggested and keep my mind clear. The inn at Lower Bound had been a grim and disconcerting place, especially when I was standing over a man's still-cooling remains. Out here on the mountain, though, it was all too easy to forget why we were here. Between the filtered sunlight and the faint rustle of a breeze among the high branches, I was very much at peace.

The name Dyrne had become synonymous in my mind with all manner of wretched and unholy things, but as we entered the town, I was struck first by its quaintness. Lower Bound proper had been all right angles and sharp corners and new paint, but the houses of Dyrne were more reminiscent of Amaya's sod-capped hut.

As we crested the last hummock before descending into the village center, I paused to admire the layout. It was easy enough to see from one end of the main road to the other; more houses stood at some remove to accommodate small plots of farmland ringed by low walls that had been built a generation or more ago. From here, I could make out a tavern, a few shops, and—at the town's far limits—an old, rambling stone building with a grave-yard out back. A church, perhaps? Although it seemed strange that a town of this size should require such a large building in which to conduct their services.

"It's charming," I said, frowning down at the village with a vague sense of betrayal.

Emerald chuckled at my obvious indignation. "Things aren't always what they seem, Crimson."

He waved me forward, but I held my ground. "What exactly do the Conjury scouts do on their rounds?"

"In theory, they make sure that the people of any given area are healthy, sound, well-nourished, and safe. In practice? They're little more than spies for the Conjury. They make sure that no one is practicing any sort of unlicensed *aidea*, and that everyone's paying their taxes. You know. The important stuff." He smiled wryly and adjusted his pack.

"And Maximilien might have learned or seen something that alarmed him while he was here. Someone is trying to keep that *something* from the Conjury." I was doing my best to not make immediate assumptions, having just had a conversation about fitting clues to a preconceived narrative, but I did not think I was overreaching.

The town, like the lake, hid something beneath its idyllic surface, although I did not yet know what that might be.

Well, there was only one way to find out.

We trudged down the hill toward the village center. A few people were outside, dressed in colorful robes that matched the ones we had seen abandoned by the lake. In Lower Bound, I had seen a variety of costumes. Both Coirpre and I had stood out from the crowd, but although my traveling dress was as sump-tuous as any of my other outfits—presumably because it cost Emerald nothing more to dress me in silk and satin than in rags

—my costume was drab when compared to the clothes worn by the people of Dyrne. Though the patterns and colors varied, all of them were dominated by lush scarlet and vivid yellow. Nearly every single person was covered head-to-toe, with their eyes obscured by thick hoods and their faces covered by veils. As we passed, most of them looked at us, and I did not have to see their faces to register their alarm at our arrival.

[Is this normal?] I asked. *[Do people often dress this way?]*

[I thought you planned to solve this mystery on your own. Do you really intend to cheat by asking me for information?]

I glared up at him. *[If I'm clever enough to ask the question, by my reckoning, I deserve an answer.]*

Emerald relented. *[If we were in a monastery on the mainland, or visiting the Sisterhood, I wouldn't find it strange. Among civilians? It's... uncommon, but these towns are isolated, and most of them keep to older traditions. Whatever god they worship out here might require it of them.]* Even through our mental link, Emerald seemed skeptical.

[Would a whole town really dress in such a uniform manner on account of religion?]

My connection to Emerald slammed shut, and he murmured aloud, "People will do any number of unlikely things if they believe their god requires it."

There was more to it, I was sure, but I couldn't fight a war on two fronts, and Emerald and I were unlikely to be parted in the near future. Whatever mysteries surrounded his person could wait for a more opportune time. I didn't relish the idea of repeating our shouting match from the day before, much less with an audience.

Apparently, I was not the only person skirting the edges of an argument. Two voices echoed down the street from what seemed to be the largest and grandest of the houses. That wasn't saying much, however. It was still a sod-capped structure built of hand-cut stone.

One of the arguing figures was that of a hunched man with a thick white beard and bushy brows. His bald head sported liver spots, and his robes were like those of the other villagers with the addition of an aging fur cape that had seen better days, although he hadn't bothered to cover his face. Despite the slight differences in dress, he obviously belonged here.

The other man was as out of place as Emerald and I were. He, too, wore no covering on his head. Despite the fact that Emerald had assured me it was a cool spring day, he wore nothing on his top half. A battered pair of leather boots rose almost to his knees, and his loose trousers ballooned over the tops. Bands of brilliant blue writing wrapped around his muscular arms and chest, and his voluminous red beard was decorated with gold embellishments that winked in the sun.

[I didn't know there were dwarves in Dyrne,] Emerald thought. *[Although it stands to reason that there are untapped mineral veins in these hills.]*

"I dunno why you're bein' so stubborn, Mayor Reade," the dwarf was saying. "The smith's guild has made good money all across the Mooncrest Highlands. The people of Dougan and Garikstown sold their mineral rights for a pretty penny, and it shouldn't matter to the village what happens underneath them."

The old man answered in a querulous voice that was no less stubborn than the dwarf's. "Shouldn't matter, right up until you're polluting our water sources with your mining and causing avalanches with your magic. You've acquired the land on the far side of the mountain, and I take no issue with that, but leave Dyrne out of it."

"You've got perfectly good minerals just sitting there goin' to waste—"

"And there they shall remain," the mayor informed him.

The dwarf looked ready to respond when he noticed Emerald and I standing there, watching with ill-disguised interest. "And who the hells are you?" he snapped.

I was prepared to sweep into a deep bow and caught myself just in time. Instead, I curtseyed, not too deeply, and smiled at both men. Being Simone required a different set of motions than Simon, but they were not entirely unalike. As a man, I would have smiled rakishly at them; as a woman, I batted my eyes a little more. I was selling something different, not out of some fundamental difference of feeling, but out of necessity.

An illusion, affecting an illusion of another sort. It was a strange sort of game, but it suited me perfectly.

"Hello, good sirs." My higher-pitched voice easily acquired a syrupy-sweet quality. "I'm so sorry to interrupt, but my companion and I have come *such* a long way, and we're hoping to obtain some information. Carry on. We shall wait our turn."

The dwarf eyed me up and down, taking my measure. "And you are?"

"I am Simone, better known as Crimson Smoke, and this is my—" *friend*, I almost said, but I caught myself there, too. As Simon, I could easily introduce Emerald as my associate, but I was not sure what to call him now that wouldn't lead people to make assumptions about the nature of our relationship. "...manservant," I finished lamely. "The Emerald Flame."

[You could just call me your assistant, you know.] Fortunately, Emerald seemed more amused than hurt by my gaffe.

"Bilk Deepvein," the dwarf grunted. "I've heard of you. Work for the Conjury, don't you?"

[I hate that everyone assumes that.] Emerald mentally growled. **[I hire myself to them occasionally, I don't work for them. I don't work for anyone but myself.]**

[Why not correct them?]

[Because the Conjury name opens certain doors.]

Mayor Reade stiffened. "Is that so?"

"It is." I folded my hands in front of me and nodded, casting my gaze toward the ground. "We are here on unhappy business, I'm afraid."

"Here to plumb the town's secrets, is that it?" Bilk cast a disgusted look toward the mayor. "I wonder what they'd do if they found anything untoward? Clear the place out, I expect. That would be a shame. A damn shame." He spat on the ground at his feet. "Might clear the way for other enterprises, though."

The mayor gripped his staff and glared at the dwarf. "We will continue this conversation later, since I assume that you are still dissatisfied with my answer. You'll get no other, but I doubt that will dissuade you from trying."

"Good day, Mayor." The dwarf bowed ironically, then waved at Emerald and me before he turned and stomped off down the street.

"Trouble with the dwarves?" Emerald asked. His eyes were fixed on the fellow's retreating back.

"The Smith's Guild acquired a mine just over the ridge, and they insist that they should be allowed to dig below the town." Mayor Reade eyed us. "Are you here to sort things out? We weren't expecting another visit from the Conjury so soon."

"Even in the wake of Maximilien's death?" I asked.

These words had an immediate effect on the mayor, and I heard a few gasps from behind us. When I turned to look, I saw that a cluster of the townsfolk had also been listening, first to Bilk Deepvein's conversation and now to ours.

"Maximilien of Leviathan Loch? He's *dead?*" The mayor swayed on his feet and his already pallid cheeks turned sallower still. He removed a purple kerchief from a fold of his robes and dabbed nervously at his forehead. "When? How?"

"Strangled in his bed two nights past," Emerald said.

"Oh." Mayor Reade swayed precariously, and Emerald rushed forward to support the old man with one outstretched arm.

"Are you ill?" I asked. "Should we fetch someone?"

"No, no." The mayor patted Emerald's arm. "Thank you, my boy. It's just such a terrible shock. I thought these dark days were behind us. That's the third scout who's been lost..." He shuddered and fell silent.

"The fourth scout in two years," I corrected.

"Of course, if you're counting Dawyd." The mayor took a deep breath and righted himself. "You can let go of me now, lad.

Shocking news. But the man did not die here, so what brings you to our village?"

He was being polite enough, although the derogatory way in which he spoke to Emerald nettled me. I wondered whether he'd be as polite if the name of the Conjury hadn't been invoked at the beginning of our conversation.

I spoke up. "From what we were told, Cassandra of Wishwind fell from a high pass not far from here. Her predecessor drowned in the spring outside of town. We've just come from there, but we weren't sure what part of the pass to investigate for Cassandra's death. Of course, those were both terrible tragedies, and it's unlucky that Maximilien's passing has followed so soon after. We're simply here to confirm that there is no connection between their deaths."

Emerald shot me an incredulous glance.

[What, did you want me to say that everyone suspects that this creepy little town is to blame? They'll shut us out at once. Let's pretend to be on their side for now. They're more likely to help us uncover the culprit that way.]

[I suppose,] Emerald thought, although his skepticism lingered.

"Of course an inquiry must be made." Mayor Reade planted his feet firmly and pointed back the way we had come. "The place where poor Cassandra fell is marked by an engraved stone along the path in the area we call The Narrows. It's only a mile or two along the road."

"I see." I placed my hand over where my heart would have been if I'd had one. "That's such a beautiful memorial. I'm sorry that I didn't get a chance to see it on our way in." I patted my eyelashes at Emerald. *[Because* **somebody** *couldn't be bothered to summon me in time...]*

"Is that all you need?" the mayor asked. It was obvious that he hoped it was, but I shattered that illusion at once.

"Where might we let a room?" I asked.

"At the bar, just there." The mayor pointed at a wooden building only a few spots down. It was much smaller than the place where we had stayed in Lower Bound, but much tidier if the exterior was anything to judge by. "The owner, Cait, has a few rooms to let, although we don't get many visitors. You can tell her that the town will cover the cost of the room, since you are our honored guests."

"That won't be necessary," I assured him. "Your town is far enough afield that I'm sure the added business wouldn't go amiss."

"As you say, miss, just as you say." A little of the tension drained from Mayor Reade's shoulders.

[I notice you're awfully quick to insist on spending my money,] Emerald pointed out.

My smile never wavered. *[What part of 'endearing ourselves to the locals' is beyond your understanding?]*

"Of course, if there is anything else we can do to accomodate you, don't hesitate to ask. Now, if you'll excuse me. I have other business to attend to." The mayor bowed deeply, then turned to make his painstaking way back into his office.

"Come, Miss Simone." Emerald gallantly waved me in the direction of the building the mayor had indicated. "Let's arrange for a room—"

[Two rooms.]

[Are you actively trying to drain my resources?]

[When I've been Simone before, have you shared a room with me?]

[Technically, no, because you don't need a room.]

[But I'm an illusion. And what illusion are you trying to sell? You want me to appear to be a refined lady, but the display is only as effective as the part you're willing to play.]

[How do you know this, but you don't know whether people dress in ceremonial robes all the damn time!?]

I was not sure how to answer that. As we passed a cluster of curious townsfolk, I watched them out of the corner of my eye. Some of what I knew about them came from deep within Emerald's psyche itself. It was more complicated than that, however.

How was it that I couldn't tell the difference between warm and cool water, but could sense the subtle divide between hostility and fear? The latter was what the residents of Dyrne felt when they looked at us, although I was not sure why.

It must be unnerving, to live in such a small, unified community and know that there is a killer in your midst. The Conjury was interested in the deaths of its scouts, but the dwarf had implied that this town had secrets. How many others had gone missing, or turned up dead in the woods? For all we knew, the clothes we had discovered that very morning had once belonged to the most recent victim of whatever evil plagued the little town. Bilk Deepvein had certainly not been afraid, but the mayor had been, and so were his constituents.

I no longer believed that we had come to Dyrne to solve a single murder. Whatever was happening here ran much deeper than either Emerald or I had suspected.

Chapter Seven

The path to which Mayor Reade directed us was a lonely one. It ran along the spine of a narrow mountain peak. On one side, a cliff wall rose straight up, although in some places the bare stone had been eaten away by endless onslaughts of wind and rain. From those vantage points, it was possible to look down on the divided valleys on either side of the winding road. The view was much the same as yesterday, although taken from a different angle, and in the sunlight the land was transformed again.

I privately marveled at the view. I had only been alive for a few days, and already I had seen so many versions of the world. This one, dotted with spots of golden sunlight in places and deeply shadowed in others, made me wonder: if Kovin Isle was as remote and dreary as everyone maintained, what greater wonders might be found on the vast reaches of the main continent?

And furthermore, what sites had I already borne witness to and instantly forgotten, before I gained my consciousness?

"What a bleeding miserable place to die." Emerald crouched down at the edge of the cliff, peering down to its base. A narrow creek wound beneath us, littered with jagged stones.

I tried to imagine what it would feel like to tumble over the edge knowing what was to come in yet unable to delay it even half a moment. My imagination failed me, in part because I could not feel even the breeze that tugged at Emerald's hair and clothing but left me undisturbed. However self-aware I might be, I was still incapable of truly comprehending physical sensation.

The place where we had stopped was one where the wall of stone blocked the view of the far valley. When Emerald had passed this way in the early morning, he had missed the carved memoriam etched into the rock behind us. Now, with the sun approaching its apex, we could make the words out clearly.

Cassandra of Wishwind—May the Gods Keep Her.

Whoever had written those words had carved them deeply, but without any great craftsmanship.

"I wonder who made this? Not a professional, surely."

Emerald stood up, although his eyes were still fixed on the stream below us. "Someone from the village, I'd guess."

"Someone who wanted to make sure she wasn't forgotten." Remembering Amaya's words, I added, "I doubt that anyone on the island would go to this trouble for Maximilien."

"Unless whoever killed them wanted a memento."

"Badly enough to draw attention to what they did?" I looked back down the path the way we had come, then forward again. From here, it was possible to see along the road toward where it met the slope of the hillside. "It seems like it must've been an accident. She would've seen someone coming if they approached."

"Unless she recognized and trusted them," Emerald pointed out.

"So you're saying they didn't sneak up on her, but traveled with her?"

"That's one possibility. She might not have been suspicious yet. If the old, long-term Conjury scout retired, and his replacement accidentally drowned, Cassandra wouldn't have any *reason* to be suspicious."

That notion struck me as particularly insidious. If Cassandra had been walking alongside someone, perhaps someone who had agreed to accompany her back to Lower Bound, she might not have been on her guard.

There were a hundred lies a murderer could tell to make that proposition inviting. *Let's walk together to pass the time... I'm heading that way anyways... The road is safer for two...* Coirpre's little trick of pretending to protect the merchants from 'attackers' didn't seem so devious now. At least he hadn't meant to harm them deliberately.

"There's no use in speculating," Emerald said. "Once you start doing that, you begin to form theories. All that leads to is confirmation bias."

I lifted my hand to smooth my already perfectly tidy hair; it was a subconscious action, and when I thought to question it, I could not tell if it was my own impulse or something Emerald had willed me to do. "Confirmation bias?"

Emerald brushed the hair out of his own eyes, seemingly unaware that I had completed that selfsame action only moments before. "You start to see patterns where there are none. You become quick to note evidence that supports your theory and ignore that which undermines it. Insignificant details rise to the surface while important clues are brushed aside. You warp the facts to fit your theory."

"Emerald." I tipped my head to one side and smiled wryly at him. "Are you giving me *helpful tips?* Won't that undermine the validity of your experiment?"

Emerald wrinkled his bulbous nose. "I'm giving you tips. If you *are* truly independent of me—and of course you aren't—then it would be unfair of me to withhold advice. Point in case: the hair was in my eyes just now, and *you* moved your hand at the very moment it occurred to me to move mine. Ergo, your subconscious and mine are inextricably linked. Ergo, I'm talking to myself right now."

I crossed my arms and scowled at him. "Fascinating. Any more sage advice, O Wise One?"

"Go with your gut."

"A useless tidbit," I snapped, "since one thing we can agree on is that I'm incorporeal. *Ergo,* I have no gut to follow."

Emerald smirked. "I guess you'll just have to follow mine, then."

"I take back what I said in Lower Bound," I muttered, tilting my nose in the air but still glaring at him from the corner of my eye. "I liked you better when you were quiet."

Emerald's smile was as close to sincere as I had ever seen it, and he relented slightly. "You might not have a gut, but if you truly are independant, perhaps you have some sort of, I don't know, feminine intuition? What can you say with any certainty?"

I relaxed my posture and looked around. This was a good question, even if it *was* asked in jest. When no further clues became readily apparent, I shuffled to the edge of the cliff and peered down into the gorge.

"It wasn't personal," I said at last. "Three murders in a year? Maximilien might have been unlikeable, as Amaya said, but that's not why he was killed."

"I agree." Emerald nodded. "Three scouts in a row. It has to be more than coincidence."

I took the high road and refrained from pointing out that to agree with me suggested that I had reached this conclusion on my own, rather than with his help. Instead, I tried to follow his advice and focus on the facts, rather than on forming a theory. To my chagrin, I found that my limited foreknowledge proved a significant handicap in that regard.

"What do the scouts carry with them?" I asked.

"Supplies, records, notes." Emerald shrugged. "Why do you ask?"

"Coirpre defrauded unwitting travelers for their money on a regular basis. Maybe whoever killed the scouts was after them for something else? Something more valuable than money, which only the scouts might have?"

"Assuming it's only the scouts that have been killed," Emerald pointed out. "It's easy enough to track their disappearances because people know what day to expect them back. For all we know, anyone who comes to this town disappears. There's no record to prove otherwise."

I raised an eyebrow at him. "That's fairly ominous, since we're the most recent arrivals."

"But we haven't given anyone a reason to hate us. We have nothing to steal, and we haven't caused problems for a single person in Dyrne." Emerald took one last look at the inscription before turning back toward the village. "If that dwarf who was arguing with the mayor turns up dead, then I'll start to worry."

The wind that whistled over the high mountain passes didn't trouble the village. It was nested in a cradle formed by the surrounding mountains, as if the land had sunk in on itself a long time ago. It was protected from the elements, but as we returned to town, it occurred to me that the place was also well-hidden from prying eyes.

It was after midday when we returned to the tavern. In many regards, it was difficult to imagine a place that differed more completely from the inn in Lower Bound. Cait's establishment was almost preternaturally clean, and boasted only three rooms for rent, two of which were now considered ours. The floorboards were freshly scrubbed, the bottles behind the bar were dusted, and the taps were polished to a brassy sheen. The place was, in a word, *respectable*.

When we first arranged for our lodgings, it had been morning and the tavern had stood nearly empty. Now, there were a few other patrons spread out at other tables, with glasses and tankards set before them. That wasn't odd.

What *was* odd was that every last one of them still wore those strange, concealing garments. I could not feel the movement of my skirts or the brush of hair below my jawline, but even without a true corporeal form, I swore I could *feel* their gazes as we passed.

[That's creepy, right?] I tried to look at our surroundings without appearing nosey, which was a trick in itself, because I absolutely was.

[Downright unsettling, I agree. Even for me.] Emerald didn't bother to conceal his frown. Given that frowning seemed to be his standard, however, I doubted that our audience noticed the difference.

Cait, the owner of the bar, dressed like all the others, with exception that her garb included breeks and high stockings rather than the flowing dress-like robes favored by the other women I had seen so far. No inch of her skin was visible, but in the slight gap formed by her heavy hood and fluttering scarf, her eyes gleamed like two bright gems, although I could not make out their color.

"What can I do for you?" she asked in a rough voice that was not entirely unkind.

"We're famished," Emerald said. "Perhaps you could..."

[How do you plan to finish that sentence?] I interrupted. *[Are you going to ask her to serve us dinner in this odd dining room, where I will be incapable of even picking at my meal in front of a wary audience? Or would you like her to send a meal up to our rooms, and either leave mine untouched, or sneak over to eat mine on your own and risk causing a scandal of some sort?]*

Emerald's eye twitched. *[If you hadn't been so picky about getting your own room, we wouldn't have this problem.]*

[If you show me up to my room, you can come back down and eat, then pretend to bring my dinner up, but just take it to your room...]

[You're making this too cursed complicated.]

[You forgot my inability to touch anything, and I forgot your need to eat. Let's stop pointing fingers and just focus on what to do now.]

Blissfully unaware of our silent squabble, the innkeeper leaned forward. "As a matter of fact, you have an invitation tonight."

Emerald and I gaped at her. "An invitation?" I asked.

"Mm." Cait's eyes gleamed from the shadows of her hood. "Kade, the town crier, stopped by to ask after you earlier. He and his wife often host venerable town guests at supper."

If I'd had a heart, it would have sunk to my toes. Figuring out how to keep my little impediment a secret was already complicated. Now I was expected to play the part of a respectful guest in the home of the man whose job was to spread gossip through the streets of Dyrne.

There was one bit of good news, however: Kade would also be able to provide a wealth of information. So long as we got on his good side, he ought to be able to tell us everything and anything we wished to know.

Chapter Eight

"Shouldn't we bring something?" I asked Emerald as we prepared to make our way down for the evening. It had taken a great deal of coercion to convince him to wash up and change into somewhat tidier clothes. He'd flat-out refused to order a bath, but after a lengthy haranguining on my part, he'd dipped a damp cloth in the washbasin and was dabbing off the worst of the dirt and sweat which caked his forehead.

"Bring something?" He rolled his eyes at me in the mirror. "You give me three hells over my appearance, and now you want me to produce a gift out of thin air?"

"To be fair, appearances are my expertise." I folded my hands in my lap and pretended to sit on the edge of his bed. It took a bit of concentration on my part, but even when Emerald was not paying me any mind, I found that I was capable of interacting with the world around me in small ways. I could not rumple the bedclothes, but I could perch upon them.

"One might argue that you're nothing *but* appearances," Emerald muttered.

"Indeed, you seem bound and determined to argue *that* at every possible juncture. Will you *please* hurry up?"

"I just have a couple more things to do." When I didn't

respond, Emerald turned to give me a pointed look. "*Alone*. If you're going to make me pay for two rooms, I at least deserve some privacy."

"Ugh." I stood up, fluffing my skirts as I did so. If I could not interact with material objects, I was still determined to kick up as much of a fuss as possible. "I don't know why you're so dramatic. If you really believed that I was part of your psyche, you wouldn't care where I manifested. At any rate, I can see where I'm not wanted." With that, I turned toward the wall that separated his room from mine and stepped through before he could belabor the point.

My rented room was not particularly remarkable. It was better-lit than the one in Lower Bound where Maximilien had died, with freshly-washed panes of glass in the window that looked out over the herb garden that supplemented the kitchens. Like everything else I had seen in Dyrne so far, the room was simple but tidy, decorated with colorful drapes in the customary yellow, purple, and white, and a welcoming bedspread under which I could never climb. If we had wandered here on our own, I believe that I would have found the village unassuming, a restful haven in a secluded spot. There was nothing particularly ominous about it as far as I could see. All those gloomy mutterings in Lower Bound seemed patently unfounded.

Emerald took his sweet time coming to retrieve me; when he opened the door, he held up a glass bottle.

"Cait sold me a bottle of..." Emerald held it up to the light and examined it. "Of *something*. Wine, presumably? Anyway, we won't arrive empty-handed."

"Wonderful." I joined him in the hall, and he shut the door behind me. "What should we ask tonight? This is a wonderful opportunity to speak to the locals."

"And somehow not give away the fact that you can't touch anything," Emerald grumbled. "That'll be a trick."

"Would it really be so bad if anyone found out that I'm intangible?" My incorporeality didn't bother me, and if Emerald was licensed by the Conjury to summon illusions—unlike certain bards one could name—I couldn't see the harm in truthfulness.

Emerald, however, was reticent. "Before, I didn't want anyone to find out that you were an illusion because I didn't want them to realize that I was lying." Emerald tucked the bottle under his arm. "Now, I don't know *what* you are, and I'm not sure what the Conjury would think if they found out about it. More importantly, I'm not sure what they would *do*."

"So you admit that something is different than before?" I asked, smiling at even this small admission.

"You're certainly more annoying than you used to be," he groused. "Come on, we're going to be late."

C ait gave us directions to the home where we were supposed to have dinner. It was not difficult to find, as it was set only a little ways back from the main road. We approached, bottle in tow. Before we could even knock on the door, it opened to admit us.

"Good evening," said a man's voice. The person who greeted us at the door sounded relatively young, but it was impossible to make out any detail of his appearance beneath the traditional robes. "You must be our new guests in town."

"And what a charming town it is," I said, taking the lead. "Forgive me, I hope that you won't be troubled by our unpious manner of dress."

"Of course not." The young man bowed, stepping aside. "We have our customs, but we don't expect anyone else to keep them. Please, come in. My name is Aindreas. My family is waiting inside. I'll introduce you."

[Not a bad welcome,] I thought. *[Perhaps we won't find it as hard as we'd feared to make connections here...]*

Before my thought was fully-formed, we stepped into the main room of the house where three other figures sat at the table. Two of them were dressed in the local fashion, while the third would not have been out of place in any other town. The latter was a sandy-haired young man with piercing blue eyes. The moment those eyes landed on Emerald, he burst out laughing. It was not a friendly laugh, either. There was a nasty note in it matched by the curl of his lip.

"Gods above and below, Aindreas, what have you brought in this time? It's bad enough when the Conjury sends scouts to make sure we pay their taxes and follow their rules, but I draw the line at taking my dinner with a *mutt*."

"Parian, please—" One of the other robe figures emitted a shocked gasp.

"What?" Parian lifted his hand toward Emerald. "Do you really mean to sit at the table with a man whose blood is tainted by the Jotunn? I would rather eat my dinner among the dogs. At least then I would not have to be ashamed of the company."

Aindreas's hands, folded in front of him, tightened over one another. "Then by all means, take your meal with the hounds. If you cannot manage common manners before our esteemed guests, then you are excused."

"I'd be more than happy to go, big brother." Parian lurched to his feet and stalked toward the stairs at the back of the building. "All of you are so quick to fall in line. Nechtan says jump, and you leap like jackrabbits. The Conjury tells you to show fealty, and you fall to your knees. Now you invite in an animal and ply him with your best hospitality? Do as you see fit, but don't expect *me* to shoulder this indignity along with you." He fled through the door and stomped up the stairs.

[What were you saying,] Emerald asked, *[about allies?]*

"Please forgive him," the third figure, presumably Parian's father, said. "My son is at a difficult point in life. He seems determined to rebel against any and everyone these days."

Emerald offered the man a bitter smile. "It's nothing I haven't heard before."

A grim silence descended on the assembled party until Aindreas cleared his throat. "My brother's manners aside, allow me to introduce my mother, Vanora, and my father, Kade."

"A pleasure." Emerald's voice could not have been more flat if he'd tried to make it so. "We brought you this." He thrust the wine toward Aindreas. "Of course, when we received your invitation, I assumed that we were welcome here. It seems there's been a misunderstanding. We should go."

"No, please!" Vanora gestured to the two empty chairs on our side of the rough wooden table. "Join us. I'll talk to Parian later. I've made you a lovely meal, and there's no reason to let a boy's outburst ruin the evening."

I hesitated, torn between loyalty and curiosity. *[We can leave if you like.]*

[No, by all means, let's stay. After a welcome like that, how could we not?] Emerald didn't look at any of us as he pulled out one of the chairs for me.

"Of course, we'd love to accept your hospitality, Vanora." I sank toward the chair, managing a rather complicated maneuver that I hoped made it seem as if I was sitting in the chair as Emerald slid it forward, although I couldn't touch it, any more than I could touch the bed in the inn. "My friend and I have traveled a long way, haven't we?"

Emerald grunted as he took his own seat.

I tried to keep my smile in place. *[What happened to making polite conversation?]*

[I'm little more than a beast, remember? Beasts can't be expected to engage in small talk.]

One might argue that you're proving Parian's point at the moment, I thought, although I was too smart to say so, even through the privacy of our connection.

"What brings you to Dyrne, if I may ask?" Kade inquired as his wife turned to the sideboard. "We so rarely get visitors."

Emerald smiled, baring the cut-down stumps of his tusks. "And when you do, they fare so poorly. We're here about the murders."

Vanora gasped and whirled toward us. "*Murders?* Whatever can you mean?"

[Emerald...]

[You wanted me to talk more, didn't you?] Rather than

biting his tongue, my companion pressed on. "I'm talking about the deaths of the Conjury scouts."

"A terrible business," Kade said, shaking his head. "But surely those were accidents."

"People keep saying so," Emerald told him. "But I fail to see how that can be the case, given that the last man was strangled in his bed."

Vanora leaned against the counter, one hand pressed to her chest. I could not see her face through her garments, but she was clearly in some distress. "It can't be..."

I wished for nothing more than to kick my companion beneath the table. Instead, I mirrored Vanora's gesture and frowned sympathetically. "I know, it's dreadful news. I'm sorry that we didn't deliver it in a *gentler* manner." **[Perhaps you should let me talk for a bit?]**

[Perhaps I should bark instead of speaking at all. I expect they would like me better if I did.]

"You are here to investigate their deaths?" Aindreas asked.

"We're here to determine *if* their deaths were accidents," I corrected.

[You know damn well they weren't,] Emerald thought at me.

[What I know is that these people will stop talking to us if we begin pointing fingers in the dark.] "Let us turn to a less distressing topic," I covered smoothly. "What do you do, Aindreas?"

"I'm an apprentice to Oidche," the young man told me. "The local trapper. He keeps to himself, for the most part, but he's apprenticing me, since he has no children of his own."

"And do you like trapping?" I asked.

"The work itself is no better or worse than any other calling," Aindreas said with a little shrug. "But I like the woods, and I like the quiet."

I was prepared to ask more when Vanora set a plate in front of me, and another in front of Emerald. "I've made you *hagbraggh*, a local delicacy. You won't find that on the mainland."

"Thank you." I smiled at her, painfully aware that I should have made some excuse for why I couldn't eat. I had been too preoccupied with Parian's slights against Emerald and his resulting churlishness to think of it. I pretended to sniff the air. "It smells, um, divine. What is it?"

"Stuffed goat intestine," she said, sounding extremely pleased with herself. "I've even used pickled beachplum imported from the mainland, a rare treat."

"Oh." I stared down at the greyish sausage resting on my plate. "Wonderful."

Vanora served the men next, then took to her own seat. Emerald grabbed his fork and knife and began cutting at the *hagbraggh*, but even as his fork squeaked against the glistening casing, Aindreas crossed his hands over his chest. Vanora and Kade made the same gesture.

"Praise be to the Lord of the Living and the Dead, He Who Beholds All." Aindrea's voice echoed through the little room. "You see us as we are, good and bad alike, and love us anyway. We ask you to keep the dead close, and to bless the living with your holy gifts. Blessed be your chosen."

"Blessed be your chosen," his parents echoed, before uncrossing their arms and reaching for their own utensils.

"Your community is strong in its faith," I observed, leaning back in my seat, careful not to pass through the wood backrest. "You don't even remove your robes in the comfort of your home. That seems like a tremendous impediment to daily life."

"We do," Vanora explained, "but not in front of guests. Our god, Dathan, loves us as we are. The robes provide us a respite from our vanity. When we are alone with our loved ones, we may put our robes aside, for the love of our families is as uncondi-tional as that of our god. Those who do not know us may be swayed by our appearance. People are so easily taken in by beauty or ugliness, but what we appear and who we are should never be conflated."

"I see." I watched as Vanora leaned forward so that her veil fell away from her face, still blocking her visage from me in its entirety, and delivered a forkful of *hagbraggh* to her mouth. The whole endeavor seemed rather involved, but rather than question their faith further, I changed tact. "If you don't mind, I'd like to ask a question about the scouts—one of them in particular."

Kade paused with his fork halfway to his mouth, his face also shrouded by the colorful cloth, even as he too leaned forward to eat. "Go on, then."

"Dawyd of Sailor's Reprieve served as a scout for many years, I believe?"

At the mention of that name, Kade relaxed. "You are correct. We loved Dawyd as though he was one of our own. We were so sorry to hear of his passing. A kinder man never lived."

"He cared so much for the wellbeing of others," Vanora gushed.

"Of all the tragedies that have occured here in my lifetime, his passing was the greatest of all," Aindreas added. "We adored him. He was like an uncle to me and Parian, and I'm sure that many others would say the same." He nodded to my untouched plate. "The conversation may be scintillating, Miss Simone, but you have not touched your food. Go on, eat. My mother worked hard to prepare this meal."

I glanced at Emerald, who was scowling down at his plate. Every time he chewed, the *hagbraggh* squeaked between his molars.

"I'm afraid I can't," I said.

Vanora turned her veiled face toward me. "I'm sorry?"

"I don't eat meat," I blurted.

"Oh, no." Sounding truly distressed, Vanora set her silverware aside. "I'm so sorry, I should have asked! I can get you something else. We have wildgrain pottage from this morning."

"That's alright," I assured her.

"It's no trouble." She moved to get up.

"No, really, I—" ***[Emerald, help.]*** I could not seem to think of a single reasonable excuse for my inability to so much as lift my fork.

Emerald only kept chewing and squeaking.

"Let me just—" Vanora began.

"No!" I held out both hands. "No. In truth, my diet is so restrictive, there is little I can eat. I don't eat anything that was once alive."

Four sets of eyes turned toward me. Emerald kept up his relentless chewing.

"*Anything?*" Vanora echoed. "Not even plants?"

"It makes meals rather complicated," I said. "I would never presume to ask anyone else to meet my requirements. I ate before we came."

"You ate before attending dinner in my home?" Vanora echoed.

"Mother—" Aindreas cut in.

Vanora huffed and reached for my plate. "You may look down on our food, Miss Simone, and that is one thing, but there is no need to *lie* to me. I can save this for Parian."

"Or perhaps for the dogs with which he prefers to dine," Emerald suggested.

It came as little surprise to me that the rest of the meal passed in stony silence.

Following our return to the inn that evening, Emerald let me into my room and shut the door with a snap behind me, returning to his own next door.

[We should talk about this,] I told him through our link, our thoughts passing through the wall as easily as I could.

[Nothing to discuss,] he retorted. *[Our hosts offended me, and we paid them back in kind.]*

[Surely there must be something useful to be learned from all that? Something that makes the endeavor worthwhile?]

[Only that the good folk of Dyrne are no better than the good folk of any other small-minded, backwater town.]

[Parian was awful, yes, but the others didn't agree with what he said. They even sent him away!]

[True, they apologized for his behavior. But they didn't deny that they felt the same way.]

I peeked my face through the wall into his room, ready to take issue with his bad mood. I could understand not knowing what to say to make up for the thoughtless words of one dear to me. I couldn't blame Vanora for feeling caught between her urge to please us and her love for her son, and Kade had hardly said two words all evening. Only Aindreas seemed willing to speak up against his brother's ravings, and he was not master of the house. What did Emerald expect?

The argument I was about to make fizzled out at the sight before me. Upon entering the room, Emerald had stripped off his vest and tunic and tossed them in a heap on the floor. He shucked off his trousers, as well, revealing the smallclothes beneath—and the scars running down his legs like notches on a wall, clean straight lines of almost exactly an inch in length, arrayed along his thighs and calves all the way to his ankles. When his arms caught the lamplight, I saw similar marks there, too; some of them were still dark against his skin, as though they had not yet healed over.

I pulled back through the wall and clasped my hands over my mouth, praying that Emerald hadn't noticed my intrusion. Surely he would not have wanted me to see those little scars. There must have been hundreds of them, some deeper than others, but all made by a similar hand.

His own, I was certain. There could be no other explanation.

His thoughts cut through my own. *[It doesn't matter, Crimson. As I said, Parian's insults were hardly innovative. I've heard worse.]*

I squeezed my eyes shut, forcing my mind blank so that he would not sense my distress. I knew that he had heard worse, because I had *heard* worse echoing through his own head. He'd not only listened to that onslaught of insults time and time again, he'd eventually come to believe them.

[Good night, Crimson.] I heard the creak of his bed through the wall.

I wanted to reply, to wish him pleasant dreams, to tell him that Parian was an idiot. I didn't trust myself to do so, however.

For a few days now, I'd believed that I was more than a rogue fragment of Emerald's psyche, but this more than anything proved me right. If I was still part of him, wouldn't I have believed that those little marks were earned? Were justified?

Instead, they elicited nothing in me but heartbreak.

Chapter Nine

The morning after our dismal dinner party, I appeared in Emerald's room. Out of habit, I glanced down at the form he'd chosen for me today, frowning when I realized that I was wearing the same dress I had worn the day before.

"Couldn't you imagine another outfit?" I asked, running my hands over the illusion of brocade. The memory of Emerald's scars flashed through my mind, but I quickly pushed it aside. He had not meant for them to be seen, and now was not the time to discuss them.

"Do you think anyone will believe that you're carrying around several changes of wardrobe?" Emerald asked.

I sniffed, rolling my shoulders back. "It costs you nothing to summon a different dress. How about something in sapphire damask?"

"You're already summoned, which is a headache even when you aren't being contrary," Emerald griped. "Green suits you. You're wearing green. End of discussion." Under his breath, but not so softly that I believed he was trying to disguise his words, he added, *"Conceited."*

I held my fist to my mouth and murmured, *"Stodgy."*

"Forget about the dress. We have our work cut out for us today. I want to get to know everyone, and how they're all connected."

"Surely there are less than three hundred people in this town. It can't be all that hard, can it?" I went over to the mirror and made a show of admiring myself, because I knew it would annoy him.

Emerald snorted. "Apparently you don't realize how close-knit communities like this can be. We could spend twenty years here and still be considered outsiders."

I turned to face him, already bored with posturing. "But there are others here who are not locals, aren't there?"

"Who have you seen who isn't wearing their robes?" Emerald asked.

I paused to consider this. Admittedly, we had only interacted with a few people, but other than Parian everyone I recalled had worn the distinctive local dress.

"We'll ask around." Emerald widened his eyes at me. "*Discreetly*. You *can* be discreet, can't you?"

"I'm offended that you have to ask." I swept toward the wall separating our rooms. "Besides, I'm wearing yesterday's dress. What's more discreet than that?"

He didn't keep me waiting this time before collecting me from my room. The two of us headed downstairs, where I slid onto a bench with more grace than I had evidently possessed the night before. Emerald left me there to approach Cait, most likely to order something. I didn't know what he was going to get, and I didn't care. As long as I could manage a little grace after the mess of the prior evening, I would be content.

I was wallowing in the unpleasant memory of our dinner when a small and rather furry face popped up over the edge of the table.

"Begging your pardon, miss," said the lambkin, blinking his large brown eyes at me. "Might I trouble you for a moment?"

I had seen lambkins in Lower Bound, but I had not stopped to look at them properly. This fellow was roughly half my height, with thick white wool atop his head, sprouting from his chin, puffing up from his short sleeves, from the collar of his partially unbuttoned shirt, and covering his long, floppy ears, one of which had sustained a rather nasty bite in the distant past.

"Of course." I gestured to the seat across from me, relieved that he hadn't tried to get my attention by tapping my shoulder. "What can I do for you?"

The lambkin pulled himself up into the chair. "I like your manners, miss. The name's Errol."

I placed my hand over my heart and bowed slightly. "You may call me Simone. Do you live in Dryne, Errol?"

"For the moment. Moved here a few months ago in search of some peace and quiet." He grinned at me, running his fingers through his beard. "You seem like a lady of good taste. Would you perhaps be interested in some..." He glanced around the room, then leaned closer, lowering his voice. "*Shine of the moon?*"

"Shine?" I repeated.

He reached into his pocket and produced a small glass vial. When he shook it, blue light emanated from the spaces between his thick, stubby fingers. "Finest on the island. In fact, I daresay you won't find another purveyor anywhere..."

"Probably true," Emerald interrupted, "given that it's *illegal*."

The lambkin whirled to face my friend, clutching the little blue bottle to his chest. "Oh!" he squealed. "Hello! And who might you be, sir?"

"A licensee of the Conjury," Emerald said. He towered over the little creature, clutching a heavy plate that he had retrieved from the bar. "I presume that you, too, are licensed to conduct your affairs. Perhaps you can show me your papers?"

"Oh, dear." My new acquaintance wilted, patting his pockets with both hands. "I'm afraid I've left them somewhere. Perhaps my room..."

Emerald set the plate on the table with a heavy thump, then crossed his arms. "Then fetch them. We can wait."

"Now that I think of it, I don't recall *when* I saw them last." Errol looked toward me for help.

"I'm sure everything is aboveboard," I said. "Master Errol was just telling me that he's new to town." *[Too new to know anything about the previous murders, but perhaps he can offer us some insight?]*

[My idea exactly. I'll intimidate him, and you charm him. And it never hurts to know people's private business, at any rate.]

I leaned forward, lacing my fingers together in front of me and letting my chin rest on them. "You don't strike me as the sort of person who would go out of their way to cause trouble, Mr. Errol."

"N-no, indeed not." The lambkin wiped one palm across his forehead. "I prefer to lie low. We lambkins are simple folk. Law-abiding."

"In that case, perhaps you can help us with something. We have some questions about what's been going on in Dyrne lately. Questions that locals might not be willing to answer."

"I don't know anything!" Errol squeaked. "I've only been here a few months. People here have been lovely, but they're not exactly forthcoming. I presume that you have some questions about..." His eyes darted around the room. "About what happened with that rider a few days back?"

"You know something about that?" Emerald asked. He took another step forward, and Errol shrank in on himself. "I would advise you, sir, to tell us everything you know, and to be honest."

I let his subtle threat sit with Errol for a second before throwing him a lifeline. "Lying is a grave matter, Emerald. I don't think Mr. Errol would do something so honorless." I let my eyes slide to the lambkin. "Especially not when he knows about our position with the Conjury."

"I'm as honest as a summer day is long!" Errol shoved the bottle of moonshine back into his pocket. "I'll tell you what little I know. I was staying in the inn when the scout, Maximilien, came through. He was pleasant enough at first, and we even played a few rounds of knucklebones one evening. Then, without so much as a goodbye, he took off for Lower Bound. I saw him from the window, riding that poor horse for all it was worth straight out of town." Errol pointed toward the road that had brought us into the settlement. "On my honor, that's everything."

"Interesting." I frowned at this little description. It matched what we already knew, with one minor exception. "Maximilien was friendly with you?"

"Not overly so," the lambkin explained. "He was a bit uptight, as all the Conjury folk tend to be, but he didn't mind talking about his adventures over a mug of ale."

"I see." *[That's not what Amaya said back in Lower Bound. She made the man sound utterly unbearable.]*

[Yes, but she met him after he'd come to Dyrne. The man was already afraid for his life.]

I pondered that for a moment. It was one thing to fear an enemy when you knew they were nearby, but Maximilien's terror had lingered even after the town was far behind him—and rightly so, seeing as the distance had bought him no safety.

"Is there anyone else new to town?" I asked.

"Other than the doctor, everyone's a local, to my knowledge, and by the sounds of it he's been here for years." Errol wiped his brow. "Except the dwarf, but he's not really staying in town. I swear to you, I'd help you if I could."

"You've been immensely helpful." I turned to Emerald. "You have a bit of coin on you still, I think? Why don't you buy a bottle of Mr. Errol's Shine of the Moon? I hear it's unrivaled on the island."

Emerald sighed, but he rooted around in the pocket of his vest in search of a few coins.

"Take it, as a gift," the lambkin said, placing the bottle on the table and hurriedly getting to his hooves.

"Nonsense. A hardworking gentleman such as yourself deserves to be paid for his labor."

Emerald shot me a nasty glare. *[What's this about?]*

[We have few enough allies here. Might as well give him

a couple of coins. If he feels kindly toward us, he may 'remember' something else later.]

[Such a soft touch,] Emerald thought, in a tone that made it quite clear that he did not intend this as a compliment.

[You catch more flies with honey than with vinegar,] I reminded him.

He snorted as he placed five copper coins in the lambkin's outstretched palm. *[A nice enough saying, but everyone knows that flies are perfectly content with shit.]*

I placed my hand over my mouth and bit back a burst of laughter as the lambkin scurried away. Emerald sat down in the seat he'd vacated and reached for the bottle. He swirled it a few times, opened the cap, and then took a swig. "Not bad," he said, with only a hint of begrudgement in his voice.

"Why is it illegal?" I asked, squinting at the bottle.

"Moonshiners in and of themselves aren't illegal," Emerald explained, tucking the unfinished bottle into a pocket. "But the Conjury keeps a close watch over any and all uses of the *aidea*. Anyone who harnesses energy without a license is in violation of the law, even when they're only bottling a mild intoxicant like Shine."

"What would happen if they found out about an infraction like this?" I asked.

Emerald waved to the plate. "Let's eat while we talk." *[I've figured out how to make this work for the moment. I'm going to create the illusion of a second plate overlaying the real one. You'll be able to interact with it like you do with your dress, and anyone watching will think we're eating together.]*

[A clever solution. My hat is off to you.] I reached for the platter of meat, cheese, and cut fruit, plucking the likeness of a sweetberry off the plate without disturbing the real one beneath it.

"A moonshiner like your friend might receive a fine. In one of the larger cities, he might even be jailed for a few days, but nothing more."

"And if someone was misusing their power on a larger scale...?"

"The larger the infraction, the higher the cost."

I paused as I reached for another fruit. "And if the scouts discovered that someone was using the *aidea* irresponsibly? Could that person be in so much trouble that they would risk taking a life to ensure the scout's silence?"

"It's one possibility," Emerald admitted. "But let me remind you not to leap to conclusions. Let's finish our breakfast, and then we'll go talk to this doctor."

I t wasn't difficult to find the town infirmary; it stood along the main road on the far end of the settlement, less than half a mile from our current location. It looked more like the sort of building we'd have found in Lower Bound than the rest of the houses, square and compact rather than rustic. All the same, the paint was scuffed in places; it had seen a few seasons of wind and rain.

"Errol said the doctor was new here, didn't he?" I asked. "This building hardly seems new."

"He said that the doctor was the only other 'outsider' in town... but I told you, he could have lived here for decades and still qualify as such." Emerald approached the house, brought his fist down twice on the little door, and then stepped back so that I stood in front.

"*Just a minute!*" a voice called from inside. "*I'm just in the middle of—oh, damn...*" The handle rattled, and a lanky man appeared at the door of the infirmary, gracing me with an easy smile. "Hello there. You must be one of the visitors in town."

"You've heard of us?" I winced, recalling the painfully awkward scene of the night before. "Nothing too terrible, I hope?"

The doctor's smile widened. It was a relief to be able to read what he was thinking in his expression. Unlike most of the other residents of Dyrnc, his countenance was unveiled, and in place of the robes—which I had come to think of almost as a uniform —he wore plain brown leggings, a rumpled shirt the color of clear sky, and a jacket adorned with buckles and straps, featuring dozens of pockets both on the coat itself and on the matching leather belt that hung across his narrow hips. His curly black hair stood up in every direction, framing a face that was the rich golden brown of a tiger's-eye gem. I had never seen a person who looked so naturally frantic and yet who exuded such natural calm.

"Nothing terrible at all," he assured me, offering a haphazard little bow in deference, presumably, to our position with the Conjury. "Visitors to this town aren't common, as you might imagine, so the presence of two new faces is..."

His eyes flicked toward Emerald, and he stopped talking altogether. His eyes widened and his mouth hung slack.

"Uncommon," he said in a strangled voice. He lifted a hand to his messy hair and mussed it some more. "Not a lot of visitors..."

I bristled automatically. Emerald might be my creator, or a father figure at the very least, but I had come to think of myself as his guardian against the iniquities of man. Parian's dreadful behavior from the night before had rekindled Emerald's self-loathing, and even if I could not take the doctor by the collar of his shirt and shake some sense into him, I would give him the tongue-lashing of his life if he dared harm my friend as that idiot boy had the night before. I glanced at Emerald out of the corner of my eye to see what he thought of this interaction.

I had seen many expressions on Emerald's face. First and foremost was annoyance, since I tended to inspire that emotion. I had seen pain and fear and anger and, once or twice, slight affection.

Even so, despite our link, I could not tell what he was feeling at that moment. Or rather, I could see his expression clearly, but I could not understand it. Tension radiated from him, but not self-defense. His mouth was pressed into a thin line, but there was something in his eyes like... not hunger, exactly. I searched for the word and could not find it. Whatever emotion had settled in his breast was unfamiliar to me.

"Please excuse me," I said in a loud voice, smiling too broadly and taking a protective step toward my friend. "I'm Simone, and this is my friend, Emerald."

As I said this, I reached out as if to pat Emerald on the arm. Of course, I could not, so instead of offering a gentle caress, my hand hovered just over his wrist; and then, imperceptibly, through it.

If I had not experienced the full depth of Emerald's emotions before, I would have been sent reeling by the strength of them. This time, I was braced for their force. Self-loathing, as always, sat at the core of his psyche, but there was no rage to accompany it this time. In that fraction of a second, I understood what Emerald's expression alone could not make clear to me.

Longing. Emerald's whole body was saturated with it. Desire, but also denial.

You want what you cannot have.

You should not be as you are.

The mind should rule the body, not the other way around. A man should only want what is necessary for survival. Everything else is a distraction.

And yet in that moment, Emerald was nothing *but* distraction.

"Emerald," the doctor repeated in a breathy tone. "Yes, lovely name." He swallowed suddenly and stood up a little straighter. "That is, it's a lovely stone. Which makes it fitting because, ah. Your eyes are..." He coughed into his fist. "I'm Tincrown of Swoop Oasis."

"A transplant," I said. ***[That's noteworthy, isn't it, Emerald? Until now, we had no proof that anyone from outside the village was allowed to carry on their affairs uninterrupted. Remember your theory from yesterday, about how anyone who came to the village might disappear in silence? Now we have two counts of evidence to the contrary.]***

Emerald did not acknowledge me at all. Even stranger, he did not seem to notice that I'd intruded on his private thoughts this time. Instead, he offered Tincrown a strained smile. "You hail from the Nomad Gamut."

Tincrown's smile returned twice as bright as before. "Have you visited the region?"

"Lovely country." Emerald's echoing smile failed to reach his eyes.

We stood there for a moment, the two of them lost in a world where I could not venture. I didn't understand what it was like to want something that anyone else could give me, with the possible exception of my autonomy.

After a moment, Tincrown stepped abruptly aside. "Come inside," he said. Then his face turned scarlet. "Inside the house," he blurted. "Step inside is what I meant, of course, because who would say... why would I... Right this way, please."

Usually, Emerald dogged my footsteps, but this time he stepped forward without paying me any heed. On his way past Tincrown, he brushed against the man's arm almost as imperceptibly as I had touched him only a moment before. Despite the brevity of their contact, Tincrown shivered.

[What am I missing?] I asked.

[Nothing.] Even through our mental connection, Emerald managed to be curt. *[It's a narrow doorway.]*

So he had noticed Tincrown's touch, even if he did not notice mine.

Feeling every bit the outsider, I followed Emerald inside. To my great relief, Tincrown made no attempt to touch me. In fact, he seemed oblivious to my presence altogether. I had to look down at myself as I stepped into the infirmary to make sure that I had not turned invisible. Sure enough, I was still present.

Curious. My whole purpose was to draw attention away from Emerald, and this was the first time I had completely failed to do so.

The house gave off much the same air as Tincrown himself did, rather chaotic and jumbled while simultaneously charming.

Two tidy beds, presumably for patients, stood in the main room, along with an enormous einwood table tapped with a diverse assortment of jars, bottles, dried herbs, and preserved wildflowers. The most impressive of all was a large bell-shaped bottle the size of my head, from which a complicated and twirly bit of glass piping extruded. Some arcane liquid sat inside.

"What is this?" I asked, squinting at the contraption.

"A distillery," Emerald said before Tincrown could answer. "It's usually used for the production of grain alcohol."

Tincrown nodded enthusiastically, his wild black hair bobbing around his ears. "Quite right, but in this case, I'm trying to perfect a disinfectant."

Emerald cocked his head. "What's the matter with lambsfoil?"

"Nothing at all, save for the fact that it doesn't grow well on the island. The lower regions are too boggy, and the soil up here is too thin and acidic to support it. It doesn't make sense to rely on bottle essence or powdered root, not when it costs a veritable fortune to acquire. I thought it prudent to find a ready source."

"Interesting." Emerald bent down to inspect the liquid. "So what are you using?"

[Awfully chatty, aren't you. Is this relevant to the case?]

His expression of intense interest never wavered. ***[I'm trying to put him at ease. He's more likely to answer our questions if he feels comfortable with us.]***

Emerald probably had a point, but even that logic could not explain his sudden loquaciousness.

The doctor continued speaking, "One of the endemic evergreens gives sap that I think might be the solution to this particular problem."

"Ah." Emerald nodded. "Clever."

The praise was lukewarm, but Tincrown's already sunny countenance turned outright radiant. "Why, thank you. Thank you very much. Of course, if you have any suggestions, I'd be happy to hear them. Are you an herbalist, Emerald?" My companion's name sounded like honey on Tincrown's tongue.

"Jotunn are by nature."

This was, to me, a further puzzle. I had never heard Emerald call himself that before. Last night, Parian had accused Emerald of being half-Jotunn, as if that was something shameful. Not so when Emerald said it; he seemed almost proud.

"You have Jotunn ancestry, then?" Tincrown beamed. "I didn't want to presume, although... would it be terrible of me to ask you a question?"

I didn't need a psychic link to Emerald to see how he shut down at these words. "Ask whatever you like," he intoned in a hollow voice. He clearly had some expectation for whatever was about to come next. I remembered the woman at the stables in Lower Bound, and how she had looked at him like he was a *thing* and not a person; and worse, how Emerald had seemed almost used to such treatment.

"One moment." Tincrown darted toward the back of the house where a narrow flight of stairs led to the second floor. For such a slight man, he certainly made a racket flying up the stairs, stomping around like mad above us, and bolting back down a moment later with a heavy book in hand. He shoved a few things aside on the large table, then flipped the book open to reveal a sketch of a plant.

"Do you know what this is?" the doctor panted, tapping one finger on the page. "It was a lovely purple with brilliant yellow stamen. I found it when I was out on the mountain last summer gathering herbs, and I've never seen the like of it before. I can't seem to find it in any books, although..." He laughed at himself and shook his head. "Well, I can't exactly ask my bookshelf to provide a list of every purple flower in existence, can I?"

Emerald stared at the man for a few seconds before glancing down at the book. He blinked a few times. "Ah... might be *panacea forndulata,* but that's only a guess..."

Tincrown immediately hurried over to a creaking bookshelf and produced a massive tome. He brought that over to the space he'd cleared and hastily began leafing through its pages.

[What did you expect him to ask?] I wondered.

Emerald crossed his arms and frowned at me behind Tincrown's back. *[Doesn't matter.]*

[You thought he was going to say something horrible, didn't you?] I pressed. *[Something about Jotunn?]*

Emerald shrugged. *[I didn't expect him to say anything worse than what Parian said last night, at any rate.]*

[I see. But it would have hurt more coming from him, wouldn't it?]

Emerald cut his eyes away from mine and did not reply.

"Aha!" Tincrown slapped the back of his hand against the open page and let the covers of the reference book slap against the table. "There it is, *p. forndulata!*" The reference book even included a handsome illumination showing the flower in bloom. It did indeed look remarkably like Tincrown's own sketch.

"I thought so," Emerald murmured.

"Thank you." Tincrown sighed happily. "You can't imagine how much that's bothered me over the last few months, and here you come, solving the puzzle the instant I put it before you."

Emerald's cheeks darkened. "Well, to be fair, it was a very good sketch."

[Hold on, is that why you're being so chatty with him? You wanted to prove that you know everything there is to know. I daresay you wanted to impress him!]

Once again, Emerald paid me no mind. I was starting to realize that nothing vexed me more fully than being ignored. Having had quite enough of their mutual admiration society, I stepped forward and clasped my hands in front of me.

"You said that you were from Swoop Oasis. When did you arrive in Dryne?"

Tincrown dragged his attention away from Emerald and refocused on me. He leaned one hip against the table and held up his hands in front of him, counting the time off on his fingers. "Goodness, nearly thirteen years ago now. I was assigned here after I completed my training on the mainland. It was supposed to be a temporary position, but—well, with one thing and another, I decided to stay."

"Who assigns physicians their posts?" I asked. "Is it the Conjury, or...?"

Tincrown's laugh cut me off. "No, no, the Conjury doesn't bother with such things. If I'd attended one of the universities, or used a biological *aidea*, that would be another matter. As it is, I took classes back home, completed an apprenticeship in Troveland Keep, and then put in for an assignment. Dyrne needed a doctor, and here I am." He held his hands out, gesturing to the little house.

I pursed my lips. "Why didn't you leave when you expected to?"

Until that very moment, Tincrown had been as easy to read as the book that lay open on the tabletop; but when I asked that question, his smile turned wooden, and his eyes darted from Emerald to me and back. "W-well, you know how it is. You get attached to a place. To the people. It all starts to feel like your responsibility." He swallowed. "At least, that's how it is for me. You start to learn about your patients' problems, their concerns, their... mm-hmm, their *way of life*..."

"Their secrets?" Emerald asked.

Tincrown ran a hand over his cleanshaven jaw. "Remind me why you're here in Dyrne?"

"We're here to look into the deaths of the Conjury scouts," I said, and added, **[Not to waste the day talking about wild-flowers,]** because Emerald seemed to have forgotten.

"Of course." Tincrown nodded, altogether gloomy now. "A sad business, that."

Emerald stared straight at him. "Do you know who might have killed them?"

Tincrown looked up to meet his gaze. "I do not."

That was surprising for a few reasons. First, because I believed him, and second, because he did not attempt to side-step the issue as so many others had. "You don't believe their deaths were accidental, then?"

Tincrown shook his head. "I saw both of the scouts after they died. Cassandra might have been an accident, but Trotter had—" Tincrown pressed his hand to his collarbone and shuddered. "He had marks on him. Bruises. No, that was no accident."

It was sad to think of a bright presence like Tincrown bending over a ruined corpse, but of course, as the town physician, he saw more than his fair share of blood and death. That came with the territory.

Emerald took half a step toward him, then stilled. *He wants to comfort Tincrown,* I realized, even as I wrapped my arms around myself. I felt almost as I had on the mountain, when I moved to smooth my hair the instant before Emerald did, but the impulse was muddled, caught between wanting to protect this near-stranger from the evils of the world, while also wanting to protect myself.

That, too, was more information than Emerald would have liked me to know. I saw the way he glanced at me out of the corner of his eye and frowned ever-so-slightly.

"It's a monstrous thing, to take a life," Tincrown murmured. He was still staring at the floorboards, lost on some awful memory. "If I knew who had done it, I would tell you."

Since Emerald did not seem inclined to speak, I continued my line of questioning. "You say that you saw both of the scouts. I presume you don't know that the third was killed in Lower Bound?"

Tincrown sighed heavily and crossed his arm. "I hadn't heard. Gods and monsters, that's an ill business. How did he die?"

"Strangled in his bed."

The doctor squeezed his eyes shut. "By the Golden Hand..."

"Has anything else like that happened?" I asked.

"Murders, you mean?" Tincrown shook his head. "No, this is a peaceful place. Quiet."

In that case, I wondered, *how did it come to have such a ghastly reputation in the port?*

"Is there any place we might go to see a list of residents?"

Emerald asked, breaking his silence at last. "Do you have a register of your patients' names?"

"I keep records, but I can't share them. Confidentiality, you understand." Tincrown offered us a weak smile. "If people can't trust their doctors, who *can* they trust? But you might wish to speak to Nechtan."

"Nechtan?" I repeated. The name sounded familiar, but I could not recall where I had heard it before.

"The high priest." Tincrown waved a hand vaguely toward the street. "You've seen the clothing everyone wears, of course, so you understand how Dyrne cleaves to its traditions. I still worship Ardus of the Golden Hand, but all the residents are devoted to the local faith."

[Except for Parian,] I thought grimly.

"Thank you." Emerald nodded to the doctor. "We'll speak to him."

"Is there anything else I can do for you?" Tincrown spoke to both of us, but he was looking at Emerald. "Anything else you want to ask?"

"Nothing at the moment." Emerald rolled his shoulders. "But if something else occurs to us..."

"You're welcome back at any time," Tincrown assured him.

"Good."

"Wonderful."

I saw that this could go on forever, so I turned toward the door. "Off we go to see Nechtan, then..."

"Right." Tincrown hurried to the door and held it open for us. I swept past him without incident. The doorframe seemed perfectly adequate to me, but somehow it seemed to shrink when Emerald got involved, and once again he couldn't manage to get through it without skimming close to our host. Emerald didn't look back at him, but I did, and found that Tincrown watched us until we were well clear of the little lane and back on the main thoroughfare once more.

[Emerald...]

[Don't. Just don't.]

I longed to demand an explanation for the strange dance I had just witnessed between the two of them, but something more important was troubling me which I could not let lie. *[You asked him if he knew who had killed the scouts… but you didn't ask if he knew why they were killed.]*

"He's not part of whatever's going on," Emerald said aloud.

I wondered which one of us he was most eager to convince.

Chapter Ten

It was not difficult to find the church. In fact, it had been one of the first things I noticed upon walking into the town, although neither Emerald nor I had paid it any particular heed at the time. It was an imposing stone structure, out of place among the quaint thatch-roofed houses, with a lofty belltower at its heart.

"We should have thought to come here earlier," I mused as we approached. "Everyone we've spoken to has been open about their deep faith. I would think a member of the clergy would be more eager than anyone to ensure the safety of the residents."

Emerald snorted. "You assume that the church cares more about its members than about maintaining control. Not all of them do."

This surprised me; we had not discussed the matter of religion in depth, but his regard for Aster was evidently abundant and deep.

"Stop looking at me," he grumbled.

I had already been nosy enough that morning, so I kept my curiosity in check for once and looked instead toward the little graveyard alongside the church.

"Funny to think that more residents of this town are dead

than alive," I observed. "There are more headstones than beds in Dyrne."

"All the more reason to keep good records of the town," Emerald said. "With so few families to choose from, you wouldn't want anyone too closely related to intermarry."

"Oh." I blinked a few times. "You wouldn't?"

"It would cause problems." When I remained silent, Emerald added, "With the children."

"Hm." I considered this, but this was one area in which my connection to Emerald did nothing to illuminate the subject. He seemed as desperate to skirt the topic in his own mind as he did in conversation. "How so?"

Emerald let out a beleaguered sigh. "I do *not* want to have this talk with you."

"What talk?"

"When a man and a woman love each other very much, they can have children." Emerald's lip curled, as if he found the entire subject distasteful. "If the couple are closely related, those children often suffer from ailments which others do not experience."

"A child can only be made by a man and woman?" I asked, more interested in the idea of origins than consequences, given that I was only a few days away from my own birth. It hadn't occurred to me to wonder where other people came from.

Emerald, who was reaching for the rusting metal gate which surrounded the graveyard, paused for a moment. "Generally speaking."

"Because when you were talking to Tincrown—"

"Let's not dawdle," Emerald said loudly, throwing the gate open. "Lots of important work to do!"

Rebuffed and annoyed, I followed Emerald inside. Since he didn't wait for me, and I had no way to close the gate myself, we left it standing open.

Most of the graves were comprised of simple headstones set over tidy plots. Aside from a few overgrown brambles around the edge of the cemetery, the place was kept neat. The newest stones were handsomely carved with the names of the deceased.

I paused before one of them and crouched down in the low grass to examine the writing. "Interesting."

Emerald was still a ways ahead of me, but he turned back to see what had drawn my attention. "*Findrel of Dyrne?* Never heard of 'em."

"Nor have I, but look." I pointed to the inscription. "Don't the letters remind you of anything?"

Emerald bent over me and squinted. "Huh. The writing looks a great deal like the inscription near where Cassandra fell."

"Do you think it was made by the same hand?"

"There's probably a stone mason who does all the carving for such things." Emerald shrugged. "That doesn't seem odd."

"But Tincrown said that the people of Dyrne worship a local god. Would you expect the church to oversee rites for outsiders?"

Emerald scratched his chin. "In Lower Bound they called in the Sisters for Maximilien, even though he wasn't from the island. Whoever's local will do what must be done, regardless of which gods the deceased followed in life."

"So Tincrown sees to the physical remains of the community, and Nechtan to the spiritual ones." I climbed slowly to my feet. "It's a closed circle."

"It certainly makes it easier to keep secrets," Emerald agreed.

[And to hide a murderer,] I added silently.

We kept walking. Soon enough, the familiar sharp hand of the newer inscription gave way to more weathered and careworn markers. Moss grew in the little cavities formed by the older letters, and pale lichen clung to the stones, which were white as sun-bleached bones. At the very back, closest to the wall of the church, stood the largest headstone of all. Unlike the others, this one was surrounded with small trinkets and wilting flowers.

"*Throop of Dunmore.*" I frowned at the dates carved under his name. "Dead more than three centuries, and yet people still honor him."

"It's the oldest stone in the cemetery," Emerald noted. "Perhaps he founded the town."

"Have you heard that name before?" It ticked something in the back of my mind, but the faint memory it sparked was not my own.

"I don't know..." Emerald rubbed his chin, frowning even more deeply than usual. "I think I've read it, but I don't remember where."

I couldn't resist a jab at his earlier display of intellect. "So the names of dead men don't come to mind as readily as the names of flowers?"

Emerald let out an annoyed puff of breath that turned smoky in the cool spring air. "I like plants more than people."

"Oh, I don't know about that. I expect it would depend on the plant—and the person." I grinned at him and ran a hand over my skirts.

Emerald was clearly prepared to respond when a low voice interrupted our conversation.

"Good afternoon, Crimson Flame. Have you found what you are looking for?"

I whirled to face a robed figure. Whoever it was was no match for Emerald's bulk, but stood as tall as my companion, made taller still by the square hat that perched atop his head. There was no mistaking this person for anyone but a citizen of Dyrne; his manner of dress was all too familiar, but the material was both more luxurious and more plentiful than that of the average citizen. His robes were a deep purple shot through with golden thread, forming writing in a language which I did not recognize. Beneath his flowing garments were white bandages, criss-crossed over his face and arms.

"Nechtan?" I guessed, curtsying in a preemptive show of respect.

"Indeed. It is a pleasure to make your acquaintance, Simone of..." Nachan paused. "Now, forgive me, but I do not know where you are from."

Emerald offered no aid, so I gave the high priest my most

winning smile. "I am uprooted, sir. I am a creature of the road. I owe no allegiance to any town. We are but servants of the people."

"I see." Nechtan clasped his hands together before him. "Let me welcome you to Dyrne, Simone of the Road. And you—" Nechtan turned to Emerald. "I sense that you are a follower of Aster?"

Emerald nodded, eying the priest mistrustfully. "I am."

"Aster is a kind and loving goddess whose acolytes are always welcome here. She smiles on you." Nechtan's voice softened. "Even in dark times."

Sensing my companion's discomfort, I interceded. "Everyone we've met here has spoken with such fervor regarding their own devotion, but I know little about the god you serve."

Nechtan bowed his head. "I am a devotee of Dathan. Are you familiar with the faith?"

Emerald shook his head.

"Dathan is a kinsman of Aster. He is a god of life, of ancestry and lineage. Lord of the past, weaver of the future." He gestured to his clothes. "We wear his colors to celebrate his many gifts."

"Right." I glanced at Emerald. "That certainly makes sense. Speaking of lineage, would it be possible to view a list of residents of the town? Genealogical records, perhaps?"

Nechtan bowed his head again. "I'm afraid that will not be possible. Such records are private. You understand, if people…"

"Can't trust the clergy, who can they trust?" I finished for him, echoing Tincrown's earlier sentiment. "Of course, I agree in full. But surely there is a record of the current townfolk? Perhaps a census?"

"The Conjury scouts took down those records, may the gods keep them." Nechtan folded his hands over chest and bowed to the earth. There was something rehearsed and theatrical about his movements that made me mistrust him, but then again, since he could not communicate through his cloth-covered expressions, body language would have to do.

"And let me guess," Emerald said. "You don't keep copies of those records for us to review?"

"I'm afraid the only records I keep are the family trees in the church. They are inscribed in the very walls of the building itself."

"Perhaps we could be let in to look at them?" I smiled hopefully.

"Impossible."

"Even if we could only get a look at them for a moment, I'm sure..."

Nechtan's voice turned icy, and his shoulders pressed back, drawing him to an even greater height. "*I said no*. Non-believers are not welcome in the House of Dathan. It would be sacrilege. Unless the Conjury intends to strong-arm its way even into the confines of our holy houses?"

I fell back a pace, even though Nechtan had not advanced. His height had not frightened me, and as far as I knew he could not strike or harm me in any way, but Nechtan was an agent of the divine. Who knew what sort of power he might wield if he wished?

"N-no, of course," I stammered. "I was only asking."

"And you have received your answer," Nechtan intoned.

We fell silent for a moment. Emerald's visage had darkened, and I had the unfortunate feeling that our conversation might come to blows if it continued in this vein. For once, however, I could not think of a single thing to say to break the tension.

Fortunately, another voice echoed across the graveyard. "Good afternoon, Holy Father!"

All three of us turned toward the nearby road, where a robed figure was waving at us. I did not know her, but she was walking arm-in-arm with Parian. He was dressed as he had been the night before: in ragged breeches and a half-unbuttoned tunic, showing as much skin as possible. He would have appeared somewhat wayward even in Lower Bound, but in rigid Dyrne, his attire bordered on scandalous.

"Ah, Kristine." Nechtan's voice turned soft, and he wandered between the headstones toward the two figures. "How lovely to see you. Will you be joining us at our services this evening?"

"Of course." She curtseyed to him. "I never miss them."

"And what about you, Parian?" Apparently the high priest was not always warm with his neighbors, either. The way he addressed Parian was not hostile, but it was not kindly, either.

"You know full well what I think of your *services*, Nechtan." Parian did nothing to hide his disdain. "Praise be to Dathan, Lord of the Living and the Dead, He Who Decides That We Must All Hide From His Holy Eye. No, thank you. I'm in no rush to fall in line and join your rites. I don't need your costumes, and I don't need your prayers."

His companion—swaddled in the garb he was so quick to decry—shook her head. "I'm sorry, Nechtan. We should be going. I'll see you this evening."

"Until then." Nechtan bowed. When the two young people set down the road again, he watched them for a time before slowly turning back to us. "Teenagers," he sighed. "I try my best, but there are always some who flout our ways. He'll come around. They always do." All his performative bravado had fallen away, and he simply seemed like a man now—a man who could use a drink and a long rest in a comfortable chair.

One must become accustomed to performance in his position, I thought. It bothered me, though, how many people we'd met who seemed adept at the art of changing faces.

"Thank you for your time, Nechtan." I bowed to him and shuffled sideways between the stones. "We won't trouble you any more. Of course we respect your faith, and your dedication both to your god and your people..." ***[Say something, Emerald. Say the*** right ***thing, because I certainly don't know what it is.]***

"Is admirable. Praise be to Dathan," Emerald said. His tone was unremarkable, but it did not escape my attention that he used the very words Parian did when insulting both Nechtan and his god.

I offered one last sickly smile and then turned on my heel, fleeing toward the gate which was, to my relief, still open.

[Gods, that was unpleasant. Do you think he knows something? Or does he simply hate the Conjury?]

[Oh, he knows something, alright. The holy always do.] Emerald slammed the gate behind us.

[You think there's something in those records we shouldn't see?]

[Without a doubt.]

[But how are we going to get it?]

Emerald bared his teeth, casting a bitter look back toward the church. *[That's the job* **you** *were made for, remember?]*

Chapter Eleven

yrne had been charming by day, but under cover of darkness it became altogether ominous. A heavy mist formed over the village at sunset, and the light of three moons cast weird shadows between the houses.

The streets were empty and the windows were dark. Other than the calls of nightjars and spring frogs, the town was silent.

[I don't know what you think I'm going to be able to do,] I thought as I followed at Emerald's heels. *[I can hardly pick the locks of the church door. Do you expect me to dictate a list of names from the wall-carvings?]*

[Even better than that. You'll see.] Emerald seemed positively gleeful about our late-night jaunt. I suspected that he was looking forward to going against Nechtan's decree. From what I could tell, Emerald took no particular offense to everyone's mistrust of the Conjury, but he clearly bore no love for other rule-makers, either.

As we walked, I went over everything we'd learned in the last two days. Emerald had told me to confine myself to the facts. So far I had done that as best I could, but the evidence was either too plentiful or too sparse, depending on what angle I examined it from. I liked Tincrown well enough, but I was certain he had not told us everything he knew, and Nechtan had outright refused to provide us with information we'd requested. There was also Parian, who clearly hated the Conjury and the church of Dathan, but other than his rash behavior, I had no evidence against him. He had been awful to Emerald, but if someone wanted to get away with murder, wouldn't they try to be a bit more covert about their intentions?

I stopped myself. That was pure speculation, based on what I thought I would do if I was the killer. The only thing I was quite sure of was that the scouts had been killed for what they uncovered on their visits. Perhaps if I could work out what that information *was*, I would be able to solve the puzzle before me. The clues would lead me to the killer.

Or else the killer would come to us.

I expected Emerald to approach the church directly, but instead he led us back into the graveyard at its side.

"What are we doing here?" I asked.

He drew up short at the spot before the monumental gravestone honoring the memory of Throop. *[I thought it would be better to come this way. I won't have* much *of an excuse if Nechtan happens to see me here, but it's better than hiding around back, anyway.]*

[Ah, so I'll be going in. You could have said so. In fact, you could have sent me alone—]

Once, back toward the beginning of my life, Emerald had compelled me to approach the innkeeper. The sensation had been disquieting, but I had not understood what I was, or what Emerald was to me.

This time was worse in every way. One moment, I was myself. The next moment, I was crushed into the back corner of my own mind. *[Stop—!]* I began, but Emerald either didn't hear me or didn't understand my fear. I could only watch helplessly as my form walked through the wall of the church, slipping between the stones. It did not *hurt* precisely, but it was immensely jarring. Whenever I shared space with a material object, that object took precedence. Being thrust between the stones made me feel small. Insignificant. Unreal. Stepping between the walls of our rooms was a choice. This was not.

I would have happily slipped into the church by this very route if Emerald had only asked; but he had not, and the difference between agreeing and being forced against my will was incalculable.

My form reached the far side of the wall and strode through a darkened chamber. Even the way I moved was wrong. Feeling present in my body was the one thing that had kept me grounded over the handful of days that comprised my life. Under Emerald's control, even my gait was his.

Stop, I cried again, *let me go,* but I knew that Emerald could not hear me. I had been forced so far out of myself that even my mind was not my own.

Emerald folded my hands behind my back and drew up short. "Interesting." He lifted my hand before us, closed my eyes, and took a deep breath that must have echoed in his own body. A moment later, a small flame flared to life in my palm. Coirpre had done the same when he was trying to escape from his disastrous performance. It had not occurred to me to wonder how either man could summon an illusion that *looked* like fire and *behaved* like fire and yet did not truly burn.

When Emerald has no more use for that little flame, he will snuff it out and think no more about it. It would be entirely too easy for him to do the same with me.

For the first time in my short life, I knew true fear.

Emerald was oblivious to my terror. He lifted my hand closer to the wall. The flame revealed an enormous relief cut into a slab of einwood, which reached from the floor almost to the vaulted ceiling. Tiny inscriptions, linked by deeply cut lines, cascaded across its surface. The words themselves were small, and their lowest point was at shoulder height. I recognized one of the names only two lines from the bottom. *Findrel of Dyrne*—we had seen that very name outside on a headstone that afternoon.

"Do you see that?" Emerald asked. The voice which emanated from our mouth was my own, but he did not speak as

I did. The rhythm was wrong, the inflection stilted. "And let me guess..."

My knees bent beneath me, and then Emerald jumped. Instead of merely hopping, I drifted up away from the floor toward the high beams of the nave, where every branching rivulet of names converged around a single point: *Throop of Dunmore.*

"Looks like he was quite the rake, eh?" Emerald chuckled. "Four wives. Woof. Seems a bit excessive, doesn't it? And look, further down, where the lines cross and converge. It seems that our little town is most unfortunately inbred. By the looks of things, they've had to bring in outsiders every few generations." My voice dropped to a growl. "And they call *me* as bad as a dog, when even a beast would leave the pack to find a mate."

I do not care what they call you, Emerald. You need to let me go!

He drifted back from the wall, squinting at the words as he went. "Do you see these little marks, beside the names? I don't know what they mean, but they appear to be intentional. Look, this one has a slash... this one an x... and this one no mark at all. I wonder what they describe. The manner of death, perhaps? No, look, even the newest names have them. Vanora and Kade are kissing cousins—well, that would explain how Parian turned out at any rate. And Vanora has an x beside her name, but Kade does not. Curious. Very curious indeed." He reached the floor and closed his palm over the little light, which was instantly snuffed out.

As he strode back through the wall, I swallowed a scream of frustration. How could he fail to understand how much this pained me, to be treated as if I was a tool and not a person, when for days I had done everything I could to convince him that I was now alive?

The moment I stepped through the wall, Emerald released me. I felt as a man must feel when he has been held underwater for so long that he fears his lungs would burst, and is finally allowed a breath of air.

"I found that rather illuminating, didn't you?" Emerald

crossed his arms and nodded at the wall of the church. "I don't know enough yet to understand the situation fully, but as we become more acquainted with the townsfolk we can always return to see what—Crimson? *Crimson!* Where are you going?"

The fourth and final moon had risen, lighting my way across the dewy grass as I fled Emerald's company. I could not bring myself to look at him. His control of my body had faded, but I still could not make myself speak. If I did, I was certain that I would scream.

[Crimson, come back here...]

I whirled to face him, still averting my eyes. "No! You don't get to talk to me as if nothing has happened! You don't have permission to reach into my head, not after what you did. I don't want to be anywhere near you!"

"After what I did?" he echoed. "What do you mean, Crim?"

"No pet names! No endearments!" I backed away from him, accidentally stepping through one of the headstones, which only made me angrier. Now that I was no longer helpless, my fear had transmuted into a fine fury. "You think you get to walk around inside me? That there's nothing wrong with donning me like a costume?"

"Is *that* what you're mad about?" Emerald threw his hands in the air. "Crimson, be reasonable." **[I needed to see what Nechtan was hiding, and that was the most expedient way...]**

"Stay out of my head!" I pressed my hands to my ears as if that would block him out. "I told you to stop, and you didn't listen."

"Cri—"

"You might have no regard for *your* body," I snarled, gesturing sharply to my arms with my fingers curled like claws, miming scratches on my arms with such violence that I frightened even myself. "That does *not* give you the right to take liberties with mine. I know that you do not see me as a person, Emerald. If I had doubted it before tonight, I would be certain of it now. I hope that whatever you learned from that gods-cursed carving was worth the loss of my sense of safety and any trust between us. Go back to your room, and I swear on my life, if you try to compel me home tonight, I will make *certain* you regret it."

I stood there, arms lifted between us, chest heaving even though I could not draw breath. I was vaguely aware that Emerald, too, was breathing hard, but I did not want to think about the thread that connected my psyche to his.

"I've done it a hundred times before," he murmured.

"Before I was a person," I shot back. "Before I told you time and time again that I am capable of feeling." I backed away another pace. "At least we have one thing in common tonight."

"And what is that?" he asked in a small voice.

"We *both* wish that we could be free of you forever."

I did not want to stand there and watch as his face crumpled, or experience the self-pity that would surely follow this pronouncement. All I wanted was to put as much distance between us as possible.

I ran. It was easy: there was no work to it. My feet seemed to fly over the packed-dirt road, past those quaint little houses, out toward the pond beyond the edge of town. I did not know how much time passed before I leapt over the pond stones and slipped silently into the water. It did not weigh my dress down. My feet did not slip in the mud of the bank. Not so much as a ripple spread out along the surface of the water as I stood there, half-submerged, gazing down at my own reflection.

"I am real," I said aloud, bending closer to the mirror of my own face. "Even if he does not see me as such, *I am real.*"

I stood there unmoving for a long time. The first of the moons set, and still I did not vanish. Emerald must be awake. Perhaps he was lying in his bed, tossing and turning, feeling unutterably small and mean.

It serves him right, I thought, although I was beginning to feel a twinge of guilt for what I snarled in the graveyard. I had said horrible things to him, yes, but what he had done to me was wrong, and I could not begin to imagine how I would forgive him.

A branch cracked behind me, and I whirled in the direction from which the sound had come. "Hello?" I called. "Is someone there?" I was suddenly aware that the song of nightbirds and courtship calls of spring peepers had cut off.

Nothing moved in the wood around me.

"Emerald?" I took a few steps into the deeper part of the pond toward the source of the noise.

I could not see anything. Perhaps some animal was on the prowl, hunting along the banks in hopes of apprehending easy prey, but I did not think so.

I took a few more steps, braced for a confrontation, fists raised out of some foolish instinct. I was only a few paces from the verge when I heard a bell, and then a bleat, and spotted a dozen pairs of silvery eyes staring at me.

"Hello, nanny," I said, relaxing as the herd of goats approached the edge of the water.

The nanny goat we had encountered the previous morning chewed a few times, snorted, and then let out another bleat. When I did nothing to hold her attention, she turned and trotted off between the trees with her herd at her heels.

In their absence, the natural sounds soon returned. I waded to the bank and sat down among the stones, drawing my knees up to my chest and watching the course of the moons marking silver trails across the water. All of them had dipped below the horizon by the time I disappeared.

Chapter Twelve

I appeared in Emerald's room late in the morning. My companion sat on the bed, hands folded in front of him, elbows resting on his knees, looking anywhere but at me. I immediately spun away from him, crossing my arms and glaring out the window.

"Sunrise must have been hours ago," I said coldly. "Were you thinking that you might be better off if you did not summon me at all?"

"No," Emerald rasped. He coughed to clear his throat. "No, that idea did not occur to me. I'm only just waking up. Last night was long. I didn't sleep well."

I snorted and glanced over my shoulder at him. "That must have been *so* hard for you."

"I'm not fishing for pity. You asked. I answered." He got to his feet and ran his hands over his wrinkled shirt. Evidently, he had slept in his clothes. There were dark circles under his eyes, and his gray-green skin had a pallid cast. My resolve to despise him wavered and cracked. He really did seem miserable.

A flash of color at my shoulder caught my eye, and I looked down at my new attire. In place of my traveling dress, Emerald had conjured me a stunning gown of the deepest blue, shot through with silver threads so that it glimmered like moonslight on the sea.

"Sapphire damask," I observed. "How tasteful. I accept your apology."

"I won't do it again," he blurted. "It didn't occur to me that it would be a problem. I thought—"

"You thought that you'd created me, and therefore you owned me. So long as it doesn't happen again, you are forgiven. As for what *I* said—"

"No need to explain." He waved one hand at me and dug the palm of the other into his eye, swallowing a yawn.

"I didn't mean it."

"Of course not. Now, let's get going before we lose any more time."

I was fairly certain that Emerald had not really listened to my words, but the conversation was clearly over. He hadn't tried to use our mental connection yet, either. I appreciated that he was respecting my wishes, but I also wondered if there was more than an apology hidden in his actions. Was it possible that he was angry with me?

You didn't like when he violated your autonomy, said a little voice in my head. *Why would he feel any differently than you do?*

I wanted to discuss the matter further, but instead I let it go for the time being. "I'm going to my room. Come collect me when you're ready."

"I'll only be a moment," he grunted, reaching for his vest.

I stepped through the wall, still wondering what to say to set things right, but when I reached the room next door all such thoughts were driven from my mind.

Someone had come into the room the night before, and presumably it hadn't been Emerald. The bedclothes were tossed onto the floor, the drawers of the little bureau stood open, and wall-hangings torn down. Muddy footprints criss-crossed the floor. I stood in the middle of what looked like a war zone. Whoever had done this had not simply been hunting for something. They had been enraged.

"By the way, I was thinking—" Emerald pushed the door open and stopped cold. "Gods above and below, what happened here?"

"Someone must have come in last night." I rotated on the spot. "You haven't been locking the door, have you?"

"No. People might find it strange that I lock you in, rather than you locking the door from the inside. Since there was nothing to steal, I didn't think to lock this room when we left yesterday." Emerald stepped inside and closed the door behind him. He knelt on the floor to examine the prints. "Whoever did this was barefoot. Odd, I wonder why?"

"They were looking for me," I murmured, too lost in the bigger picture to properly absorb the details.

"Evidently." Emerald glanced up. "They couldn't harm you, though, Crim."

"But they intended to." I waved a hand to encompass the damage. "Whoever did this wasn't here to ask after my health."

"True enough." Emerald placed one hand on the floor, still studying the damage.

"We should ask Cait if anyone heard a racket last night."

Emerald sighed and got to his feet. "And how would we explain the fact that you didn't notice it earlier?"

"I'll tell her the truth: that we fought last night, and I slept elsewhere."

"Of course." Emerald nodded. "And that will *certainly* convince them that we're not a couple."

"Who cares about that?" I demanded, gesturing to the room. "Emerald, what if this person had come to *your* room last night? What if they'd hurt *you?*"

His eyes found mine, and his lip curled ever so slightly. "Then we would both have gotten our wish."

"Don't you *dare*—"

"I'll tell her about it." Emerald turned toward the door. "And we'll stay in one room tonight, as we should have all along. This farce isn't only expensive, it's impractical." He stalked out of the room toward the stairs.

I wished, not for the first time, that I could knock some sense into him through one means or another. On the other hand, I was relieved that Emerald had not been hurt. The words I had spoken in anger the night prior were patently untrue. If anything happened to him, I would be distraught.

Furthermore, if he vanished, what would become of me?

Cait apologized profusely for the damage to the room and insisted on moving our quarters at no cost.

"This is terrible," she fretted. "Who would come into my business to harm someone?"

"The same person who's already killed at least three others?" I suggested.

Cait shook her head. "Of course the whole situation is terrible, but to think that something might have happened here, under my own roof, is beyond belief. I will pray to Dathan for guidance and for your safety. In the meantime, take the room above mine. There are two beds, and I'll be just below you if anything more should happen. I can hear everything that takes place in the room above me."

Emerald and I exchanged a look.

"I'll mind my own business, of course," Cait hurried on. "I won't listen in on any personal matters."

I held up a quelling hand. "That will be perfect. Thank you."

Cait bowed at the waist. "I'll have your things moved."

We left the inn, lost in our own thoughts. Emerald had a strange look on his face, and I wondered if he'd put something together that I'd missed. In the light of day, now that I'd had a little time to clear my head, I puzzled over what we'd learned in the church the night before. People in this village were closely related, but I wasn't sure that was particularly odd in a little settlement like this. It did explain one thing, however. Whoever was guilty had ties within the community, and everyone would be eager to shield them from discovery.

"Who should we seek out today?" I asked.

"I was thinking that we should talk to Kristine," Emerald

said.

"Parian's girlfriend?" Our brief encounter the day before hadn't told me much about her.

"She seems like a nice young woman. Devoted to her faith." Emerald snorted and rolled his shoulders. "I can't imagine what she's doing with a boy like that, but such things aren't for me to understand, I suppose."

I looked around, then leaned closer to him. "Do you think he might be the one responsible for everything?"

"I have no proof," Emerald said.

"But you have a, how did you put it? A gut feeling?"

"Only two people in this town have been outright hostile to us, and Parian is one of them." Emerald lowered his voice. "Nechtan is the other."

[Ah,] I thought, reasoning that we had better be covert when it came to this particular subject. If the people of Dyrne were protective of their kinsmen, I could only imagine how they would react to accusations regarding their religious leader. *[So you don't trust the high priest, either?]*

[I never trust leaders,] Emerald replied, *[especially religious ones.]*

At that moment, a flash of color caught my eye. The robes of every person in Dryne were of a similar style, but I was coming to realize that they were not quite the same. It was possible to identify each person by the hue and pattern of their attire. In a town where one could not recognize one's neighbor based on their face, it would be helpful to recognize the cut and color of their garments instead. Already I could have picked Cait out of a crowd, because she preferred trousers and high white stockings rather than a more traditionally feminine skirt. Nechtan, of course, wore the most ornate outfit of all. The man we were walking past just now seemed familiar, if only because his clothing was dominated by a pastel blue tone. I stopped abruptly and turned to him.

"Hello, there!" I called. "Pardon me, sir, but might I have a moment of your time?"

The man looked around as if to see who I might be flagging down. Realizing that I was indeed focused on him, he trotted over and dipped into a little bow.

"Good morning, miss. How can I help you?"

[Yes,] Emerald thought, frowning slantwise at me. *[I'd like to know that, too.]*

I smiled at the stranger. "Are you by any chance a goatherd? I believe we met your flock on our way into town." *[I'm quite sure he's wearing the outfit we saw thrown over the tree in the woods that first morning.]*

[I believe you're right.] Emerald nodded, clearly impressed.

The man laughed. "You did indeed! I'm sorry that I didn't greet you back then."

"You saw us by the lake?" I asked. "We noticed your clothes, but nothing else."

"That's as I intended," the man chuckled. "I'm afraid that you came upon me in a rather, ah, *vulnerable* position. You see, I was skinny-dipping in the lake when I heard you approach. I slipped off into the woods to hide my shame, as it were."

"Leaving your goats at our mercy?" Emerald raised both eyebrows in a show of utter skepticism.

"I wasn't far away," the man said. "I'd have intervened if necessary, and I daresay that if you'd had any ill intention toward them, you'd have gotten the shock of your life to have a stranger charge toward you with their niblets flappin' in the breeze." He chuckled again. "Begging your pardon, miss, but I thought it best to spare you the sight."

"In that case, I am grateful to have been spared the company of your... niblets." *[Do I want to know?]*

Emerald laughed and quickly turned it into a cough. *[Doubtful.]*

"At any rate, it's a pleasure to meet you now." The man bowed deeply. "The name is Dun."

"Simone," I told him, curtsying in return.

"Lovely name. I'm at your service, Miss Simone." I was

certain that Dun was smiling at me, but since I could not see, my eyes were drawn to his waist, specifically to the slingshot hung at his belt. Amaya had told us that the babblebird Maximilien had tried to send to the mainland was brought down by one.

[You don't suppose we should look into him more, do you?] I asked.

[What do you intend to ask him now? If he trashed your room last night?] Emerald clicked his tongue. *[We already had a plan. Let's not deviate from it now. We can always track him down later if we deem it necessary.]*

"I'm so glad that we were able to meet at last," I told Dun, curtseying again. "Could you by any chance tell me where I might find Kristine?"

"The schoolmarm's daughter?" Dun shrugged. "I don't know for sure, but it must be nearly lunchtime. Her mother, Davina, will be in the schoolhouse at this hour. You could try asking her." He pointed up the road to one of the buildings. "Just there. I can walk you, if you like."

"I would appreciate it, truly." I cast him what I hoped was another charming smile.

"Are you coming, too?" Dun turned his attention to Emerald.

"Where she goes, I go," my friend grunted.

[How charmingly proprietary.]

"As you say, sir. Come along, then!" Dun struck up a cheerful whistle and led us down the street toward the schoolhouse. Just as we approached the neat, single-floored building, a cluster of schoolchildren in child-sized versions of their parents' outfits burst forth from its interior and ran giggling through the street. A few of them produced slingshots much like Dun's and began whirling them over their heads.

"Do many people in town use slingshots?" I asked, pointing toward a knot of children who had knelt down to gather pebbles from the street.

"Oh, nearly everyone," he said. "In fact, I can't think of anyone who doesn't. They're a popular toy and a useful tool. Personally, I don't know what I'd do without mine. I've defended my flock from many a weirling without shedding a drop of blood, and those of us who keep gardens use 'em to scare off the crows."

"Where is your flock now?" I asked.

Dun waved back up the street. "I brought 'em in this morning and penned them just outside of town." He leaned closer and lowered his voice conspiratorially. "Used to bring 'em with me, but last year my nanny got into Davina's garden plot and et the tops off all of her carrots. I thought she was going to skin me alive."

I laughed at the idea of the goats running amok in town. "It's a good thing you penned them, then."

"I've got to," Dun said. "She got so mad about it, the mayor wrote up an ordinance."

"In that case," Emerald said, "perhaps we'd better go in and talk to her on our own."

"A wise choice." Dun nodded. "Lest the memory of her mangled tubers cause her any undue distress. On that note, I'll leave you here. Good luck, Simone! May you find Davina's good side, assuming she still has one." He waved and set off again, leaving us outside the schoolhouse.

[I don't like when men do that,] I thought, turning toward the schoolhouse door. *[The men of Dyrne seem to think that women should be compliant and subservient.]*

[How do you gather that?]

[You saw how Aindreas and Kade treated Vanora the other night. She was expected to do everything. She cooked, she served the meal, she even tidied up the dishes.] I stopped just shy of the schoolhouse door. *[And all the leaders we've met are men. Granted, that's only Mayor Reade and Nechtan, but I suspect there's a fair bit of suppression at play in Dyrne. I become more and more certain that our culprit is a man.]*

Emerald chuckled and raised his fist to knock at the door. *[Because men are taught that they are entitled to commit violence when it suits them? It's possible, Crimson, but I*

wouldn't write off the possibility that a woman is our culprit just yet. The female of the species is often just as dangerous as the male, and frequently moreso.]

"Come in," called a brusque voice from the far side of the door.

With a wink in my direction, Emerald pushed the door open. Inside, a woman sat scribbling on a sheaf of paper, seated at a desk at the head of the open room.

She wore the colors of the town, but her hood had been set aside, and her pale blue gloves lay folded on the top corner of the desk. Her fingertips were stained black with ink; evidently, her quill had leaked onto them.

The woman glanced up as we entered. Scarlet, white, and vivid yellow made up the primary colors of her unusually simple garments, but the yellow was echoed in the curtain of golden hair spilling over her shoulders. Precious gems gleamed at her throat, and a series of small silver hoops adorned her ears. She fixed her eyes on us as we approached.

"I beg your pardon," she said in an arctic tone. "I thought you were my daughter stopping by with lunch. You've caught me in a rather compromising situation." She gestured to her uncovered face and bared her teeth in a mirthless smile. "Please be so kind as to refrain from mentioning this to anyone. It isn't good form to show one's face to strangers."

"Don't worry, I do it all the time," I assured her.

The woman did not so much as crack a smile.

With a distressed glance toward Emerald, I curtseyed to the seated woman. "You must be Davina. My associate and I hoped to have a few words with you."

Davina nodded and set her pen aside. She reached for her gloves and tugged them on in one smooth motion. "You're here about the Conjury scouts. Word travels fast in this town. You also insulted Vanora, I hear?"

"Unintentionally," I said. "And only after her son was—" I caught myself before I could say anything unkind about one of

Davina's neighbors, a man who was most likely a not-so-distant kinsman.

To my surprise, however, Davina's lips quirked into a small smile. "I assume that you're referring to Parian? I've known him since he was a student of mine. The boy has always been a handful. I believe he said some untoward things about you, sir." She nodded to Emerald. "I did my best to teach him manners, but I believe you can intuit how successful *that* was."

"Would you call it 'bad manners' to say aloud what everyone is already thinking?" Emerald asked.

Davina leaned back in her seat as she examined him. "That depends on what everyone is thinking, I suppose. But you are right, I misspoke. What I failed to teach the boy was the ability to think for himself. He still believes that going against the grain is the mark of an independent mind, when in fact he is as shackled to public opinion as those who buy into it without question."

Emerald's eyebrows rose. "And you believe yourself liberated from such things?"

Davina threw back her head and let out a bark of bitter laughter. "Believe me, I know enough to understand that the monsters who pass as decent men are more insidious than those who we label outsiders based on race or creed. I have earned the right to think for myself, and I will not let social mores dictate who I respect and who I hold in low regard."

Davina's countenance was cold, but I liked her attitude. It was clear that she had seen more than her fair share of difficulties over the course of her life, and they had only served to make her stronger.

The door behind us creaked open, and Kristine stepped in. I knew it was her by the large puffs her sleeves formed around her shoulders, and the bell-shaped blue hems of both her sleeves and skirt. She was carrying a covered basket on one arm. When she saw Davina's face, she cried out and rushed to her mother's side.

"Why aren't you wearing your veil, Mama? Did something happen?"

"No, dear." Davina sighed. "I simply found it stifling, and once our guests had seen my face, there was no point in rushing to hide it, was there?"

"Please, Mama." Kristine lifted the cast-off garments and held them out to her mother. "You *know* what Nechtan says."

"Do you see what I mean about thinking for oneself?" Davina asked us. She accepted the hood and veil from her daughter's outstretched hands and pulled them into place. "There, are you content, my dearest?"

Kristine did not answer, and I wondered what expression she wore beneath her veil.

"These are the visitors Parian managed to offend within moments of their arrival." Davina waved toward us.

"Oh, I know it." Kristine placed one hand over her heart and got to her feet. "I am so sorry, sir. I love Parian dearly, but he is so obsessed with the surface of things, and he forgets Dathan's mandate to look deeper."

Emerald did not seem impressed by this display of regret. He lifted one dark eyebrow. "You mean to say that he should have given me the benefit of the doubt, despite my lineage?"

"Yes, exactly." Kristine nodded. "We cannot help what we are, Nechtan is always saying so."

[So Parian cannot help that he is an ass, and she cannot help that she is more condescending than she realizes,] I observed. ***[Truly, they make a fine and willfully ignorant pair.]***

Emerald cracked a smile at my thought.

Davina drummed her fingers on the desktop. "Has it occurred to you, my love, that our new friends might be offended by the notion that their identities could be a burden, rather than a treasure?"

"Whatever do you mean, Mama?" Kristine turned toward her. "They understood me quite plainly."

"I'm sure they did." Davina waved one hand to us. "Perhaps

we should move on from this subject. You wanted to ask us something?"

"We wondered if you could tell us anything about the Conjury scouts who perished," I said.

"Oh, isn't it *awful?*" Kristine cried. "Nechtan says that we must pray for their souls, may Dathan keep them." She crossed her arms over her chest and bowed her head, much as our hosts had done while saying prayers over that ill-fated dinner on the night of our arrival.

"I never met any of the Conjury scouts, other than Dawyd," Davina said. "Everyone adored him, and he came to feel like one of our own. He got to know people. The island was his home, and he understood how difficult it can be to make a good life out here. The others had no time for us and no respect for our traditions."

"That's not entirely true," Kristine said. When her mother looked up at her in surprise the girl went on. "The woman, Cassandra, *she* was alright. I spoke to her a few times while she was here. She was pleasant enough, and she showed a true interest in our way of life." She turned to us before elaborating. "Sheiling was sweet on her. They spent a great deal of time together."

"Sheiling?" I frowned at the sound of yet another unfamiliar name. "Who is that?"

"The shopkeeper in town," Davina explained. "He owns the general store. It doesn't surprise me that he flirted with her. I'm sure that if you go to speak to him, he'll shower you with affection, too. He chases after every foreign girl, and Dathan knows that there are few enough of them that come out this way."

"This was different," Kristine insisted. "They spoke at length. I think he really liked her. I believe that he may even have made... *advances*. She seemed to want to understand our traditions, and Sheiling convinced Nechtan to have a long talk with her before she left to finish her route. It's such a pity what became of her. I think she might have come to live here on the island, with Sheiling. But she never got the chance." Kristine sighed, and her shoulders drooped.

"Did you speak with either of the others?" I asked.

"Of the men? Of course not, other than for what was strictly necessary. The first one was all business, and the last one left before he even had a chance to complete his rounds."

"In that case, I suppose we should be headed out to have a word with the shopkeeper," Emerald said.

"Thank you very much for your help." I curtseyed to both women. "Before we leave, however, I have one more question for you. Kristine, your devotion to Dathan seems strong, and your respect for Nechtan is obvious. Why are you with Parian?" I wondered if it had anything to do with that branching family tree. Perhaps she had so few options within the village that she was more or less stuck with him.

Kristine twisted her fingers together, and I wondered how many times she had asked herself that very question. "Parian and I have adored each other since we were small. His convictions are not always in agreement with mine, it's true, but he is loyal and kind. He would do anything for me. I believe that he would even wear the robes, if I asked it of him, but I hope that he will come to Dathan of his own free will one day."

"Isn't young love divine?" asked Davina in a clipped voice.

"Speaking of love, isn't Papa due home today?" Krisitine asked.

"I believe he is." Davina's tone made her feelings toward her husband entirely too clear.

"Papa left the day before the scout set out," Kristine explained. Unlike her mother, she sounded delighted by the prospect of the man's return. "I hope he's alright... oh, but I'm sure he is. He knows the roads like the back of his hand."

This piqued my interest. Someone had left the village the day before Maximilien, only to return now that he was dead? We had assumed that Maximilien was running away from something when he fled the town, but what if we were wrong? What if he had been trying to catch up with someone, and had failed to find them on the road?

"Where exactly would your father have gone?" I asked.

"To the port, of course," Kristine said. "He's the village trader. His earliest trips out of town are usually at the spring equinox. Before then, the roads are too dangerous for him to take the cart."

"You mean to the port in Upper Bound?" Emerald asked. He did not look at me, but his nervous energy flickered through our connection.

It seemed we had found not one lead in the schoolhouse, but two.

[*Consider it,*] I told Emerald as we approached the store. [*What if someone in Dyrne is using the aidea toward a mischievous end? Perhaps Nechtan is doing something that the scouts found out about... like the Shine Errol makes in secret, but bigger? If he wanted to sell the fruits of his labors outside of the town, he would need someone to carry them to the port. For all we know, there is a black-market trade going on right under our noses. It's possible that Maximilien learned of it after the trader had already gone and rushed to catch up with him. Oh, and remember what we said at the high pass? If Cassandra agreed to travel alongside him, it would have afforded him the perfect opportunity to throw her over the ledge when she wasn't paying attention!*]

"Too many variables," Emerald grumbled. "Too many *maybe*s and *what if*s. So far, we have no proof of anything."

"You told me to follow my instincts," I reminded him. [*My instincts say that there is something to this.*]

[*Instinct isn't enough to try someone on.*]

[*I thought you hated the clergy! Now I have a theory, and suddenly you're defending the head of the local church? Look around, Emerald. People in this town would happily go wherever Nechtan commanded. He may not literally*]

***have the same power over them that you have over me, but
he can still steer them in one direction or another, as easily
as Dun steers his flock. The faithful rely on Nechtan for
guidance.]***

Emerald stopped short and held up his hands. "I'm not
defending anyone. I'm only saying that we need proof." Something just beyond me caught his eye, and he leaned to one side,
craning his neck to look over my shoulder. "Hold on. Don't we
know that man?"

I turned to see who he meant. Sure enough, the squat,
muscular figure of a figured trudging toward a heavily-laden cart
reminded me of someone. I stared at him for a moment before I
realized where I'd seen him.

"He was in the inn the night Maximilien died," I said.

"Yes, he was." Emerald's frown deepened. "In fact, I think he
followed us to the room afterwards. I believe that we corrected
his grammar."

"*Their money spends as good as anyone else's,*" I murmured,
recalling what the merchant had told us. "Funny, he didn't
mention the fact that he *lived* here."

"One might even go so far as to say that he went out of his
way to hide that fact." Emerald stepped around me and set off
toward the cart.

I had not asked the merchant's name the night of the
murder, but it was most certainly the same man. A few other
facts were obvious from his appearance alone. His height and
figure were a great deal like that of Bilk Deepvein's, while his
clothes were a more casual iteration of those worn by his wife
and daughter. He was a dwarf, but he was also a Dyrnian.

*I wonder if that puts him in a difficult position, now that his
kinsmen are making trouble for the town? Even if his loyalties aren't
divided, I'm sure that the likes of Parian have opinions about his presence
here.*

The moment he laid eyes on us, the merchant frowned.

"Good day," I said, curtseying before him. "Funny to see you
again, all things considered."

The merchant leaned against a box on the side of his wagon. "H'lo. Can't say I know you, though, miss. Now, your friend, *he* looks familiar."

For a fraction of a second, my pride was deeply wounded. How could he forget me, after the performance I'd put on in Lower Bound? He might have been distracted by the death, of course, but what about my confrontation with Coirpre? I daresay that must have been the most interesting thing to happen in that little town for quite some time.

Fortunately, Emerald was paying more attention than I was. He stepped forward and bowed to the dwarf. "We met in passing. Miss Simone wasn't feeling well that evening, and she was *quite* overcome when she heard about the unfortunate matter of the murder. Her brother and I investigated while she recovered. I believe we crossed paths outside the dead man's bedroom?"

"Oh, yes, I remember." The merchant lifted his flat-topped cap off of his balding pate and scratched idly at the shiny patch atop his head, of which—given the disparity in our heights—I had an excellent view. "Your brother was the loud, flashy so-and-so who put on that show with the bard, I take it?" He chuckled to himself. "Nothing funnier than watching two self-absorbed lads like that locked in a battle of halfwits, tryin' to outdo one another. Like watching two peacocks fight, innit? I doubt you were the only delicate female who was *quite overcome* that day."

My smile froze on my face in what I'm sure looked more like a grimace than anything else. ***[Halfwits? Delicate female!?]***

Emerald snorted and quickly covered it with a cough.

I was so put out, the thought I aimed at Emerald was loud even in my own mind. ***[He's married to Davina, the most sensible person we've met since we arrived! How can she tolerate him?]***

[Her tone when speaking of him suggested that 'tolerance' was the warmest emotion they shared,] Emerald reminded me. ***[Maybe she preferred to marry him than settle for wedding her cousin?]***

Perhaps he had a point, but it did little to soothe my

wounded pride. *[I should rather marry my own* **brother** *than tolerate a man like him.]*

[Yes, but in this case you are *your 'brother,' and judging by how much time you spend looking in the mirror each morning, it comes as little surprise to me that you think yourself the most attractive person in the region.]* Before I could protest this dig at my vanity, Emerald nodded to the merchant. "The two of them squabbling was rather an absurd sight, wasn't it?"

[Squabbling? How dare you reduce my finest performance into terms that make it sound like a mere cockfight!]

At my choice of words, Emerald choked back another laugh, which was lost in the burst of merriment which erupted from the dwarf.

"Oh, you are quite right!" the merchant cackled. "Like two matchbirds fighting over a mate!"

"An apt comparison, since matchbirds and bards are both more interested in showing off than in accomplishing anything." Emerald had clearly warmed to his subject. "If they hadn't been interrupted, I daresay they might have resorted to puffing up their chests and dancing around the table."

"While singing!" The merchant beat his fist against the side of his cart while tears of mirth spilled over his cheeks. "Quite right, quite right! I can see it now."

[I want you to know that I hate this,] I told my friend.

[Why? I'm doing exactly what you asked, aren't I? Talking more, forming bonds with the locals, warming them to my company...] A wicked twinkle had come into Emerald's eye.

I was prepared to protest, but in some regards he was quite right. This was, in fact, what I had asked for. Moreover, this was the first time since our fight the previous evening in which Emerald had truly felt at ease through our connection. If having a little fun at my expense was all that was required to smooth things over between us, I would bear his teasing nobly.

Still, I was determined to pay him back for it at some future date.

"Ah, I haven't laughed so heartily in months." The merchant wiped his palms across his face, smearing away his tears of laughter. "Dathan be praised, what a sight *that* would be. And after all that, the three of you find yourselves in Dyrne?"

"Only the two of us," I corrected. "My brother, Simon, left for the mainland by boat, while the two of us came here."

The merchant raised one shaggy red eyebrow at me. "Sounds as if *you* should have been sent to the mainland, Little Miss, if the sight of a dead body was too much for you."

"I believe I can stand my own," I said aloud. With every word, the man solidified himself in my mind as an undesirable personage. "I'm fully recovered from my... *swoon*." Oh, Emerald was going to pay for this, alright.

"In that case, I suppose you're here to poke your noses about the town." The merchant dropped his hat back into place and straightened up. The gloomy, sour air he'd affected earlier returned at once.

I nodded. "Indeed, we just came from speaking to your wife, although she didn't mention your name."

I hadn't intended this comment as a jab at the man's family life, but at the reference to Davina, his scowl turned into a sneer. "That doesn't surprise me, although I'm sure she had a lot to say about me anyway. The name's Shale."

"Shale of Dyrne?" I asked.

"Never thought of myself that way." He shook his head and directed his next comment to Emerald. "I moved here to marry the prettiest girl I'd ever met. I was young and foolish in those days. I thought beauty trumped everything—and the fact that her beauty was only for my eyes made it feel precious. So much for that. You see what a tough old bird she's become. Beauty never lasts, eh? Keep that in mind and don't involve yourself overmuch with pretty girls."

[What a wretched little man.] I squinted at him. *[And he says that he was young and foolish, but he can't have been that young. He must be older than Davina, mustn't he?]*

[By two decades, give or take,] Emerald agreed.

If Shale had married Davina for her looks, I couldn't imagine what Davina's motives for marrying *him* had been. Emerald had been quick to call me proud on more than one occasion, but I had seen the way Tincrown looked at him. Emerald might not be a great beauty, at least not by general consensus, but the attraction between them had been instantaneous. It was hard to imagine a similar chemistry between Shale and Davina, since he evidently had neither charm nor wit enough to recommend him.

"I see that you're wearing the local style, or at least a version of it." I gestured toward his colorful clothes. "Is that at your daughter's behest?"

"Ah, Kristine." Shale's expression softened. "That girl's the best thing about this town, and no mistake. She's got my brains, bless her." Shale snorted, and his mouth twisted into a wry smile. "Although her looks come from her mother's side of the family."

"The best of both worlds, then," Emerald said.

"That's one way of puttin' it. If it weren't for her, I'd be hard-pressed to think of a reason for coming back to this wretched town."

"A town which you failed to mention you called home," I pointed out.

Shale spat in the dust at his feet and stroked his beard absently. "Oh, come now, you've heard how the folks on the island talk about this place, as though it's cursed or haunted. If I'd come in boasting about the place, trying to tell them it was alright... well, they get funny ideas in the lowlands. We like our privacy here, so I keep my trap shut, don't I?"

I pursed my lips. **_[I'd find that more believable if we didn't know the full story. All these murders and disappearances add up to more than just 'the funny ideas of the lowlanders.']_**

"So there's nothing odd about Dyrne?" Emerald asked. "Nothing unusual?"

"Nothing more than in any other small town." Shale shook

his head and reached for a crate. "Pardon me, folks, but I've got work to do. Sheiling is expecting this delivery in a timely fashion."

"One more thing," I said hastily as he hoisted the nearest crate into his arms. "The other dwarves, from the Smith's Guild. Do you know anything about them?"

[Because all dwarves know one another?] Emerald asked. *[Look at you, making brazen assumptions about interrelations.]*

"You're asking about Bilk, I take it?" Shale grunted as he lifted the crate onto his shoulder. "He's my cousin's cousin, if you must know. We moved to the island together back in the day. I told him to leave this town alone, but he saw how well I've done for myself, and he wouldn't be deterred. Greedy wretch, he has no regard for privacy, even though I warned him—" Shale snapped his mouth shut.

"Warned him what?" I asked as we followed him to the door of the shop.

"My family lives here," Shale muttered. "And if he and those boys of his end up polluting our water supply with their digging, there will be hell after hell to pay." He elbowed the door of the shop open and stepped through.

Emerald caught the door before it swung closed.

[See, aren't you glad I asked about the connection between the dwarves? Now we know that there's a link between Shale and Bilk Deepvein—]

[Stop!] Emerald's voice echoed through my head, a harsh reminder of the night before when I had exclaimed that very word in an attempt to forestall his intrusion into my mind. Unlike him, I took this warning seriously and froze with one foot above the ground.

[What? What's the matter?]

[Look where you're stepping,] Emerald said.

I glanced down to the floor of the shop, only to find that there was none there. Or rather, there were no boards as I had expected. Instead, a thick layer of white sand stood in its place.

Emerald slipped around me, still holding the door open. *[If you step on the sand, you won't leave footprints,]* he explained. *[It will look strange. Let me go first, and follow where I've stepped.]*

[What is the purpose of such a floor?] I wondered irritably. Other than to inconvenience me, I could see no reason for keeping a floor like this inside a shop.

[No idea, but we'll work with it for the time being.] Emerald went ahead of me, dragging his heels through the sand as he made his way to the counter where Shale, with the help of a figure in full Dyrnian robes, had set to work unpacking the crate he'd carried in.

Another person was already waiting at the desk, wearing another set of robes that was familiar to me.

"Good afternoon, Aindreas," I said.

He turned to look at me, then nodded his head. "Good afternoon, Miss Simone."

"Simone and Simon?" Shale looked up from his work and guffawed. "Gods above and below, your parents must have hated you."

"It does feel that way sometimes," I said, staring pointedly at the back of Emerald's head. "I'm glad to see you again, Aindreas. I'm sorry about the other night. I'm afraid that I offended your family terribly."

"You only finished what my brother started," Aindreas said. "I apologize again for his behavior. He's erratic. He doesn't know what to do with his anger, and until he finds an outlet for it, I'm afraid he will continue to lash out at anyone who comes within reach."

"Yes, he does seem to have a lot of unresolved rage," I murmured. Enough rage to destroy my room, perhaps?

Enough rage to kill anyone who represented the Conjury, an institution which he so clearly hated?

Emerald had warned me about speculation, so I let this pass for the moment. The shop owner turned from his work and came over to the desk carrying something he'd unearthed from the chest.

"Here we are," he said, in a voice muffled by the veil of his religious garb, as he handed over a bag. "I knew we were expecting a new shipment of flamestones today, and you're just in time. Is that everything?"

[Flamestones?] I asked.

[Stones imbued with the* aidea *that make it easy to start fires, even in damp conditions,] Emerald explained. ***[Like the Ignius I showed you.]***

[Wouldn't those require a license?]

As if he could read my mind, Shale looked up from his work and scowled at us. "Before you get a bug up your butt, you should know that I have records for everything." When the shop owner turned to him, Shale nodded in our direction. "Conjury folk. I don't want 'em trying to stick you with a fine, not when I pay a premium on import tariffs for even the smallest item."

"Oh. *Oh.*" The shopkeeper turned back to us. "Why, *hello,*" he purred. He leaned one elbow against the counter and nodded to me. "I'll be ready to help *you* in a moment, my dear. Just let me finish this little transaction and you'll have my undivided attention."

I couldn't see Aindreas's face, but there was little doubt in my mind that his expression mirrored Shale's, as the merchant rolled his eyes behind the shopkeeper's back.

"There are ten stones in there," the shopkeeper told Aindreas, getting back to the business matter at hand. "Is that enough? How many days will you be gone this time?"

"A week," Aindreas told him. "This should be sufficient."

"Another week? Oidche is working you to the bone. Didn't you just get back?"

"Indeed we did. We were gone for two weeks this time. There's an early migration of griffons near the mining encampment, and he was worried how their flight path would impact the local wildlife populations. They're ruthless when they're young."

"Just what we need. More trouble." The shopkeeper sighed. "As if this year hasn't been bad enough."

Aindreas nodded. "At least they're on the far side of the mountains. The town should be safe, although we may find ourselves with less meat on our plates." He looked over his shoulder at me, and I was certain that he was smiling under his veil. "Which means less *hagbraggh* to go around."

"That would be a shame," Emerald said in a flat voice.

Aindreas chuckled and fished a few coins out of the pouch at his waist, dropping them on the counter. "At any rate, Oidche will be in town for a few more days, while I'll be on my own for once. These are all I need, Sheiling. I'll step aside so that you can give our guests your... undivided attention." Lifting the little bag of imbued stones, he turned to leave. As he walked past, he murmured in a low voice, "Good luck, Miss Simone. You're going to need it."

Sure enough, now that this business was concluded, shopkeeper Sheiling turned the full force of his charm on me. "Simone, is it? What a *lovely* name. We don't get many foreigners around these parts. Are you really employed with the Conjury?"

"Indirectly," I hedged. I stepped out of Emerald's shadow into the smudges in the sand left by Aindreas's passing. My feet were sufficiently smaller than his that I could walk in his footprints without difficulty. "We're here to investigate the deaths of the prior scouts."

"Ah... yes." Sheiling's shoulders slumped.

"Did you know them?" I asked.

"I didn't speak much to the men, but Cassandra was something special." Sheiling's voice turned dreamy and tragic. "I really thought we had a chance. She was so wonderful. She'd been all over the continent, and she had so many interesting stories. When I heard what had happened to her, it broke my heart."

"Accident?" Shale repeated, getting to his feet. He hooked a thumb toward us. "Not to hear these two tell it. Not after what happened to the fellow in Lower Bound. According to them, it was a murder."

[Wasn't Shale one of the people who insisted that Maximilien's death was an accident?] I thought.

[Maybe he's come around to our way of thinking,] Emerald mused.

As Shale stomped through the sand toward the door, Sheiling collapsed against the counter, cradling his head. "No, no. So you truly mean to say that someone *killed* Cassandra? Who would do such a thing? Everyone loved her! Even Nechtan—" He stopped short and let out a shuddering breath.

"What about Nechtan?" I pressed.

Sheiling drummed his gloved fingers against the countertop. "Nechtan has to approve of any relationship that takes place in Dyrne. I had asked Cassandra to stay, or at least to come back when her route was finished. She and Nechtan spoke at length the day before she left, and I hoped that it meant she was considering my offer."

"You proposed to her?" I asked, puzzled. Based on the records we had seen, Cassandra couldn't have been in town for more than a few days.

"Not exactly," Sheiling explained. "At least, not yet. I didn't know her well enough, but I had hoped that she might be willing to discuss the matter somewhere down the road. She liked the island, and our old scout, Dawyd, had lived on the Western shore. It wasn't as if I wanted her to sacrifice her career for me. She could have kept up with her duties on the route twice a year and spent the rest of her time here." He sighed heavily. "If she'd chosen to leave, I would have understood, but to think that she died so horribly is a nightmare in and of itself. And to think that someone did that to her? On *purpose?*" Sheiling shuddered and clenched his hand into a fist. "I hope that you find whoever did it. She deserved better."

"You don't know who might have killed her, then?" I asked.

Sheiling was silent for a long time. Once again, I wished that I could see his face. Perhaps, if I'd been able to look into his eyes, I would have seen something there, some truth that he hoped to keep obscured from me.

"I know a few people I might ask," he said at last. "Believe me, Miss Simone, I'll let you know the instant I learn anything of use."

"And I shall be grateful if you do," I assured him.

He sniffled and nodded, but his romantic bravado from earlier was gone.

"May I ask you one more thing?" Emerald cut in. "The sand on the floor. What's the purpose of that?"

Sheiling straightened up and spoke more formally, as if trying to put aside the emotions that now plagued him. "We've had something of a pest problem lately. Ever since those dwarves started their mining operations, we've had shrewbugs popping up all over the place. They can chew through wood like it's paper, and I can't afford to put in a stone floor. The sand keeps them out and stops up the mouths of any burrows they try to dig. If I didn't keep them in check, they'd ruin the goods." He waved across the floor toward the door. "It doesn't fix the problem, but it helps."

I looked around at the room he indicated. It was a small store, but marvelously well-stocked. Presumably fresh produce didn't ship well, and Davina and Dun had already mentioned that the locals kept private gardens. Aindreas and Oidche provided the town with meat and Dun the milk, while Sheiling's store was filled with everything else a town might require. Pickled produce from around the continent, colorfully-wrapped candies, bolts of dyed cloth, thread, tools, dried grains, pots, pans, liquor, spices, and tea filled the shelves, which groaned under their weight. He must have a small fortune in supplies here. I could see why he'd want to protect his investments.

"It's a beautiful store," I told him.

"Thank you, you're too kind. I'm sure it pales in comparison to anything you'd find on the mainland, but I'm proud of it." Sheiling looked around, nodding in approval. "I make a decent living. It's not a grand life, but with Cassandra, it might have been a wonderful little adventure."

"I'm sorry for your loss," I told him, although the words

didn't seem quite right. Sheiling had been quick to flirt with me before we broached the topic of Cassandra. For all I knew, he was overselling the significance of their connection.

As we turned to the door, I found myself puzzling over something Sheiling had said. It made sense, I supposed, to ask the priest before agreeing to a marriage, but to seek religious counsel before entering into even a casual relationship seemed extreme. Then again, if Cassandra had any intention of staying in Dyrne, wouldn't it impact the whole community?

I was still wondering about this when Emerald reached the door, and Sheiling picked up a broom from behind the counter. He began to sweep away the tracks which Emerald, Shale, and Aindreas had left behind.

I thought suddenly of the muddy footprints someone had left in my room the night before. Sheiling may have blamed an infestation of shrewbugs, but perhaps there was another reason to keep sand on the floor. If someone entered the store in the night, Sheiling would know they had been there, even if the streets were dry.

Did he know more about Cassandra's death than he had let on? It was possible, but then again he'd seemed genuinely upset about her passing.

I was still torn in two directions over this when we emerged into the weak sunlight. Shale was grumbling to himself and swatting his arms around the wagon as though swatting away a cloud of gnats. When he saw us, he bared his teeth in an unfriendly smile.

[Today has been endless,] I complained as we walked along the road back toward the inn. ***[We've talked to half a dozen people and haven't learned a thing.]***

[Haven't we?] Emerald asked, stroking his chin.

I waited for him to elaborate, but he said nothing for a while. Before I could press him for an answer, a woman came bolting out of a nearby house. Panic was evident in every jerky movement of her limbs, and she spun in a circle crying, "Lidia? *Lidia?*"

At once, Emerald straightened and strode over to her.

"Ma'am? What's the matter?"

The woman began to tremble and sob, almost collapsing against him. Emerald was clearly startled by her touch, but he held the woman up as she pressed her hands to her veiled face and sobbed.

"My little girl, my Lidia! She's gone!"

Chapter Thirteen

❧

It did not take long for a crowd to gather around the woman. Shale strode over, followed by worried neighbors who appeared from the surrounding houses.

"What's the matter?" demanded one of the men, balling his gloved hands into fists. He turned his face toward Emerald as if preparing for a fight. "Did this big fella hurt you, Moira?"

"No," the woman wailed. "I'm fine, it's my Lidia. She's gone missing!"

The man backed off, although I saw that Emerald's lip curled back at the accusation. *[She's the one who grabbed onto me. Of course, they'd blame me for upsetting her.]*

[He acted on what he could see,] I reminded him. Emerald jumped, and I suspected that he had not meant for me to overhear that last thought.

[And on what he assumed,] Emerald added. *[Everyone's quick to blame the Jotunn.]*

[A girl is missing,] I reminded him. *[Who would you rush to blame? We're the outsiders, Emerald. It's natural to blame a stranger when trouble arrives in town.]*

I could tell that he wasn't entirely won over by my logic, but at least his defensiveness dissipated a bit. He patted Moira's back, and she hiccuped through her tears.

We had not been standing there long when Mayor Reade emerged from his offices alongside the violet-swathed figure of Nechtan. Both men strode over to where we stood, the mayor with his cane clutched tightly in one fist, the priest with his hands clasped before him.

"What's the matter, Moira?" the mayor asked.

"It's my daughter," Moira moaned. "She's gone. I thought she was asleep in her bed, but when I went to wake her from her nap, there was no sign of her."

Mayor Reade sighed and squeezed her shoulder. "There, there, Moira. We'll find your little girl, don't worry."

"Someone send for Oidche at once." Nechtan nodded to one of the nearby men, who hurried off along the main road in search of the Huntsman.

"Does this happen often?" Emerald asked the mayor.

Reade shook his head and leaned heavily on his cane. "There's nothing to be alarmed about, Master Emerald. You know how children are. It's not uncommon for them to go missing now and again, but they always turn up safe and sound."

[Not drowned in a lake? Or fallen from a cliffside?] I kept my skeptical musings silent so as not to alarm Moira. She was still in great distress, but the rest of the crowd had relaxed a great deal. I could not make sense of that. It was almost as if they thought Moira was overreacting. But who would feel such dispassion for a woman whose child had disappeared? It was almost as if they'd *expected* her to disappear.

"Perhaps we should search for her," Emerald suggested.

"That will not be necessary," Nechtan informed him. "I'm sure that we are all moved by your offer of assistance."

"No disrespect intended, sir," Emerald said, in a tone that suggested that it very much was, "but isn't that for the child's mother to decide?"

Moira stepped away from Emerald, doing her utmost to compose herself. "I agree," she said, swallowing her tears. "I'm sure Nechtan is right. Oidche will have no trouble tracking her down, and we'll soon be reunited." Unless I was very much mistaken, she was watching Nechtan to make sure he approved of her response.

Emerald returned to my side, absently running his palm over the front of his tunic and vest, smoothing away the wrinkles left where the woman had clung to him. "If you're certain."

Moira nodded. "I'm overwrought," she said. "I'm sure she's safe."

Three people are dead, I thought in bewilderment. *Is she a fool?* But Moira, I was certain, had chosen to tell herself this story for the same reason that I did not voice my concerns aloud. It would be monsterous to insist that the child had met an ill fate when there was still hope of her recovery. Although, if whoever had visited my room in the night had chosen to visit Lidia today, who knew what they might have done to her?

No, I would not think of it. The thought was too terrible, and it served no purpose to entertain it now.

I was still wracked with dismay when the man Nechtan had sent away returned. In his wake came an enormous figure which I at first mistook for a bear. On closer inspection, I realized that it was a man, but a man who draped himself in pelts with the same enthusiasm that the rest of the town donned cotton and silk. A whole skinned weirling was wrapped around him like a cape, with its head forming the hood and its paws crossed below his throat; the striped pelt of a badger girdled his waist like a loincloth, overlaying a heavy coat made of goatskin and mayhound hide; and beneath it all, the smooth silvery pelage of a mooncat formed his trousers, disappearing into the tops of his black leather boots.

"Nechtan," he grumbled, "what seems to be the trouble?" He looked as he sounded, as much like a wild animal as a man. He put Emerald's strong and silent act to shame.

"Moira's little girl, Lidia, has gone missing. She disappeared from her bed," the priest explained.

"Hmm." Oidche nodded. "I will go at once." Without

waiting for further explanation, he turned and lumbered down the street.

"There, you see?" Nechtan nodded to Moira. "All will be well, my child."

"Yes, of course." Moira let out a shuddering breath. "I'll await their return. Thank you, Nechtan." With that, she turned on her heel and withdrew to the house.

The crowd dispersed, with the neighbors returning to their homes as if nothing had happened. Emerald and I watched as they went back about their business. Nechtan and the mayor returned to the mayoral offices, although I noticed that they both looked back at us. Reade's face was as unreadable as Nechtan's, which took some doing, given that the latter was entirely obscured.

[This is odd, isn't it?] I turned in a circle as the observers withdrew. *[It's as if they don't care about the child at all.]*

Emerald nodded and turned to walk back toward the inn. *[It certainly is strange, but never fear, we shall get to the bottom of this.]*

[How?]

[If you're willing to assist, I have a suggestion. Once we can safely get out of sight, you can tail Oidche. You won't leave a footprint or accidentally step on a branch, so it shouldn't be difficult for you to follow him.]

I looked down at my highly visible brocade dress. *[I'm not exactly dressed for subtlety.]*

[Don't worry,] Emerald thought. *[I have a plan for that, too, if you'll trust me with an experiment.]*

The memory of the prior night came back with sickening clarity, and although we walked in broad daylight and the houses around me were as charming and solid as always, I couldn't help but recoil.

[If you're willing, I'll do something I've done before —without entering your consciousness. If it doesn't work, I'll put you back at once, just as you are now.]

We reached the door of the inn, which Emerald opened to

admit me. I did not answer him as we mounted the stairs to our new quarters, in part because I didn't know what my answer would be. I trusted Emerald not to do as he had done the night before... *mostly.* He claimed not to understand how awful an experience that had been, even though I had tried to stop him. How would he know if this new experiment 'worked?' Or did he simply mean that he would try it and see if the results suited him, with no regard for my own well-being?

Once we were back in the room, with the door closed behind us, I turned to take his measure. He was visibly weary and down at the mouth, but in every other regard he was the same as he had always been.

"How will you know if your experiment works?" I asked him.

Emerald rubbed his palms over his face and took a deep breath. "Last night, did you try to communicate with me at all? Through the link?"

"I kept telling you to stop." I crossed my arms over my chest and turned my face away from his. "I *begged* you. It was like you turned off my connection to myself. Everything about it felt wrong. Like you *unmade me.*"

"Oh, Crim." Emerald dropped into the edge of the bed nearest the window and hid his face in his hands. His shoulders trembled as he continued. "I know what it's like when others make you feel small."

"Not like this." I sat on the side of the bed facing him and folded my hands in my lap. "You might know things that I don't understand, about how people look at you and assume the worst, but you *don't* know what it's like to have someone else use your body like that. To make you walk in a way that doesn't feel right, to speak in a tone that you would never use, to compel you against your will. You *don't* know."

Emerald took a few deep breaths. "You might be surprised," he murmured. "But that was never my intention, Crimson."

"And yet, it was the result."

He dug through the pocket of his vest and produced the

bottle that Errol the lambkin had sold him. Uncorking the bottle, he took a deep swig of the Shine of the Moon.

Watching him, my heart broke a little. Emerald had made me, and we were connected on a deeper level than any two people alive, but that did not mean that I understood him. Sometimes, I doubted that he understood himself. There were so many parts of himself that he denied, or hid from, or shut out as best he could, even when they seeped in at the edges of his consciousness. Emerald thought himself ugly, but I was certain that the ugliness was inside him, planted in his psyche by some traumatic experience that he had tried to bury in the deep corners of his mind.

That is not your responsibility, I told myself. *It is not on you to fix every wrong that he has suffered.* And yet, he was my other half, my progenitor, the one who had brought me into the world on the strength of his imagination. I had assumed for some time that he had pictured Coirpre when he summoned me, imagining the perfect person, someone he longed for.

I had been wrong. He summoned the person whom he wished to be, someone beautiful and compelling, someone instantly accepted everywhere I went.

He wished to be me, and yet could not see the limitations he had set on me by making me everything that he desired. And all that was, still, his problem rather than mine. He envied me and loved me in equal measure.

Did he hurt me on purpose last night? Did he wish me to suffer as punishment for becoming independent?

Or did he simply want to be someone else, if only for a moment?

I swallowed hard and gripped my hands around fistfuls of my dress. "If you're going to try your experiment, you should do it now."

Emerald let his hands fall to his knees as he examined me. "Are you sure?"

"If you don't, we'll lose Oidche's trail." I rolled my shoulders back and lifted my chin. "Go on, try it."

Emerald fished a chain from within his shirt as he mirrored

my posture, closing his eyes and breathing deeply. For a fraction of a second, I could feel what he felt: a loosening of the muscles, the rush of air into his lungs, the calm of dipping into the *aidea* and reshaping one tiny fragment of the universe to fit his will. Power surged through him, and I bore witness to it, riding out the wave of energy that coursed through him. We were one creature, with all the force of the *aidea* at our fingertips.

Then, quite suddenly, I was myself again, although I did not recognize what I saw. I seemed to have grown quite small, since the bedclothes were now nearby and Emerald had tripled or quadrupled in size. I looked down at myself and found not a human body, but the shimmering black feathers of a bird, and spindly black legs to match.

[What am I?] I asked.

[A red-winged blackbird. They're a common songbird all across the continent.] Something on Emerald's end of our link relaxed. *[I take it that you're still Crimson?]*

I twisted my neck around to look at my wings. Sure enough, they were capped with a cluster of brilliant red feathers. *[So it seems.]*

[And it doesn't hurt?]

[No. Not in the slightest.]

Emerald ran his hand through his hair, then got up and walked to the window of the room. Undoing the latch, he flung it open. *[Well, go on then. Report back when you can. You've got a Huntsman to track.]*

Flight did not come naturally to me. When I first jumped off the edge of the bed I simply hovered in midair. After a few beats of my wings, however, I managed it; after all, the air pressure had no effect on me. I only had to envision myself in motion and it was done. I sailed out of the window over the rooftops of Dyrne.

[I'll let you know what I find!] I thought back.

[Be careful,] Emerald thought in reply. *[If you pass beyond a certain range, I'll lose you.]*

I understood his warning, but I was too preoccupied with the glories of flight to worry about what would happen to me if I passed outside those bounds. From up here, I could make out every detail of the town from a perspective I had never witnessed before. Dyrne was laid out below me like a map in miniature.

I wheeled over the town, searching for the bestial figure of Oidche. It took a moment for me to get my bearings from this unfamiliar angle, but soon enough I recognized the mayor's residence, and then Moira's home. From there, I followed the path that Oidche had taken.

A few people were out on the street, and my first impulse was to hide. But why should I? They could not guess who or what I was simply by looking at me. Nechtan was not the only one who could hide behind a disguise. To everyone else, I was nothing more than a bird. They could not see me as I was. It was *my* turn to hide in plain sight.

It took me longer than I had anticipated to find Oidche, and I would have lost him altogether if he hadn't emerged from a familiar house just as I passed overhead. Tincrown's residence, from this angle, looked like any house in Dyrne aside from the shingles which covered its roof in place of thatch.

I circled back and perched on the gutter; it was more difficult, in this form, to respect the bounds of tangible objects, and I nearly fell through the wooden trough before I managed to right myself.

"You're quite sure that the midwife has them?" Oidche asked.

Tincrown nodded, crossing his arms over his chest. "She needed them last."

Oidche grunted an affirmation and lifted a leather-clad hand to the brim of his weirling-skin hood, nodding to Tincrown. "May Dathan keep you, Doctor."

"And you as well." Tincrown nodded before closing the door behind him.

[Where are you?] Emerald asked. *[Are you safe?]*
[Oidche has just left the home of your doctor.]

I was not sure how Emerald managed it, but even through the mental link, he spluttered. *[He is not my doctor…]*

I ignored his protests and took flight again, following Oidche through the town as he traced the streets to another familiar home. It had never occurred to me to ask what Vanora's profession was, but the matter was soon settled. Oidche thumped a heavy fist upon her door until she answered. It swung wide, revealing the familiar figure whom I had unintentionally insulted more than once.

"Aindreas isn't here," Vanora said. "As a matter of fact, I believe that he left town already."

"I need the goggles," Oidche interrupted.

"The Dawyd-goggles?" Vanora asked. "Whatever for?"

"Girl went missing," Oidche grunted. "Doctor says *you* have them."

"I certainly do." Vanora stepped aside, permitting the Huntsman entrance to her home. "Whose child has run off this time?"

"Moira's," the Hunstman grunted.

"Little Lidia?" Vanora shook her head. "Well, *that's* no surprise. Moira's never been the careful sort."

I could not very well follow them through the front door, so instead I slipped through the roof as the pair stepped inside. I peered through the wall before flitting through and found Parian lounging on his bed on the second floor, flipping through the pages of a book. Passing him by, I swooped lower through the wall until I could see Vanora and Oidche moving about in the kitchen.

"I put them in the desk for safekeeping," Vanora was saying. "If I have to deliver a baby blind, I'll be giving Moira a piece of my mind big enough to choke her until fourth moonrise... it's a blessing that no one is due until the end of the month." She whipped out a small rectangular box and slapped it into Oidche's hand. "There you are. I knew I'd put them away safely."

Oidche opened the box and removed a pair of goggles. He slid the strap over the back of his hood and positioned the lenses over his eyes. "Thank you," he said. "I'll return them when I've found the girl."

Vanora waved a hand. "Take them to Tincrown and have him look the girl over. I'll retrieve them when I need them."

Oidche nodded and turned back to the door.

[Interesting,] I thought to Emerald. *[Oidche's just retrieved a pair of goggles from Vanora. Did you know that she was the midwife of Dyrne?]*

[Didn't think to ask,] he replied. *[Did they say what these goggles do?]*

[Only that she'd be blind without them. Oidche assumed that Tincrown had them, but he was wrong.]

As Oidche headed down the street, I left the wall and soared after him, altering my course periodically so that I would appear aimless if anyone happened to notice me. It was a long shot, but *someone* had deemed it a worthwhile effort to shoot down a babblebird. A slingshot wouldn't harm me even if I was spotted, but my imperviousness to stones might raise some questions.

Emerald kept his own counsel as I wove after Oidche. He left in the direction opposite of the pond, farther down the road than I had ever been.

Before long, the houses of Dyrne were left behind. Oidche moved at a steady clip, covering more ground than I would have believed possible given the measured motion of his limbs.

As we quit the edges of town, I became aware of the distant sound of hammers striking stone and voices raised in a rhythmic chant. The Smith's Guild, I assumed; their mining operation must lie in this direction.

Is that so strange? After all, they did threaten the mayor that something bad would happen if he continued to defy them. What could be worse than children disappearing from their beds?

The thought was not yet fully formed when my body gave out quite suddenly. I had the strange sensation of being stretched along my meridians, drawn out to the very limits of my physical abilities, and then being sucked backwards against my will, condensed to a pinprick of light.

The next thing I knew, I was on my hands and knees, shuddering against the floorboards of our rented room. My deep blue skirts billowed around me. I was Simone once more.

"Crimson?" Emerald fell to his knees beside me, reaching out to touch my back before realizing, just in time, that I was intangible.

"I'm alright," I panted. My body had reformed in its proper order, but I was shaken to the core. "Give me a moment, I'm startled, that's all."

"Of course." Emerald sat back on his heels. "It's the tether. You can't get too far away from me. I've never tested the limits before. It didn't hurt, did it?"

I shook my head. "No, it didn't."

"Thank Aster." He ran his hands through his short hair. "Did you learn anything else?"

Once I was able to compose myself, I explained to Emerald everything I had heard from him over the course of my excursion. I had assumed that my findings might have shed some light on a few things, but my companion seemed as puzzled before my explanation as after it.

"Do you have the faintest idea what any of it means?" I asked.

Emerald stroked his chin. "I'm beginning to get a sense of the larger picture, but I am still waiting for the last pieces to fall into place."

Forgetting my discomfort, I leapt to my feet. "You cannot possibly have solved the whole mystery already, can you?"

"Not entirely," Emerald admitted. "But some things are beginning to make sense, don't you think?"

"I couldn't disagree more! If anything, the facts are becoming more and more muddled in my view." I tapped my palm to my forehead. "Do you truly mean to say that things are beginning to make sense to you?"

"Incrementally, yes."

"So you know who has taken Lidia?" I demanded.

"That, I don't know," Emerald admitted. "But it's possible that she is still in town. If Oidche cannot find her, then perhaps we may locate her yet. In the meantime, we shall keep our eyes open. Lidia's disappearance is linked to the matter of the Conjury deaths, but I'm hopeful that she is alive and well—unlike the Scouts."

I gaped at Emerald in consternation. He seemed more at ease than before, and like the witnesses who had crowded around Moira earlier, he did not seem to be worried about little Lidia's fate.

The answer to the mystery in Dyrne, it seemed, lay before me. All I had to do was decipher the clues we had gathered.

So far, I was doing a terrible job.

Chapter Fourteen

"Tell me what you've worked out," I begged, dogging Emerald's steps as we headed back out into the street.

"What about our deal?" In the time we'd been together, I'd never seen Emerald looking so smug, so confident, so... *cocky*. "I thought that you wanted to solve this mystery on your own, to prove your point."

I groaned in frustration and ran my hands through my hair, pulling my braid loose so that my scarlet locks fell around my shoulder. I would just as soon have pulled it out. "You are so patently *vexing*. I have never so much as *tried* to keep a secret from you." **[In fact, I've been open with you about everything, and helpful, and...]**

Emerald raised a hand to cut me off. "I'm not debating either your intellect or your honesty, Crim." **[Think of it this way: we're partners. We've seen the same evidence, we've spoken to the same people, and it would put my mind at ease to know that we've drawn the same conclusions. If I tell you what I think, you're more likely to be swayed by my opinion. If, on the other hand, we reach the same conclusion independently, won't that do a great deal to validate your confidence in our findings?]**

[I suppose.] Part of me was still convinced that he was holding back information just to torment me, but his argument was sound. Irritatingly, this meant that I was now more annoyed with myself than with him. If I had everything I needed to know to start making sense of this town's secrets, why couldn't I unjumble the facts?

As we strolled along the main street, I looked around and reviewed what I knew, but nothing quite fit together.

[Tell me who you suspect so far,] Emerald suggested. *[And why. Your reasons will be the most important.]*

[It's a long list.] I frowned at the door of Vanora and Kade's house as we passed. *[Parian is the obvious choice, I suppose. He's openly hostile, and his behavior is erratic.]*

Emerald nodded approvingly. *[These are the main things to consider from where we stand: opportunity and motive. The means of killing we already know, and they vary from case to case. The motive, we are still working out. Carry on.]*

[After Parian, there's Shale. Shale had an opportunity, especially if he offered to travel with the Scouts, but I'm not sure what his motives would have been. Unless he's hiding something in his business? Speaking of which, I suppose I must include Errol on this list as well, since we can consider his illicit Shine of the Moon sales as motive. It's hard for me to imagine that he could be responsible, but I suppose he might be more powerful than he looks. Then there are the members of the Smith's Guild, one of whom openly threatened the mayor.]

Emerald had begun to strut a little as he walked, clearly amused by my growing list of suspects. *[Is that everyone?]*

[No, because there are things involving Oidche, Tincrown, and Vanora I don't understand. What should I make of those goggles? Sheiling strikes me as a bit suspicious. And then—]

I stopped in the road alongside the church, staring out over the graveyard peppered with its silent tombs. *[And then, there is Nechtan.]*

"Ah, yes. Nechtan." Emerald crossed his arms. "The leader of the faithful, the devout follower of Dathan, Lord of the Living and the Dead."

[His power gives him opportunity, and he has motive. The Conjury presents a threat to his power over the citizens of Dyrne. They can't even form romantic partnerships without his say-so. I can't imagine that he likes it when an outside force comes in to challenge him.] I stopped to consider my own words, then turned to face my companion. *[Nearly every person we've spoken to has mentioned Nechtan in one capacity or another, haven't they? Because he involves himself in everything. He has the people of Dyrne under his thumb, or at least he would like to. That's why he wasn't concerned when he found out that Lidia was gone—because he didn't hurt her. Or he did, and he doesn't want anyone to panic!]*

A half-smile slid onto Emerald's face. "That's certainly one theory."

"You can mock me all you want, but tell me if I'm right!"

"I told you, Crim, you need evidence. What does the evidence suggest?"

"That Nechtan lies at the center of this web." I crossed my arms and glared at the venerable old church. *[That the worship of Dathan reaches into every corner of this town, with Nechtan at its helm.]*

"And if I asked you to produce evidence for the Conjury, what would you say?"

That stopped me short. "What do you mean, evidence for the Conjury?"

"We're talking about more than mere whims, Crimson. We're talking about a trial that could change a man's life, and the whole course of this town. If you accused him and he was found guilty, he could spend his whole life imprisoned in the magistrate's jails. He would be taken away from the island. He would lose his freedom, and the town would lose their religious leader. If he's guilty of the crime, so be it, but—" Emerald held up one finger and wagged it at me. "What if he was innocent? All that would happen, and the true culprit would walk free."

"But the Conjury would gather more evidence to back up my accusation, surely?" I asked.

"Do you really think that every person who languishes behind bars is guilty?" Emerald snorted. "Hardly. And what if Nechtan was taken to trial, and found innocent? How would he and his flock view the Conjury from that point forward?"

"I didn't think of that," I admitted, shrinking away from him.

"A job like this is a matter of life and death," Emerald said more gently. "If the wrong person is charged, the effects ripple outwards. How much sleep do you think a member of the Conjury would lose over imprisoning the wrong man and washing their hands of this matter? They never have to face the everyday consequences of their actions. None of them have ever set foot in Dyrne. They wouldn't care what became of those who look up to Dathan... or Nechtan. They would simply do what seemed best to them and move on."

My eyes widened. "And such people are responsible for making the laws?"

"It's what happens when you consolidate power into the hands of a few individuals," Emerald said.

I pressed my palm to my forehead. *[No wonder Parian hates the Conjury. No wonder people have been so cold to us when they learn who we're working for!]* This revelation introduced another problem as well. If the people of Dyrne learned that their high priest had been killing Conjury scouts, they might not even think that he'd done something wrong. In fact, they might be supportive.

"It doesn't bode well for us if you're right," I murmured. "But if Nechtan is responsible, why resort to such violence? If he spoke to Cassandra on his own, like Sheiling said, he could have used that opportunity to harm her."

"Let me pose another leading question," Emerald said. "The last scout, Dawyd of Sailor's Reprieve, visited on his regular route for many years. Everyone who's mentioned the deaths of the scouts has excluded Dawyd from their number. Why wouldn't Nechtan—or whoever killed the other scouts—target him? Why would they suddenly take exception to the Conjury's presence?"

"Because something changed?" I suggested. "Or... or because someone new arrived, and Nechtan isn't responsible at all." I gripped my head in my hands and shut my eyes, trying to think. Somehow, it was all related: those marks on the church walls, the footprints in my room, the panic with which Maximilien had fled the village, the babblebird felled by a well-timed stone, *all* of it meant something.

Emerald grunted abruptly. ***[Look up. You'll find this interesting.]***

I did as he suggested, only to find the bulky, fur-swaddled figure of Oidche making his way up the street. He was carrying an object in his arms, and for a moment I was convinced that it was the little girl's body; but then the object stirred, and I realized that she was alive, wrapped in the cloak taken from Oidche's back so completely that I could barely make out her shape. He was still wearing the goggles he'd borrowed from Vanora.

"You found her!" I exclaimed.

"Indeed." Oidche nodded, clutching the child to his chest. "She wandered off on her own, poor thing. Terribly cold. Gonna ask the doc to check her." He didn't stop walking as he passed us, but Emerald and I turned to follow him nonetheless.

"Nechtan said that children often go missing," I observed, lifting my skirts a little as I bustled along beside them. I could not see the girl, although she did indeed appear to be shivering. It must be cold today, at least for a girl of her size.

Despite her chill, it was the child who replied. "Didn't go missing. I runned away. Mama won't let me play outside!"

"Spring fever," Oidche grunted. "Little ones get tired of being indoors all winter. Another boy did the same last week."

"I wanted to see the giffins!" Lidia added.

"Are you always the one who goes after children when they vanish?" Emerald asked.

Oidche shrugged. "When I'm here. It's easier for me. I know the land better."

His path led us straight to the doctor's door. Emerald did not speak, but the sense of anticipation passed through our connection. It nearly drove me up the steps before him, but I was able to resist.

[Stop pushing me,] I told him irritably.

[I'm not pushing you.] He glared at me behind Oidche's back. *[I'm not even touching you.]* The pressure in our connection slackened anyway. He stepped past me, sidling between me and Oidche so that he could be the one to knock on the door.

I couldn't resist teasing him. *[I know that you're eager to be reunited with your doctor, but there's no need to shove.]*

[He is not my—] Emerald's mind went blank as the door opened, and the now-familiar, tousled figure of Tincrown appeared in the doorway. "Doctor," Emerald said.

"Why, if it isn't my botanist." Tincrown went pink around the ears. When he glanced away, he registered Oidche and the girl, and cried out, holding both arms toward Lidia. "Oh, you're alright! Thank goodness." He took the child from Oidche and braced her against his hip. "May I have the goggles, please?"

Oidche lifted them from his head and passed them over without a word. From another man, his silence might have contained a hint of disapproval, but silence seemed to be Oidche's natural state.

"Will you please ask Moira to come by with a set of Lidia's clothes? I'll get the cloak back to you later once she's properly warmed up." Tincrown nodded to all of us, letting his eyes linger a little longer on Emerald's than anyone else. "I must see to my patient. Isn't that right, Miss Lidia? What were you thinking?"

"I wanted to see the baby giffins!" Lidia explained as the doctor closed the door behind him.

Oidche grunted and backed up. His eyes gleamed from the

shadows of his weirling-skin hood. "Bye," he growled and set off again, this time in the direction of Moira's home.

The light was beginning to fail, and I was distantly aware of a growing pang in Emerald's belly and an ache in his head. Ever since he had re-cast me into my bird form, I had become more aware of his physical needs. I wasn't sure if that was because our connection had shifted, or if his hunger and weariness had grown so pronounced that they were bleeding into our bond.

"*My botanist*," I repeated aloud. "He may not be your doctor, but he has a use in mind for you, it seems."

"Shut up," Emerald grumbled, but his ears darkened a shade.

"Don't be coy, Em. It's obvious that you wouldn't object to a bit of the doctor's... undivided attention." I imitated the tone Sheiling had used with me in the shop this morning.

"You're in a good mood, aren't you? Feeling smug?" He rubbed his temples, but he didn't look entirely displeased with my ribbing.

"Of course!" I swished my skirts around my ankles. "Lidia is safe. That's the best news we've gotten since we arrived in Dyrne."

"And that's all you've learned?" Emerald asked.

"I suppose that *you*'ve pieced together the identity of our killer." I rolled my eyes.

"Not quite. I still require proof."

"Wait." I hurried my pace until I was able to step in front of him and block his path. "You must be joking. In the course of the last hour you've managed not only to uncover this town's secrets but also the identity of our suspect by mere deduction? How can that be?"

Emerald winked at me with all the confidence of a rake. "If you weren't so preoccupied with the botanical pursuits of *my* doctor, you might have done a better job noting the identity of *my* current suspect."

"But when—!? How—!?"

"Someone lied to us today, Crimson," Emerald said. "And I can think of no innocent reason for it."

"Oh, so one of the two-dozen people we've spoken to is your suspect? Well, *that* narrows it down." I placed my hands on my hips, made the appearance of tapping my toe against the road, and glared at him.

"There's no point in pouting, Crim. I've given you the only hint I intend to pass along." With that, Emerald sauntered away, leaving me to mull over the conversations we'd endured throughout the day. I was so distracted that I forgot to pretend to eat over dinner, and when we retired to our new quarters, I silently paced the boards running everything over in my mind again and again.

Could Oidche be his suspect? Or Sheiling? Surely not Tincrown. He wouldn't be smug if his doctor was involved, would he?

I still suspected Nechtan, but I couldn't think what lie he might have told us.

As Emerald nestled against the pillows, I returned to our conversation with Shale.

Shale's reasons for lying about his connection with Dyrne rang false. And he told us that he isn't close to the dwarves in the mining camp, but the little girl was headed toward the camp because she wanted to see the griffins. So maybe the dwarves—!

Before the thought could fully take shape in my mind, Emerald fell asleep, and I blinked out.

Chapter Fifteen

I rematerialized with a question on my lips, but Emerald—disheveled and still lying in bed, with his clothing askew—held up a warning finger.

"Do you hear that?" he whispered.

I inclined my head toward the window, listening to the voices that wafted up from the street.

"*Mayor Reade!*" someone shouted. "*Mayor Reade? Show your face, you old coward. There's been a murder...*"

"I'm not imagining that, am I?" Emerald rubbed his eyes. "Unless I'm mistaken, that's our calling-card." He swung his heavy feet out of the bed and stretched, looking about for his boots.

"If you already know who the killer is, why are you so excited?" I asked moodily, crossing to the window to give him a bit of privacy. To my surprise, although robed figures were already emerging from the thatch-roofed houses, the person wailing in distress was not one of the Dyrnians, but a bearded, tattooed fellow of middling height. I did not recognize this particular dwarf, but judging from what Shale had told us the day before, he was likely one of Bilk Deepvein's crew.

I turned back to Emerald, who seemed ready to depart

despite the fact that his black hair was still sticking out from his head at all angles.

"Are you coming?" he asked, throwing the door ajar.

"You didn't answer my question."

"Is it so wrong to relish a bit of confirmation?" he asked. "This might provide you with some necessary clues... and me, with proof."

"Someone is *dead*," I reminded him. "It's nothing to be smug about."

That wiped the smile from Emerald's face, and he turned to the door so that he would not have to meet my gaze.

"Some of us find death more disturbing than others," he said in a low voice.

"And yet, we all find it equally permanent," I reminded him.

"Oh, you sweet child of spring." Emerald shook his head. "Not everything dies."

"I'll be asking more about that later," I informed him as I slipped past him toward the door. "And don't worry, I may be a mere babe, but I recognize condescension when I hear it."

Emerald muttered something under his breath, and I turned back to glare at him.

"What was that?"

"Nothing," he said hastily. "Hurry up, we've got a murder to investigate."

By the time we made it to the street, most of Dyrne was gathered in a murmuring cluster outside of the mayor's office. Moving between them was difficult, since I couldn't risk passing directly through anyone without exposing us. We were forced to hover on the edges of the crowd. There was something uncanny about all those people in one spot, all speaking in lowered voices and with only a few of their faces visible.

"I can't hear anything," I complained, craning to see the dwarf who was now deep in conversation with both the mayor and the priest. Nechtan was in his robes, although the elaborate bandages beneath were slightly askew. **[Goodness, does he sleep *in them?*]**

"Does who do what?" Emerald asked in a dreamy voice.

I turned to him in frustration. When I did, the source of his distraction became evident. Tincrown, wearing a loose night-shirt and ill-fitting trousers that only reached his knees, was approaching along the edge of the crowd.

[Really? At a time like this, can't we focus on the issue at hand?]

[We have one local contact who actually likes me—er, likes us. Let's not drive him away.]

[You are besotted,] I informed him. *[And since I have never in my life heard anyone use that word, I can only assume that it comes from your head, which by logical extension makes it true.]*

"Good morning," Emerald said, ignoring my sulky diatribe.

"Not sure it's a good one." Tincrown was a bit down in the mouth. He rubbed one knuckle in his eye as he spoke. Like Emerald, he had the appearance of a man who had just rolled out of bed. I disapproved, but only because Emerald so wholeheart-edly did not. How were we supposed to get any work done when Tincrown's nightshirt had slipped off his narrow shoulder, and Emerald had no eyes for anything else?

Clues, for example.

We should *really* be focusing on clues.

For reasons I could not understand, I, too, was staring at Tincrown's shoulder. Of *course* our connection would be strongest at a moment like this. I couldn't care less about the smooth, umbre skin of his neck, the freckles dotting his collar-bone, the curl of hair that framed his ear so invitingly, the soft patch of stubble beneath his jaw just begging to be kissed...

[EMERALD.]

My companion jumped and crossed his arms, turning to face the mayor. "So," he said gruffly. "What do you think they're waiting for? We've yet to see a sheriff in Dyrne."

"Oh, there's no sheriff." Tincrown yawned and stretched, and Emerald's eyes slid toward him almost against his will. "Nechtan is the law around here."

"Is he now?" Emerald cocked his head. "In that case, I suppose *we* represent the Conjury, so *we'll* have to go investigate." He nodded to Tincrown. "And they'll want a doctor on-site, so you'll have to go, too."

[We need to work on your flirting.] I did everything in my power to imbue my thoughts with the maximum dose of disdain. *[If you want to spend time with him, have you considered asking him to join you for a drink?]*

[I'm not flirting. This is work.] That wall in his mind slammed closed again, and the half-smile slipped off of his face.

There was only so much nonsense that I could stomach in a morning, and this ranked quite highly. Fortunately for Emerald, Nechtan raised his hands and drew our attention back to the matter of some poor fellow's untimely death.

"People of Dyrne, please join me in a prayer for the poor soul who has been lost this day."

All around us, robed villagers crossed their arms over their chests and bowed their shrouded faces toward the earth.

"Praise be to Dathan, Lord of the Living and the Dead. May the lost spirit find peace, and may the gods keep him." Nechtan's voice boomed out over the square.

"Praise be to Dathan," the crowd echoed.

Emerald might have shut me out of his mind, but I was aware of a strange sensation along my spine, and since I had no flesh of my own, I was certain that *his* was crawling. It did not escape my notice that Tincrown had lowered his head in an imitation of local piety, but he kept his lips pressed into a thin, tight line, and his dark eyes were troubled.

Nechtan lowered his arms and clasped his hands over his bosom. "Friends and acolytes, I must ask you to return to your homes. This is a serious matter, and a dark accusation."

"Accusation?" the dwarf spat. "Bilk is *dead.* Killed in our own encampment."

[Bilk?] I glanced toward Emerald. *[Bilk Deepvein? The mining boss?]*

[I wish I could say that I was surprised.]

Emerald might be able to take this revelation in stride, but I was deeply disturbed. It did not fit the pattern of known attacks, although it *did* reinforce my suspicion that outsiders of any kind were in danger here. My companion misliked religious enclaves, but the fear that accompanied this news was entirely my own. If someone could attack Bilk in the safety of his encampment, and that same brazen person had been willing to launch an attack on my room at the inn, then Emerald truly was in danger.

"I do not mean to belittle your loss." Nechtan inclined his head toward the dwarf. "You wish to protect your own, as do I. We will come at once to see what we can learn. Doctor?" He scanned the crowd in search of Tincrown, then waved him over when he spotted him. "Come with us. The rest of you, please, stay inside. Keep your children close."

Near my right, Moira emitted a small, frightened sound and hurried back to her house. The rest of the villagers followed at a more measured pace, mumbling among themselves.

Tincrown made his way to where the dwarf, the mayor, and the high priest waited, and Emerald followed on his heels. I came last, where I would be the least likely to run into anyone— or pass through them unexpectedly, as the case may be.

I could only imagine how Nechtan felt about our presence, since I could not see his expression. To my surprise, however, neither he nor the mayor protested our company.

"I'll need a moment to collect my things," Tincrown told them.

"Make haste, then," Nechtan replied.

"And perhaps you should change into something more suited to the daytime while you're at it?" I added.

Tincrown jogged off toward his house, and Emerald followed after shooting me a suspicious glance, but for once I held my ground. Instead, I turned to the dwarf.

"I'm sorry for your loss," I told him.

The dwarf scowled and made what I assumed was a rude gesture. "Save your platitudes. *Sorry* won't bring him back. Bilk knew that there was something rotten in this town, and now he's paid the price."

I frowned. "If you believe that, why come here for help?"

The dwarf sucked his sand-color mustache into his mouth and chewed on it, glaring at each of us in turn. "Because—"

"If I may, Simone of the Road, I do not think that you are familiar with how things work on the island." The mayor stroked his bald head as he considered me. "Bilk and I were hardly great friends, but out here, in the wilds, we must rely on our neighbors to look out for our safety."

Even when those neighbors are blackmailing you? I thought, but I kept my peace.

The dwarf did not. "What a crock of pig swill. I came to you because I hoped that you'd own up to whatever you've done, and turn over the coward responsible! I don't care what's going on between you cultists and the Conjury, they're no friends of *ours*, but Bilk was a dwarf of his word. Whatever he knew about this town, he kept it under his beard. He didn't even tell *me!* And I've no doubt it cost him his life."

The four of us fell into grim silence until Tincrown and Emerald returned. The doctor had a brown leather satchel slung over his now fully-clad shoulder and a pair of inscribed gloves covering his hands.

"I'm ready," he said.

Nechtan bowed to the dwarf. "Very well. In that case, *neighbor*, lead the way."

The mining encampment was on the other side of the ridge from Dyrne, but the only road between the two was a treacherous, rocky slope. The dwarf took the lead, picking his way along the path as though he was part of the mountainside itself. The mayor followed, with frequent assistance from Nechtan, who held out a hand more than once to steady the old man as we went. Then came Tincrown, who for once was not in a talking mood. Emerald followed on his heels, and I came last of all. I made a great show of watching my step, although in truth I was in no danger of slipping.

Dark clouds above threatened rain, and before long a fine mist gathered around us, obscuring the camp from view and making the already perilous passage that much riskier.

Roughly halfway down, a stone beneath Tincrown's foot slid free, and the doctor's arm spun wildly in an attempt to keep him upright. Emerald caught him about the waist and set him back on solid ground.

"Thank you," Tincrown said breathlessly, clinging to Emerald's shoulder.

"It's nothing." Emerald took an awfully long time to unhand him. "I would hate to see you come to harm."

I rolled my eyes behind their backs and pretended to trip, landing—by all appearances—on my hands and knees.

"Oh!" Tincrown spun toward me. "Simone! Are you alright?"

"It's nothing." I stuck out my bottom lip as I got back to my feet. "A little tumble, but I shall persevere."

Emerald glared at me. Since Tincrown stood a pace below him on the path, he could not make out my companion's peeved features. "What a miracle," my friend intoned in an emotionless voice. "There's not a scratch on her. Why, not even a hair out of place. How *lucky* you are, Simone."

I batted my eyelashes in feigned relief as I examined my palms. "You are quite right. I do appear to live a charmed life."

Tincrown's shoulders relaxed. "We should both be more careful in the future." He returned his attention to the descent, and Emerald shook his head at me before following.

[You simply cannot stand to be upstaged, even for a moment, can you?]

[I'll admit my appreciation of high drama when you admit your appreciation of the doctor. I felt your heart lurch when you caught him, and not only out of concern for his well-being...]

Emerald growled without looking back.

At long last, we reached the floor of the little valley. It was not as picturesque as Dyrne, although it might have begun that way. The same rugged trees and abundant greenery lined the outskirts of the camp, but where the Dyrnians had incorporated elements of the landscape into their architecture and the contours of their streets, the dwarves had shaped the camp to suit *their* needs. Bare gray stones comprised the majority of the plateau, upon which an assortment of tents and temporary structures had been erected. The mouth of the mine, set at the intersection of the high cliff which we had just traversed and another wall of rock, was a wound in the earth. The gaping chasm drew my attention, but I had no desire to explore it further.

All around us were stacks of oilcloth-covered chests and crates. Two dozen surly dwarves milled around, watching us with beady eyes and curled lips. They made no attempt to hide their hostility.

"This way," our guide said, gesturing toward the mouth of the cave.

I wondered how far inside we would have to go, but descending into the mine itself was not necessary. We rounded a stack of crates, and Mayor Reade gagged.

Bilk Deepvein had not been strangled or drowned. He had been torn apart.

The mining boss lay on his back with his arms splayed wide and his empty eyes staring toward the sky. Blood smeared his parted lips, and his beard was soaked with red.

I had never encountered viscera before. My only experience with the inner workings of the body were all the confusing aches and lurchings that came through my connection with Emerald. Bilk's, however, were on full display. Other jagged cuts crisscrossed the remains. Around him, a burst of white-and-black ribbed feathers lay among the stones where his blood had congealed.

The mayor averted his eyes, but Nechtan took a step closer. "These are griffin feathers," he observed.

The dwarf bristled. "Yes, this looks like it might be the work of griffins. I'm sure that he was attacked by a flock of them in his tent last night and dragged out without waking any of us up, only to have his guts torn out and *left behind*." The dwarf snorted deeply before spitting at his feet. "Why didn't I think of that? Ah, right, because it's *bollocks*."

"I only observed what I saw," Nechtan said. "Can we at least agree that they *are* griffin feathers?"

The dwarf glowered, and a low mutter of disapproval passed among the observers.

"No need to talk down to us," one of the others snapped. "We can see what they are plain enough."

Tincrown handed his bag to Emerald and crouched next to the body. He crossed his gloved hands across each other, palms apart, so that the inscriptions on the back flared to life, emitting a faint blue glow. He passed his hands over the body, brushing his palms against the exposed viscera, the weeping wounds, and the dark bruises on what was left of Bilk's flesh. The inscriptions faded from pale blue to a deep yellow.

"He's right," Tincrown murmured. "Nothing was taken. If it was an animal attack, I would expect them to have eaten him."

"I've seen what griffins leave behind," Emerald added. "They carry their prey back to their eyries and strip away any scrap of meat."

"Meat," the dwarf grunted. "He wasn't *meat*. He was our *kinsman*."

"If a griffin had killed him, he *would* have been meat," Emerald clarified.

Tincrown was still moving. "Odd, though. All of these wounds were inflicted *after* his death."

The dwarves struck me as a stoic lot, but at these words, a few of them sighed aloud and they all made small, respectful gestures toward the earth with their hands.

"Glad to hear it," our guide said. "I had imagined..." He ran a rough hand over his mouth. "I had imagined that he suffered terribly."

Tincrown glanced over his shoulder. "What is your name?"

"Carthen Deepvein," our guide said. "That *meat* you're examining is my father."

Emerald grimaced. "I didn't mean—"

"I know what you meant." Carthen scuffed the toe of a nail-studded boot in the stones. "A griffin would have eaten him. But this wasn't a feeding. It was a warning."

"Perhaps you wish to leave while I finish this?" Tincrown suggested.

Carthen shook his head. "No. I want to make sure it's done right, doctor."

Tincrown nodded and returned to his work. All eyes were on him, but this time I did not feel the faintest scrap of jealousy. The gentle way he handled the body made me think that much better of him. I didn't get the feeling that it was just for show, either. His respect for the dead moved me.

Emerald had once told me to trust my gut, despite my definite lack of them. The way Bilk's body had been handled after death was far more horrific than anything we had seen thus far. It would have been the work of a moment to push Cassandra to her death, and one might hold a man beneath the waters of the pond in a fit of passion, but to desecrate a corpse after the fact required a different sort of anger.

My *gut* told me that Tincrown was not our killer. His expressions were too unguarded, and there was no hint of delight or even dispassion on them.

I could not say the same for Nechtan. The way his eyes glittered as he took in the dead man's remains belied a shade too much interest in the proceedings.

Tincrown pushed Bilk's blood-soaked beard aside, revealing a deep gash across his throat through which the white of his spine was visible. Carthan let out a guttural moan at the sight.

"There we are," the doctor sighed. The inscriptions on his glove flared red as he probed the wound with his fingertips. "This is what killed him. Everything else was done later, presumably to make it look like a griffin attack. It's a clean cut. He must have died quickly."

"*Quickly?* Drowning in his own blood?" Carthan snarled in a quaking voice. "Is that the kind of death *you* would choose, doctor?"

Tincrown let the dead dwarf's beard fall back into place. "There are worse ones."

I cut in before Carthan could reply. "You said that you found him this morning? That he was dragged from his bed?"

"Aye." The younger Deepvein gestured to the nearest tent. "He was in there. But I was sleeping not ten feet away! Why didn't we hear him?"

Emerald strode away to investigate the tent, but I was more interested in what Tincrown was doing. As I watched, he prised open Bilk's mouth to reveal a blood-soaked wad of cloth.

"I don't think a griffin left *this* behind," he murmured. The cloth unfurled to reveal a deep sapphire color I knew well. It was the same color worn by many of the Dyrnians. "Whoever did this must have stuffed it into his mouth to silence his cries."

"You know what *else* a griffin didn't leave?" Emerald asked. He was holding the tent flap aside. I approached to see what had caught his eye.

Among the tangle of blankets were a trail of footprints too large to have been made by any dwarf.

They were, however, exactly the size of those left in my room at the inn the night it was ransacked.

Whoever had come for Bilk Deepvein had already come for me.

Chapter Sixteen

Our trip back to town was completely silent. Nechtan and the mayor fell behind as we took the longer but less dangerous track that led us on a roundabout track to Dyrne. They spoke in low voices, but every time I dawdled to close the distance between us, they stopped talking.

Emerald was immersed in his own thoughts, which he took pains to hide from me, while Tincrown walked with his head down, gripping the strap of his medical bag.

For my part, I turned over the evidence in my mind. Someone had snuck into Bilk's tent last night. That person had stuffed a wad of cloth in his mouth to keep him silent, then hauled him out of the tent to cut his throat. Or—and this was somehow more horrifying to me—they had cut his throat *inside* the tent and stood over him while he died before dragging him out into the open to complete their wicked work. I presumed that it must be the former, since we had found few traces of blood inside, but for all I knew the killer had disposed of that evidence after committing the crime.

At any rate, it was careless to have left the cloth in the dead dwarf's mouth, unless their aim had been to send the dwarves a message about keeping their silence. There was a deep contradiction in that, but I was already beginning to suspect that our culprit was becoming more unhinged with each killing. The attempt to make the murder look like a griffin attack had been haphazard at best, but perhaps they were taunting us.

Which would mean that whoever did it is waiting to see how we will respond.

Our longer route brought us into town from the opposite direction of the main road. Nechtan and the mayor took their leave without bothering to bid us farewell, while Emerald and I followed Tincrown.

As Tincrown mounted the steps to his home, Emerald cleared his throat. "Would you mind if I came in for a while?"

"Oh." Tincrown paused with the door half-open. "Of course. You're both more than welcome."

"Not both. Just me." Emerald stuffed his hands into the pockets of his trousers.

A sweet, bemused smile bloomed on Tincrown's face. "To discuss the case?"

"Of course. What other motive could I have?" Emerald's face was far less openly expressive, but a fizzy, bubbly emotion echoed through me.

"I can't imagine." Tincrown stepped inside, leaving the door open.

[What about me?*]* I demanded. *[What am I supposed to do?]*

[I don't know what your problem is.] Emerald flashed me a smile over his shoulder and opened his jacket just wide enough that I could make out the glowing bottle of Shine of the Moon in his inner pocket. *[It was your idea for me to suggest that we have a drink together.]* Aloud he added, "Simone, why don't you see if you can gather any further information? There might be witnesses worth speaking to. See what you can learn." *[You know, since I've already solved the mystery. I'm collecting my proof, which means that you're now two steps behind. Try to keep up.]*

"I would love..." *[...to know what you're really up to right *now, and...]* "...do a bit of investigating on my own." I offered my companion a small and rather ironic salute. *[And please keep in mind that if you let your guard down, I shall know exactly what you're doing. Mind your manners. I don't wish to be traumatized.]*

"I'll see you back at the inn," he said. With that, he stepped inside the doctor's house and slammed the door in my indignant face.

I scowled at the painted wood. Let him have his afternoon away with the doctor. I would use the time to do some exploring of my own.

I wandered through the town, rubbing my palms together as I thought. The people of Dyrne had been asked to stay inside, which meant that there was very little I could do in terms of visiting. I couldn't very well go about knocking on doors; my hand would simply pass through. Short of standing in the street and shouting for people to come out, my options were few and far between.

Oh. I could pass through *walls.* Emerald had used that particular ability of mine to his advantage that awful night in the churchyard, but I could use it, too. To my own advantage this time.

I chose a house on the outskirts of town, set close to the woods. A familiar jangling from out back caught my attention as I slipped around the side of the house, and I peered over a wooden fence to find several dozen pairs of eyes watching me with interest. The blonde nanny-goat poked her face through the slats and attempted to grab my dress with her pink tongue.

"Sorry, sweetheart," I whispered, taking a step closer. "That won't do you any good."

The fence abutted the house, and the brush surrounding it offered me some cover from the road. Every twig within reach of the fence had been stripped clean by the goats, although there was plenty of fresh hay piled in a little shed out back, which the goats had chosen to ignore in favor of the harder-to-reach morsels outside the pen.

I passed through the wooden barrier and part of the nanny-goat as well. An intense but patient longing for everything I could not have shivered through me. The goat returned to her task of stripping the tops from the nearby grass stalks while I slipped toward the wall of the house.

There was no window into the living quarters, so I took one last survey of my environs before sticking my face directly into the wall. I tilted my head sideways, hoping to get a good look at the room without alarming Dun or any guests he might be hosting.

If he's within, I'll leave him be. I'll only take a quick peek, like I did with Emerald the other day.

The room within was modest but relatively tidy. The floor-plan was open, and the whole place was visible. On the far side of the room, the front door would have opened to reveal the kitchen table. A small kitchen setup stood on the wall to my right, while to my left stood an unmade bed.

There was no one inside, and after a moment I stepped through to get a better look at the place. *After all, it's not spying if there's nobody about, is it? It's* investigating. *He'll never know I was here, unless I find something that proves his involvement, and in* that *case I'll have been more than justified.* My logic was perhaps on the dubious end of the spectrum, but surely this small incursion on Dun's privacy was worth it, for the greater good?

Never mind that my excuses sounded remarkably similar to Emerald's. He craved the doctor's company, and I wanted to solve this mystery for Cassandra, Trotter, Maximilien, and Bilk's sake. And yes, for my own as well.

The house stood empty, but it must have recently been occupied. The table was set, and a rough clay plate sat in front of the only chair, piled with potatoes and carrots and two fried eggs.

I stared down at the plate of steaming food in bewilderment. I knew enough about Dyrne to understand that, while its residents were far from poor, food was highly valued. Vanora had been a shade beyond offended when I refused to eat her questionable meal. Why would someone prepare a meal like this and then leave?

Out of curiosity, I approached the cookstove stove, crouched down before it, and pressed my face through the metal. Sure enough, the coals still glowed. I could not be certain that the food was hot, but whoever had cooked it had been present recently enough that the fire had not died.

Interesting. I was tempted to reach out and tell Emerald what I had seen, but he was otherwise occupied. Besides, this was my chance to solve the mystery without his help.

I straightened up. The circumstances of the house were interesting, but I couldn't see how it related to the murders. Let the goatherd have his privacy, no matter how odd his habits. I walked back through the wall and out into the goatpen, slipping like a shadow into the forest beyond.

Vanora and Kade's house was only three homes away. I stopped to examine it through the leaves, pondering my next course of action. Dun wasn't really a suspect as far as I was concerned, but Parian was young and angry and brash. What did *he* do alone in his room?

Investigating presented an added challenge. His room was on the second floor, and Emerald was not here to grant me the gift of flight. I squinted up at the second-story window, recalling how Emerald had made me float up to examine the inscriptions in the House of Dathan. At the time, I had not been truly present within myself, and I could not recall how he had done it. Likewise, my brief time as a bird had not prepared me for flight in my current form.

It must be the same. You don't require wings to fly, the wings only made it easier to grasp the idea *of flying.* I spread my arms and tried to flex whatever power I had used in my form as a blackbird, but it had no effect at all.

Feeling rather foolish, I lowered my arms and frowned down at my feet.

When you mount stairs, the steps aren't what's important. Your feet aren't properly touching them. What if you pretended *you were climbing a flight of stairs?*

Hesitantly, I lifted one foot and lowered it again, imagining that I was stepping up onto an invisible box. There was nothing to stop my foot at the proper height, and yet my foot stopped anyway. I tried again, lifting myself with the leg that now stood in empty air.

It worked. I now stood well above the ground, floating on nothing.

Excellent! Now, what happens if I jump and assume that the air will catch me?

I bent my knees and pushed off, floating up into the open air among the tree branches. I passed through a nest filled with eggs, and for a few seconds I was filled with the desire to stretch and expand and grow, to burst out of my confinement. Then the sensation slipped away, and I found myself at eye-level with Parian's room.

Unfortunately, I was still several strides away from the wall. Once I'd made sure that there was no one else in sight, I pressed off against the empty air behind me until I reached it, where I "caught" myself with my hands.

The whole experience was somewhat strange and awkward, lacking all the fluid ease with which Emerald had manipulated me, and Aster only knew what anyone walking by would think if they saw me hovering in midair. All the same, I was proud of myself. I had figured it all out without Emerald's help—or coercion.

What else could I do that hadn't occurred to me yet? In fact, there might be things that hadn't occurred to *Emerald* yet, either. That was an intriguing notion, one that I would have to explore more once the matter in Dyrne was settled.

For the time being, I repeated my examination of the room from outside. Finding it empty, I slipped in.

The place was not as inviting as Dun's. An air of gloom pervaded the space. I stood in the middle of the floor, rotating on the spot, but there was nothing much to see: a half-empty bookshelf boasting unmarked covers, a narrow bed draped in a faded handmade blanket, a dresser whose partially opened drawers revealed a heap of hastily folded clothes, and a small writing desk just below the only window. A leather-bound journal set on the corner of the table, looking ever-so-inviting. Unfortunately, I could not open it, and when I passed my hand through it in the hopes of catching a *feeling* from the pages, as I had when touching Emerald, the goat, and the bird's eggs, I received nothing.

It would be a lot easier to spy if I could go through people's things, I mused, but that would make me little better than Emerald on the night that he invaded my mind. I had not enjoyed having my privacy violated. Why would the residents of Dyrne feel any differently?

Dissatisfied, but finding nothing else of interest, I stepped back out of the room and drifted down to ground-level. Perhaps I should find other ways to occupy myself.

I mused on this topic as I rounded the side of Vanora's house, and only barely avoided a disastrous collision with a man walking along the street.

To my consternation, it was Dun.

"Er, hello," I said, quickly stepping aside. "Funny running into you, Dun. How are you?"

"Solid and whole," Dun replied. "Which is more than I can say for that poor dwarf. I was just about to sit down to dinner when I heard the news—been in the woods all morning. I went off to see if there was anything that was needed of me. What about you? Mislaid your big green friend, have you?"

"I know exactly where's he's laid... where's he's been laid... where I *left* him." *Gods above and below, what's wrong with you, Crimson? Be normal!* "He's busy, and I thought, um. I thought... I thought I would go to the pond. It's so lovely."

"Nicest spot in town," Dun agreed. "Well, I'm off to finish my dinner before it goes stone-cold. Be careful, Miss Simone. There's been one accident too many in these woods. I know you're just passing through, but I'd hate to see anything happen to you."

I'm not aware of any accidents. Only murders.

I forced a polite smile and curtseyed to him. "Well, off I go then."

"Off you go," he agreed.

I set off in the direction of the pond. Now that I'd told him I was going there, I couldn't think where else to go. I'd already been too careless.

I trooped off down the path. The sun was still hidden behind clouds, and the mist lingered, hanging like smoke over the landscape and turning the woods, which had struck me as singularly lovely upon our arrival, into an eerie network of black-and-grey shadows and silhouettes.

I had intended to approach the pond and then turn back once I was sure that I had lost Dun, but just as I was about to retrace my steps, a distant cry echoed out between the trees.

For a moment, I hesitated, but another sound followed soon after.

Perhaps I had finally stumbled upon a clue after all.

The footpath leading to the lake bore fresh bootprints. I kept my steps slow and measured, hoping not to attract attention. The mist was thick enough to hide me, but that also made it difficult for me to see whatever awaited me in the water.

Near the boulders beside the road, I passed two sets of clothes hanging from the trees. One was Parian's dull tunic and brown britches. The other looked as though it might be Kristine's full religious regalia, judging by the colors and fine fabrics and those singularly puffy sleeves.

Perhaps Emerald and Tincrown aren't the only ones who have found pleasant ways to occupy their time. I smirked to myself and drew a little closer.

The sight that greeted me was anything but pleasant, however. The warm waters of the hot spring burned away the mist over the water. Through the steam, I saw two figures. They were indeed Kristine and Parian.

It took me a long, horrified moment to process what I was seeing. Parian stood waist-deep in the water with his back to me, the lean planes and angles of his body on full display. His hair was plastered to his face, as if he had just emerged from the water.

Beside him, floating on her back, was Kristine. Or rather, what was left of her.

The corpse had no hair. Her skin had been stripped away, leaving only bone and muscle behind. Her eyeballs were entirely exposed; her scalp had been peeled away to reveal the pale dome of her skull. The red meat of her muscles, mottled in places with stores of yellow fat, held her skeleton together, but Parian had been precise in his awful work. Even her fingers had been de-fleshed, leaving the nails behind.

"There," Parian said, bending slightly toward the body and caressing one hand across her fleshless belly. "Didn't I tell you how freeing this could be, my love? If only you'd listened to me months ago."

The corpse stirred.

I had been wrong. Parian had not granted Kristine the same mercy he had granted Bilk Deepvein. He had not killed her before the torture began. The poor girl was still *alive*.

I could not stop the piercing scream that tore out of me and echoed across the water. Parian whirled toward me. His eyes widened as he beheld me.

[Emerald. Emerald. EMERALD!] I covered my eyes, unable to stop screaming. What pain, what profound and unutterable pain that poor girl must have endured.

"Crimson?" Emerald asked.

I trailed off in a sob and lowered my hands. The forest was gone. Parian and Kristine had vanished. I now stood in Tincrown's laboratory. The two men were seated on either side of the little table. Emerald still gripped a mostly empty glass of Shine of the Moon, but Tincrown's slipped from his fingers as he stared at me, open-mouthed.

"How...?" the doctor wheezed.

Emerald huffed and scowled at me. "I can explain."

"There is no time to *explain!*" I shrilled. "I know who is responsible for everything. I know who has done all of it! Parian is to blame—and Kristine has just become his next victim!"

Chapter Seventeen

My untimely arrival in Tincrown's house was followed by a whirlwind of activity. The explanation of what I had seen at the lake tumbled out in confused detail. Emerald tried to calm me, while Tincrown paced behind him, muttering to himself under his breath.

When the pieces of the story were finally out, in a jumbled sequence that Emerald's puzzle-solving mind managed to reassemble, he turned to the doctor. "I should go investigate. I'll come back later and explain—"

"You intend to *leave me here?*" Tincrown exclaimed. "I still don't understand what's happened here tonight, but if one of my patients is indeed dead in the woods..." He pinched the bridge of his nose between his thumb and forefinger. "Oh, by the Golden Hand."

"Don't pretend that I'm the only one keeping secrets," Emerald replied.

"Can't this wait?" I gestured between the two of them. Perhaps you didn't hear me when I said that *Kristine was still alive!?*"

Emerald raised his eyebrows at Tincrown. "Seems to me that for a young woman to survive such a vicious attack would take nothing short of a miracle. Divine intervention. Wouldn't you agree?"

Was he not hearing me? Or am I missing something? "We need to go!"

Neither responded to my comment. Tincrown seemed locked onto Emerald's last words. His mouth opened, and he held out his hands toward Emerald. Twice he tried to speak, but words eluded him.

"Fine," he said at last. "Let me get my bag."

Dusk was approaching by the time we stepped out of the house. Tincrown took his time locking the door and all but dragged his feet as we made our way down the road. I turned so that I could walk backwards, urging the two men onward.

"Hurry, hurry!" I exclaimed. "We need to get there before he hides the evidence!"

Emerald stopped in his tracks, peering over my shoulder.

"Emerald, that's the *opposite of faster...*"

"And where, pray tell, are you going in such haste?" asked a deep voice from several paces away.

I turned to find Nechtan blocking the road.

"Parian killed Kristine!" I blurted.

Nechtan straightened, and his usual calm demeanor was replaced with one of nervous energy. "Are you certain?"

"I saw them, just now, at the pond. She was flayed."

"Just now?" he echoed. "Only moments ago? It must have taken you some time to make the return journey."

I took a step closer to the high priest. "Fear made me swift. Is that enough of an answer for you? Why is it that every man I encounter seems unconcerned with the suffering of a young woman? What if, instead of questioning what I saw with my own eyes, we hurry back so that you can see the truth for yourselves?" My voice rose with each utterance, until my words echoed off of the houses.

Nechtan raised both hands. "Forgive me, Simone of the Road. Let us return with all haste. Please, lead the way." He stepped aside to let me pass, and I hurried down the road, checking back from time to time to make sure that my companions had not wandered off to speculate on my perceived hysteria.

If they had seen what *I* had witnessed, I was certain that they would not waste half as much time asking useless questions. The sick, tender way that Parian had caressed the dying girl came back to me. What had he done to her that I had *not* witnessed? If I had arrived earlier, I might have been able to frighten him away and give her a chance to flee. If I had not wasted time spying on Dun, I could have saved her.

Instead, I had been able to do nothing but scream. Worst of all, I had abandoned her, so that her final moments were spent in the company of the man who had stolen her life.

My guilt consumed me as we approached the pond. No doubt Parian had fled when he realized what was going on, but poor Kristine might yet be floating in the hot spring just as the Conjury scout, Trotter of Shantytown, had been left almost precisely a year ago. In the last few paces, my courage nearly failed. I did not want to see her again, not like that, not reduced to mere *meat* as Emerald would say.

The first sign that something was amiss came a few seconds later. Both sets of clothes had been collected from the boulders, and new tracks covered the ones that had stood out so clearly against the damp soil.

As for the pond itself, it was empty. There was no sign that anything was amiss. Not so much as a ripple marred its surface, and the fading light revealed not a single grisly clue along the shoreline.

"They were here," I murmured.

"Are you certain?" Nechtan asked. "The mind can play tricks on people, and you have already seen one awful death today. Perhaps you were simply overcome with emotions."

I spun toward him. "Ex*cuse* me?"

"Some women have more, ah, *delicate* constitutions." Nechtan folded his hands before him.

"Do I *look* delicate to you?" I growled, baring my teeth at him. "They were here. I didn't imagine it. Parian stared *right at me*."

Nechtan turned to Tincrown. "You might wish to examine her, just to be sure."

Tincrown held up a quelling hand. "She believes what she is saying, Nechtan. I have no doubt of that." He turned to me, using a gentle tone that, although not as degrading as Nechtan's, still smacked of condescension. "Is there somewhere else we should look? Surely flaying someone would leave a trace. The human body contains twelve pints of blood and is covered in nearly eight silvers of skin. It would be difficult to remove all that without leaving a trace of evidence."

I turned away and jogged along the deertrail circumnavigating the pond. There was no sign of Kristine anywhere: no blood, no skin, no *corpse,* not even a break in the brush to indicate that a body might have been dragged through the branches. I all but flew around the hot spring, where I rejoined the group of men. None of them had moved more than a few paces, although Emerald and Tincrown were at least *pretending* to search for evidence. Emerald had waded into the water while Tincrown scoured the shore.

Nechtan turned to face me as I approached. "Fear does *indeed* make you swift, Simone. What have you found?"

"Nothing," I muttered sullenly.

Emerald emerged from the water. "Well, she didn't sink. Which begs the question: what *exactly* did you see?"

"Yes." Tincrown tugged at the fingers of his inscribed gloves. "Although that is not my *only* question."

Nechtan raised one bandaged finger. "I have an idea. Since we have found nothing here, there *is* someplace else we might search. We could ask her parents when they saw her last."

"Fine." I rubbed my forehead. "Maybe you'll believe me *then*." I stomped past him, wishing that my feet could land on the ground and make a proper sound so that he would know the depth and breadth of my irritation.

[Crimson.] Emerald hurried after me. ***[Crimson, listen to me. Nechtan is being awful, but I believe you.]***

[Then why don't you defend me? You already know that Parian is guilty! I don't know how you put it together, but we need to stop this guessing game, Emerald.] I cut my hand sharply through the air. ***[Two more people are dead. What good does our coming here do if we cannot save an innocent girl?]***

Tincrown hurried to catch up with us, although Nechtan took his time.

"Does anyone care to explain to me what happened in my house earlier?" the doctor mumbled. "Because I'm still lost."

Emerald scratched his nose. "Can't we settle this matter first?"

"I suppose we could." Tincrown huffed. "Or perhaps I should discuss the matter with the high priest and get his opinion."

"No." Emerald's voice came out gravelly and desperate. "Wait until tomorrow. Please. Once we have proof of what has become of Kristine, I'll answer all your questions... if you're willing to answer mine."

Tincrown bit his lip and took a long moment to consider this offer.

"Please." Emerald reached out to touch the doctor's forearm, but pulled back before making contact. "I promise you, I'll tell you everything."

The plea was raw and desperate, but even beyond the tone of his words, his urgency was enough to distract me from what I had witnessed in the water. When he said *everything,* he meant it. I suspected that this included even secrets that I was not privy to.

Tincrown extended his arm so that his fingers brushed the back of Emerald's palm. "Alright," he murmured. "I'll wait. Until tomorrow."

We were back within the boundaries of the town, and Tincrown led us to one of the little houses, which I had yet to visit. He knocked three times upon the door and stepped aside, so that we formed a semi-circle before the lintel.

A moment later, the door opened, spilling golden light out into the twilight. Davina, the schoolteacher, examined us with her cold blue eyes. When she saw Nechtan, she bowed her head and reached for a hook beside the door to retrieve her hood and veil.

"Forgive me, Nechtan, I meant no disrespect." Pulling the hood into place, she ushered us inside. "Come in, please. We were just sitting down to dinner, but the meal can wait."

The four of us trooped inside. The thought of imparting the dire news to Kristine's parents brought me no pleasure, so I bit my tongue and waited until we were all inside. Nechtan led the way, while the doctor followed. Emerald brought up the rear.

As we stepped into the kitchen, Nechtan coughed significantly. "Good evening, Shale. How are you this evening?"

"Hungry," came the gruff reply. "What's all this about?"

I steeled myself to deliver grim tidings, but as I rounded the corner, I let out a yelp of surprise. Kristine sat at the table, hands folded before her in an attitude of prayer.

"Please forgive my father, High Priest," she said in her honey-sweet, musical voice, unmistakable despite her shrouded face. "We have so few nights together as a family, and we cherish them, but the will of Dathan always comes first."

"So it does, my child." Nechtan gestured to me. "I hope that we will be able to keep this brief. Simone, will you please state the nature of our business here this evening?"

"I... well, that is, I..." I gaped at the assembled company. "I thought I saw you by the pond less than an hour ago."

"Impossible," Davina said. She walked around behind Kristine's chair and laid her hands upon her daughter's shoulders. "She has been here all night, helping me prepare the evening meal and prepare for tomorrow's lessons. Isn't that right, my love?"

"Yes, Mai-mai." Kristine nodded.

"You all came here because you thought you saw my daughter somewhere else?" Shale cocked an eyebrow. His red-faced sneer could not have been more at odds with the open piety of his wife and child. "Haven't you got something better to do? Solve the murder of my distant cousin, for example?"

"We simply wished to verify Kristine's safety," Nechtan assured him. "Are we all satisfied on that front?"

"Yes," I whispered. I was glad that the girl was alright, but I could not make sense of what I had seen at the lake, and Nechtan's smug attitude left me incensed.

"Then we shall take our leave and allow your family to enjoy the evening meal in peace." Nechtan bowed and led our retreat.

Perhaps it was another girl. Perhaps you only assumed *it was Kristine because you saw her with Parian.* The thought made me anxious again, but I lingered long enough to examine her robes. Sure enough, they were the same colors and design as the clothing I had seen beside the water.

"Come on," Emerald said gently, waving me toward the door.

I went with him, scouring the rooms for any sign that I was not going mad. Kristine had been on the verge of death; Kristine was now alive and in perfect health. I believed both things with the same unshakeable certainty, and yet one fact so blatantly contradicted the other that I could not explain how both statements could be true.

I stopped inside, however, as my eye snagged on a pair of boots. They were the smallest of the three pairs that stood in a row, and were freshly-spattered with mud, the leather near the sole dark with water damage. Almost as if they'd been pulled on hastily at the lakeshore. I glanced around in search of other clues.

"I'm going home." Nechtan paused outside the front door. "We have enough troubles in Dyrne without any need to invent more. Good night, doctor."

"Good night," Tincrown replied.

I stood in the doorway, frozen stiff, unable to take a step.

[Crimson?] Emerald gave me a gentle push through our connection. **[What's the matter?]**

I did not speak. Mere words were not enough. Instead, as Nechtan wandered off into the night and Tincrown waited for us to emerge, I lifted one finger to point to Shale's coat, which hung on one of half a dozen pegs beside the door, above the row of boots. The coat itself was the one he'd been wearing when I met him, but now a handful of black-and-white striped feathers peeked out of the pockets.

Griffin feathers.

Exactly like the ones that had surrounded Bilk Deepvein's desecrated remains.

Chapter Eighteen

Nothing I had seen the day before made sense.

Bilk's ruined body. The feathers in Shale's pocket. Kristine, flayed and bloodless. Kristine again, sitting down to dinner with her parents. Nechtan's smug certainty that everything was alright. Parian's horrified expression when he realized that he was not alone.

Some parts, admittedly, made sense together, but taken as a whole, I could not see the bigger picture.

It was not until very late that evening, well into the Sacred Hours, that I realized what we were up against.

A cult.

There was a cult in Dyrne.

As tempting as it was to blurt out my suspicions, I kept my own council. I had already caused one false alarm the day before. But what if it hadn't been a false alarm at all?

So as not to disturb Emerald, I ducked through the wall into the hall, where I began to pace from our old rooms on the far end and back. No wonder I couldn't figure out the person responsible. There was more than one. In fact...

I stopped short. What if the whole *town* was in on it?

"Dathan is the Lord of the Living and the Dead," I whispered, keeping my voice so low that I was sure no one would hear me, even if they were to stumble upon me in the dark. "His followers worship him in all his forms. What if the dead in Dyrne don't *stay* dead?" Emerald had implied as much the morning before. We knew about the murder of the mining boss and the wholesale slaughter of the Conjury scouts because they had not been followers of Dathan, but Kristine was pious. Perhaps that was why she had still been alive when I'd stumbled across her at the pond.

I had never seen her face beneath the robes, and Nechtan wore wrappings that covered him from head to toe, with ceremonial garb draped over that.

May the gods keep them. How many times had I heard those very words since entering the town of Dyrne? There might be more power in that incantation that I had presupposed. What if Dathan kept his most ardent followers neither living *nor* dead? Bilk must have worked it out first and threatened to expose the town's terrible secret.

What if every religious person in this town wore their robes not for modesty, but to cover the marks of their decay? The whole town might be walking around with their flesh sloughing off their bones, caught in limbo for eternity while the animus of Dathan kept them going, never able to show their faces—

I stopped short, clenched my hands into fists, and uttered a minor curse. I had seen Davina's face only the night before. The mayor, who had been arguing with Bilk on the day we arrived, had never *once* hidden his face.

Bit by bit, my whole theory fell apart. The feathers in Shale's pockets didn't fit. Nor did the fact that Parian had made it quite clear that he had no interest in paying homage to Dathan. That being the case, why would he be the one taking part in the gruesome events I had seen by the lake?

Not to give overmuch credit to Emerald's taste in men, either, but I didn't think that Tincrown would be eager to protect a town full of murderers and monsters.

Dammit. I had been so certain that I was onto something.

Alright, then, scrap the idea that the whole town is involved. I tried to see how my theory might apply to only a few select individuals, but it was like grasping at smoke. Every handful came back empty.

I was back where I'd begun, with only vague suspicions, too many suspects, and no idea where to turn my attention next.

My frustration was short-lived, because Emerald finally found a comfortable position in the bed, and before I could speculate anymore, I blinked out.

When Emerald summoned me the next morning, we did not speak right away. He took a long time pulling on his boots, while I examined myself in the mirror.

"You've given me quite an ugly dress today," I observed at last.

Emerald glanced up at my rough, homespun dress that looked as if it had been made out of old curtains and tough leather. "I didn't mean to. I wasn't thinking about it. Just summoned you, is all."

"Maybe you shouldn't summon me when you're feeling so sorry for yourself." I ran my palms over the bodice of my dress. "Also, I'm fairly certain that this bit is supposed to go *under* the others. Has your upcoming conversation with Tincrown got you so out of sorts?"

"Well, to be fair, I have to explain to him why we started out having a perfectly nice drink and genial conversation by ourselves, only to be interrupted by my screaming female companion who appeared from *nowhere* yelling about a flaying that we cannot prove ever happened." Emerald rubbed his temples. "So, yes, I've been concerned about how that will go."

I took a step closer, deciding to let the matter of my unsatisfactory appearance lie for the moment. "You said that you believed me about Kristine. So how do you explain the fact that she is alive?"

Emerald lifted both hands in surrender. "I don't understand

what you saw last night. I promise you that if I could, I would tell you everything. It's obvious that you were frightened when you manifested in the room. That's never happened before. You've never reappeared like that, unless you went too far away from me."

I perched on the edge of the bed and tapped one finger against my lips as I considered this. The day before, I had taught myself how to fly by imagining that I was climbing stairs and pretending to jump. At the lakeside, I had wanted nothing more in the world than to return to Emerald.

Did I somehow conjure myself back into his presence? As theories went, it was unlikely, but not impossible.

"Not that it matters," Emerald said quickly. He thumped his palm against his forehead and closed his eyes. "Only, it could cause real trouble if the wrong person had seen you appear out of nowhere."

"Is Tincrown the *right* person, then?"

"Perhaps. I trust him more than any other person in Dyrne."

"Excluding me, presumably." I offered my companion a crooked smile. "Since I was born out of your own mind, I'd like to think that you can believe what I tell you."

"Are you joking?" Emerald retorted. "That's the one fact that makes me think I *can't*. Like Nechtan said, the mind plays tricks."

"Like when it tells you that your life has no value?" I suggested.

Emerald's jaw tightened, and he crossed his arms defensively over his chest. "Now's not the time, Crim."

"When *is* the time?" I asked. "When are you going to tell me what happened the night I was born?"

If Emerald had reached out and struck me a blow in the chest with his enormous fist, it would not have sent me reeling, but the force of his emotional response to this question was another matter. For a moment, I thought that he had tried to push me away, either physically through compulsion, or emotionally through our mental link.

No, I realized. *He didn't strike a blow against you.* You *hit* him.

"The night you were *born,* as you put it, I conjured you in the woods outside of a tavern," he growled, not meeting my eye. "And may I be the first to point out that you have been a royal pain in my ass ever since?"

I stared down at my hands, then turned them over to examine my palms. For a fraction of a second, I did not see *my* hands, with their pale slender fingers and narrow wrists. I was looking down at broad, moss-green palms, with thick knuckles and square fingertips, cracked nails, and deep blue veins pulsing under the thick flesh just below the joint—

The image vanished as quickly as it had come. Perhaps I *was* going mad. Perhaps I *had* imagined Parian at the lake the night before.

No. Last night was real. This... this was a memory.

"Not that night, then," I said slowly. "The night before. What happened the night *before* I was born? On the equinox?"

"*Crimson.*" Emerald spun toward me, pinching his features together as he loomed over me. A white-hot bolt of anger flashed between us, only to be doused by the memory of water. I shrank before him, made small by the tidal wave of resentment and disgust.

I've never seen him look at anyone that way. He's never shown his anger, or tried to frighten anyone.

As I cowered, Emerald stepped back, and the wall between us went up again. He hugged his arms around his chest for a moment, and I recognized the gesture as one I had made before when I was trying to protect myself. "Sorry," he grunted. "Didn't mean to frighten you. Just drop it, alright? Let it go."

His anger hadn't been meant for me, then. Now that our emotions were distinct again it occurred to me that Emerald was always trying to make himself smaller. I'd seen him crotchety and bitter, but never truly enraged. If I hadn't had my window into his mind, I might not have realized that he was anything more than fed up with my constant needling.

As always, his ugliest emotions were reserved for himself.

"You didn't frighten me," I said, which was mostly true. At the very least, I wasn't frightened for my own sake. "I was just taken aback." Since I had nothing helpful to say, I decided to dispel the tension between us. I flipped my hair over my shoulder and pouted. "First you summon me in a tatty old inside-out dress, then you yell at me for asking questions. The doctor really *does* have you out of sorts."

"It's a perfectly fine dress, Crimson." Emerald rolled his eyes and moved toward the door. "Come on, it's getting late. Like you said last night, we don't want anyone else dying on our watch." He let out a pained sigh. "I'm going to have words with Tincrown. Depending on how much he's willing to help us, we might finally be able to close this case and stop the killings in Dyrne once and for all."

"And if I haven't figured it out by that time?" I asked. "What will become of our bet?"

"It will prove nothing one way or the other." Emerald reached for the door. "I'm not going to drag this out to give you more time."

"No," I agreed. "No, you certainly should not."

Which meant that if I was going to have any hope of working the case out on my own, I would have to accomplish it today.

Chapter Nineteen

It was difficult for me to leave the inn on my own in daylight hours, since I could not open the doors, and could not reasonably rely on asking others to do so for me. I waited until Emerald was ready to depart and let him lead the way.

As we passed through the main room of the tavern, the suspicious gazes of townsfolk followed us. We were almost to the door when a wooly white head appeared at Emerald's elbow.

"Begging your pa-a-ardon, good people, but I've heard some dreadful rumors." Errol the lambkin dabbed his brow with a lace kerchief. "Another murder? Perhaps two?"

"Not sure it counts as a rumor when it was shouted in the streets," Emerald retorted. "But, yes, someone was killed at the mine."

"Oh dear." Errol patted his neck with the kerchief. "What an awful turn of events! I thought I'd find myself a home in the quietest town on the island. Oh dear, oh dear…"

Emerald bent down and lowered his voice. "There is a bit of good news. That liquor of yours is the best of its kind I've ever had."

"Really?" Errol crumpled the kerchief against his palm, and a shy smile overtook his features. "Why, I'm sure it's very kind of you to say so!"

"I don't suppose you have another bottle handy?"

The lambkin's childlike features were not suited to skulduggery, but he peered about the room before slipping a bottle out of his pocket and into Emerald's palm. Emerald passed him a few coins and straightened up.

"Dangerous times, I'm afraid," he intoned. "Watch your back, Master Lambkin. I hope to put this matter to rest as soon as possible, but in the meantime, keep your eyes open."

"Yes, sir." Errol bowed to us both and hurried away.

I glared at Emerald. "Really?"

[What?] The bottle had already vanished into some hidden pocket of his vest.

[Last time you blackmailed him for a bottle of that stuff. Now you're doing business with him?]

[What can I say? I've developed a taste for it. Besides, as I've said, this will be a rather difficult conversation.]

[Which is why you need liquor to smooth things over, of course.] I rolled my eyes at his back as he pushed through the door.

[Of course.]

I followed him out into the street. The sky above us was overcast, and although I could not feel the air on my skin, I shivered and wrapped my arms around myself.

"There's a chill, isn't there?" I murmured.

[How would you know? Because of the clouds?] Emerald made a gesture toward the sky that would have looked like an idle wave of the hand to any unknowing passersby.

[The leaves. The other day, when it was raining, they turned over.]

Emerald hummed and shot me a sideways glance. *[You're observant. And you're right. There is an ominous chill in the air today. I wouldn't be surprised if it rains before nightfall.]*

We walked by the hall, and then the familiar bulk of the

church. My suspicions from the prior night returned. Every time I passed the temple, it seemed to have grown larger, like some lazy, sluggish predator that swallowed its prey whole.

My theory about ghouls and ghasts might not hold water, but I had put the matter of the markings by each name out of my mind following the traumatic evening under Emerald's control. They meant something, but whether they had anything to do with our case, I could not begin to say.

This town is riddled with festering secrets, I thought. *Its residents are tight-lipped. They know more than they say. Perhaps that's why Emerald's hesitant to point a finger. If Nechtan is to blame, the people will not want to see him carted off, because he stands upright on the altar of their blind faith.*

The same altar, I was beginning to suspect, upon which others lives had been given in sacrifice.

I stopped in front of the Church of Dathan, and Emerald took a few more steps. When he realized that I had fallen behind, he turned back to me. "Are you coming?" he asked.

"No," I murmured. "No, I don't think so." I ran my palms over my bare arms, lost in thought. Emerald already had answers, which meant that *I* had all the answers, too. I just hadn't put them together yet.

But maybe there's another way. After all, my deal with Emerald had never specified *how* I would solve the mystery on my own, only that I would. A few nights ago, someone had come to my room to look for me. I was already a target.

That realization had troubled me on Emerald's account. If someone had attacked him while he slept, he might have suffered grievous harm.

But if someone attacked *me*, I would not be in any danger—and I might manage to look into the eyes of a killer without being in any real danger.

"You go on," I said. "Talk to Tincrown. I'll find ways to occupy myself."

"As you wish." Emerald dipped into an ironic bow and left me standing there, alone, before the temple of Lord of the Living and the Dead.

I retreated a few dozen paces toward the black iron fence that surrounded the graveyard. Nechtan stood before the oldest grave, his bandaged arms folded over his chest and his head bowed in thought. When he registered my presence, he turned and bowed to me with a great deal more solemnity than Emerald had shown upon his departure.

"Good morning, Simone of the Road. How do you fare today?"

"Quite well." I lifted my chin proudly, despite my homely outfit, and pressed my shoulders back. "And I have good news. We have discovered the identity of the killer."

"Is that so?" Nechtan's face was, as always, hidden and inscrutable, but the note of surprise in his voice was obvious. "And what have you learned?"

"That... is a secret." I paused to give myself time to formulate the lie. "We've sent for an official Conjury scout, who will meet me on the high road at midday. Near the spot where Cassandra of Wishwind died. That seems only fitting, doesn't it?"

"So there is to be a formal inquiry?" Nechtan asked.

"There must be." I forced a grim smile onto my lips. "So many people have died, Nechtan. It is *such* a tragedy. Things cannot be allowed to go on like this. The Conjury has to be informed."

"Of course." Short of flying into a murderous rage, Nechtan made every appearance of accepting this news as inevitable. "It is a terrible sequence of events, Miss Simone. So much death leaves a mark on a place, even one as peaceful as our little hamlet."

I nodded. "I'm glad you understand. After today, the matter will be out of my hands."

There was nothing more to say, and with that I turned on my heel and strode away, trembling with anticipation. Three Conjury scouts had been slain in service of concealing the information which I now claimed to have. A babblebird had been struck from the sky. In my conversation with Nechtan, I had named *myself* as the messenger, and provided both the motive and opportunity to bring the full force of the killer's wrath down upon my own head.

Unlike some hapless bird, however, I could not be felled by a well-placed stone, and our murderer would be hard-pressed to send me tumbling over the mountainside.

It was not enough to tell Nechtan, however. I needed to provide all of my suspects with the same information to ensure that the responsible party would make himself known.

I spotted Shale outside of the general store not far away, waving his fists in the air.

"Enough of that! Hands off, I warn you, or I'll have your sorry hides!" He spun around, swatting at nothing, until he saw me. When he did, his face pinched in a frown, and he turned back to the cart.

Who is he fighting? I wondered. *Apparitions? Or a guilty conscience?*

"Good afternoon, Shale," I said.

"Come to hover around me again, have you?" he snapped.

"Hardly. I have good news... my associate and I have worked out who is responsible for your kinsman's murder."

Shale straightened up. "Murder, was it? I thought the lad might be delirious with grief. I heard it was griffins that did it."

That's right, keep blaming the griffins... as if the beasts were responsible for stuffing Bilk's mouth with silk. I shook my head sadly and told him, "I'm afraid it was murder, and we know who. We'll be meeting with an emissary for the Conjury at midday on the pass where Cassandra died. Before long, the matter will be put to rest."

Shale's discomfort was easier to observe than Nechtan's. He wiped the back of his palm across his forehead, and his eyes darted nervously around the town. "Er, is that so? Messy business, that. Glad to see justice gettin' dispensed, and all. I just hope that whoever's responsible doesn't, ah, cause any more trouble in the meantime."

I nodded to his mostly empty cart. "Preparing to leave town, then?"

"Oh, aye, just unloading the last of it. Depends what the weather does." Shale squinted up at the darkening sky. "Those paths are treacherous in the rain, so I might wait a day before setting out. Mind your footing out there, Miss Simone."

"I'll be careful. Thank you for your concern." Assuming, of course, that Shale meant his words as a friendly warning and not a dire threat.

"Shale?" Sheiling, the shopkeeper, appeared in the door of the general store. "Is there anything else?"

"Yup." Shale hoisted the last crate and shot me one last wary glare. "Just one more bit of luggage to unload, and then it'll all be taken care of."

With that, my trap was baited and set. That left only one more suspect to inform. I waved farewell to the shopkeeper and turned back the way I'd come.

Vanora and Kade's house was the liveliest on the street when I arrived. Dun stood out front, along with three of his goats: the blonde nanny, a white billy, and a small and rather pudgy black one with brown patches on her face that looked for all the world like eyebrows. All three goats were placidly smacking their lips with a deeply self-satisfied air.

Vanora, Aindreas, and a figure I didn't recognize stood in front of them. The third person clothed was in mismatched articles of the village garb that were too tight in some places and too loose in others. Vanora wagged a gloved finger in Dun's face, while Aindreas seemed to be trying to placate her.

"All of my lettuces!" Vanora screeched. "Every last one! Some goatherd you are, letting these dirty beasts wander through town in the night, wreaking havoc on people's garden beds!"

"They're not dirty," Dun retorted. "Say what you like about *me*, Vanora, but leave the goats out of it!"

"*Mah-ah-ah*," the black goat interjected, and went back to smacking her lips.

"It's only lettuce, Mother. We can plant more." Aindreas

gestured to the unfamiliar robes worn by his companion. "Parian will turn the bed and reseed it."

If I'd been a flesh-and-blood person, his words would have floored me. I gaped at the unrecognizable form in front of me.

Was this really *Parian?* The young man who'd made his disdain for the Church of Dathan and his high priest apparent at every opportunity?

Vanora crossed her arms in annoyance, but Aindreas and Dun spotted me at the same time.

"Oh, begging your pardon, Miss Simone." Dun bowed. "I'm afraid you've caught us at a bad time. My fence broke last night, and my goats went running all over the gods' creation. Caused a bit of a stir, I'm afraid."

Remembering my brush with the nanny goat the day before, and her aching need for any tasty morsel beyond the fence, I could only imagine how happy she must have been to see the fence come down.

"Was there something you wanted, Miss Simone?" Vanora asked. She smoothed out her robes, evidently somewhat ashamed to be caught in the act of a scolding.

"I was only heading out of town. I'm to meet with a Conjury agent on the pass at midday. We've figured out who's to blame for the murders."

If I had hoped that this announcement would be met with a sigh of relief, I would have been sorely disappointed. All four stayed silent for a long moment.

To my surprise, it was Parian who spoke first. "They'll take whoever did it and leave this town in peace, won't they?"

"I should think so," I replied. *What's that, Parian? Is your guilty conscience prompting you to confess so that the rest of Dyrne won't be forced to pay for your crimes?*

"Good," Dun said. "Best that the matter be put to rest once and for all."

"Indeed," Aindreas added.

"It'll be good to have that settled." Vanora turned her back on Dun and took Parian's arm. "Let's go around back, dear, and fix the damage Dun and his wastrel beasts had wrought."

The two of them went around back, and Dun set about herding his goats away down the road.

"Miss Simone?" Aindreas's already deep voice dropped lower still. "May I ask you something? I think I might know who's responsible for all this mess."

"Oh?" I smiled up at his shrouded face. "And who might that be?"

"The merchant, Shale." Aindreas sighed heavily. "He's spent a great deal of time here, and his family is dear to all of us, but I've heard rumors." He took a step closer, speaking even more softly. "He might have a license for his Flamestones, but that's not all he sells. He travels all over the island. The Conjury scouts must have found out more than the rest of us suspect... and I believe that his kinsman was blackmailing him. Outsiders like him can easily tarnish the reputation of a small town like ours."

I was not often tempted to reach out and touch people, but as Aindreas spoke, I longed to do just that. It would be illuminating to know whether he really believed everything that he was saying, or if he simply hoped to cover for his brother or the high priest by casting suspicions on Shale. I had wondered about that very subject, and I had seen the griffin feathers in his pocket with my own eyes.

If my plan worked, however, I would know the truth soon enough, and I could solve the mystery *without* having to invade the minds of every person on the street.

"I appreciate your candor," I told him. "Would you mind if I asked *you* a question?"

Aindreas spread his gloved hands. "By all means."

"Your brother, Parian." I gestured toward the back garden, then folded my hands in front of my inside-out bodice arrangement. "Has he had a religious conversion in the night?"

I must have tipped my hand a little too fully, because Aindreas went very still.

"I don't mean to imply anything," I added hastily. "But only yesterday, he showed nothing but disdain for Dathan and his... accessories. Now, he's dressed the same as the rest of you."

"The decision to accept our customs was his choice, and his alone," Aindreas replied stiffly.

"Of course." I dipped into an awkward curtsy. "Forgive me, I meant no offense."

"Faith is a mysterious thing, Miss Simone. An intangible thing. It defies all natural laws." Aindreas bowed his head. "Forgive me. My mother was quite upset about her lettuces. I should check on her."

I winced as he followed his mother and brother. He'd been trying to help me, and I'd thrown his help back in his face with a thinly veiled insinuation, so to speak.

Or he was trying to steer suspicion away from his brother, and realized that he had not succeeded entirely.

I would find out soon enough.

⚜

Shale had been right to warn me about the dangers of the high pass in the rain. Shortly before the sun reached its zenith, its already dim light was subsumed by the louring sky and the whole world was cast into shades of black and white. The rain followed soon after, falling with even greater fury than it had during our first climb into the mountains. If I had been anyone else, I would have given up and turned back to avoid risking my life on that windy precipice.

At that distance from town, I was stretching the limits of my bond with Emerald. I could *feel* the invisible tether between us, and it tugged me with ever-greater urgency as I approached the carving that signified where Cassandra of Wishwind had lost her life. The sensation was an altogether strange one, the first external force that had acted upon me in such a manner.

If this is what Emerald feels for Tincrown, no wonder he's helpless to resist.

At last, I reached the outlying spot, where that steady hand had carved out the dead woman's name. It occurred to me that the weather might deter my would-be assailant, but that didn't worry me too much. Whoever had killed Bilk Deepvein so ruthlessly would have no qualms about braving the weather if they thought it would achieve their ends.

Once there, I had no recourse but to wait until the murderer showed his face.

Without Emerald to alter my appearance, I must have cut a strange figure on the cliffside, with my bright red hair loose and soft against my shoulders despite the driving rain.

I held out my hand, watching the water pass through it as I waited. It was not fair that only Emerald could affect me. Yes, he'd made me, but why should I be bound to him?

You can fly, Crimson. You can walk through walls. You can read emotions. You even cast a shadow. Why shouldn't you be able to make yourself look however you please?

I twisted one lock of scarlet hair around my finger, trying to imagine it wet.

What is the purpose of coming into my own power, of having consciousness and sentient thoughts, when I do not have autonomy over my own body?

I was still lost in thought when a few fragments of slate lining the path slid loose and tumbled over the ravine. I jumped in alarm and turned toward Dyrne in the direction from which the disturbance had come.

"Hello?" I called.

The rain fell so thick and fast that I could not see anyone on the road. I took a step back, scanning the path in its entirety.

No one was there.

The rocks might have slipped free on their own, driven loose by the rain, but I kept staring at the empty stretch of road. Some instinct, what Emerald might have called *my gut*, drew my eye again and again to the same place a few yards away from me. I tried lifting my hand to shield my eyes, a singularly silly impulse.

There was nothing to see. And still, I could not look away.

Then, just when I was beginning to question my own sanity, something moved.

Or rather, *nothing* moved. There was an empty space amid the raindrops, a place where they did not fall. The drops pinged off a silhouette, the outline of a man, and yet there was no man there.

"Who are you?" I whispered.

I got no answer, but the shape advanced. I could not tell its exact distance, but it was close, close enough to see the outline despite the rain.

I retreated another step, trying to make sense of the *nothingness* before me. The tether that bound me to Emerald yanked at my core, almost knocking me out of existence and pulling me back to him, as it had when I was a bird following Oidche too far past the edges of town.

The shape moved, and I took one final step back. This would have to be the last one, or I would no longer be able to resist that lodestone pull to my creator.

"You are like me," I murmured to the empty space. "You are as I am, but inverted. We are not real, not the way other people are. I see you. You are empty air, and yes, *I see you.* I won't ask again. Who *are* you?"

Something passed through my throat. A faint shiver of contact between two unreal beings.

He's trying to strangle me, I thought, and I would have been afraid, but there was no room left inside me for any of my own feelings. I was full to overflowing with *his.*

Rage. That was all he felt. A hollow, blinding, aching rage, a fury with no clear direction.

This is it. This is the kind of anger it took to tear Bilk Deepvein apart and cut his throat to the bone. This wrath was visited on Maximilien, when he was strangled until his eyes protruded and his tongue turned all but black.

The sensation was a nightmare, worse than anything that I had ever felt, more vindictive and malicious than even Emerald's feelings toward himself. And worse of all, at the heart of that white hot core of anger, was another emotion so bound up with my attacker's fury that it was functionally indistinguishable from his ire:

Love.

His rage was rooted in love, a corruption so deepseated that it turned what should have been a bright and joyous emotion into a blight that spread through every corner of his mind.

I tried to pull away, desperate to distance myself from that awful, sickening emotion, and as I moved, I fell.

I landed without a sound on the floor of the inn, beside the bed where Emerald sat staring down at some object in his hands.

"Crimson?" he asked in surprise. "Where have you been? What happened?"

I let out a sob as I reached for him. My attacker no longer had me in his grasp, but his hideous fury still clutched at me. It *hurt*. I had not understood pain before that moment, but in the aftermath of that assault, I was wounded.

So much for your clever little plan. So much for being invincible.

Emerald fell to the floor beside me and made a vain but well-intended attempt to wrap his arms around me. We passed through one another, overlapping at a dozen different points.

As I sobbed out my distress, Emerald's emotions flowed into me, replacing the scourge that had been planted in my mind by the unseen assailant. Emerald had his flaws, but he loved fiercely, and his love was without malice.

"You're alright, Crim. I'm here now, and you're alright." He whispered the words over and over again like a mantra.

And he was right.

I was.

Chapter Twenty

❧

It took me a long time to explain what had happened, mostly because every time I stopped crying, I remembered how it had felt to be battered by the would-be murderer's onslaught, and that set me off all over again. When I finally stopped bawling like an intangible baby, Emerald sat back on his heels.

"Well, I'm sorry to hear that was the outcome," he said. "But it was a good idea, even if it didn't work out the way you thought it would."

I sniffed as I struggled to my feet. "I didn't learn who was after me, but I did learn one thing—something that explains a lot of what hasn't been making sense to me."

"Oh?" Emerald rose, too, and leaned back against the bedpost. "Which is?"

I rubbed one eye. My face felt puffy and hot beneath my own palm, and my tears were wet against my cheek, even if only I could feel them.

"I have learned," I pronounced, "that our murderer is invisible."

"Ah, yes." Emerald's worried features relaxed into a smile. "I wondered when you'd get there."

"What does that mean?" I demanded. "Hold on. How long have you known that?"

Emerald gave a poorly-timed wink, considering my emotional state. "You tell me what you think, and I'll tell you what I *know*."

"Gods." I stamped my foot and glared at him. "You're unbearable. After everything I've been through today, couldn't you at least *try* to be nice?"

"I'm being nice. You asked for a chance to prove yourself, and I'm letting you speak your piece."

I glowered at him and wiped away the last of my tears. "Thank you. I think."

"Present your case, Crimson." Emerald leaned back and fixed me with his verdant gaze. "Who is Dyrne's killer?"

I didn't like being tested—but that said, now that he had determined to test me, I was equally determined to pass. I folded my hands behind my back and took a hesitating step. As I did so, a flash of something shiny caught my eye on the bed.

A pair of leather and crystal goggles.

That must have been what Emerald was holding when I first appeared in the room. They represented, I supposed, some portion of what Emerald *knew*.

I would ask about them later. For the time being, I began to pace.

"The figure who came after me was invisible. That makes sense, and it explains how he was able to move about so easily. And why his feet were bare!" I whirled toward Emerald. "My room, Bilk's tent... he *had* to be naked, because whatever turns him invisible must only apply to him." I lifted both hands as clue after clue fell into place. "When we were in Lower Bound, the innkeeper opened Maximilien's door, and something... something *passed* me in the hall. I thought it might be a ghost or something—"

"You noticed that?" Emerald smirked. "And you thought it was a ghost."

"In my defense, I was very young at the time." I turned back to my pacing. "That also explains some of the strange things I've witnessed. When I went out to the lake the night after you violated my freewill—"

"I'm still sorry about that," Emerald murmured.

"I know, I know. Stop interrupting! There was someone at the lakeside, watching me." I clapped my hands to either side of my face and stopped again. "*Dun!* When I went to his house, he wasn't there, but I was so sure someone must have been. But he *was* there, I just couldn't see him!" I paused and wrinkled my nose as the implications sank in. "Wait. Was he wandering the house *naked?*"

"Presumably," Emerald said.

"Ew." Despite all the violence I had witnessed at the hands of our killer, that detail still troubled me. "He sits on the furniture naked?"

"And cooks naked, by the sounds of it." Emerald lowered himself to the edge of the bed. "Let me add, from personal experience, that cooking with your *niblets flapping* presents a great deal of personal risk."

"So Dun is our killer?"

"You tell me," Emerald said. "Is he?"

"I suppose that he might have planted the feathers in Shale's pocket. And it explains some things, like why we didn't see him at the lake that first day, but..." I closed my eyes and massaged my temples as I thought. "But it doesn't explain everything. And, pardon me, he strikes me as an oaf. Not that oafs can't be killers, but I don't think he is."

Emerald waited, still wearing that smug grin. Only a few minutes ago, his presence had been such a great comfort. Now, I wished that I could manifest a physical form long enough to slap the smirk off his face.

"Alright, *don't* give me a clue. Let me think." I tapped my finger in the middle of my forehead. "If Dun is invisible, but he's *not* the killer, that means that he's also not the only one who can turn invisible."

My theory from the night before had been demonstrably

wrong, and yet, as I considered this new angle, it shifted slightly and came into focus. The people of Dyrne were not ghouls lifted up from the grave by Nechtan's twisted misuse of the *aidea*.

"That's why Nechtan wears the robes," I said. "That's why all of them do. Because some people in this town can turn *invisible*. That's why the little girl disappeared! When Oidche brought her back, he had her wrapped in that cloak to hide her. Tincrown told Oidche to send for Moira, and to bring the child's clothes." I clapped my palm to my forehead. "*Tincrown knows!*"

Emerald offered a modest and somewhat condescending round of applause. "If anything, Crimson, this proves that you are at least *somewhat* distinct from me."

"Because I figured it out on my own?" I asked.

He lifted one shoulder and bobbled his head back and forth. "Debatable. I meant because I'd worked this all out on the first day."

I stamped my foot on the floor, although of course it made no sound. "I am only a week old, Emerald! How quickly could you solve a mystery when you were my age?"

He chuckled at my tantrum. "In that case, you are a star pupil, but your age is showing."

"Ugh." I ran my hand through my hair and turned away from him. The rain had let up. It now came as a slow drizzle, forming little rivulets against the windowpane. It was late afternoon, and the light in the sky was already fading. My little farce had cost me a great deal of time. It had yielded some answers, but the most important one of all still eluded me.

The dark exterior meant that, rather than seeing plainly into the distance, the window reflected the light of Emerald's bedside lantern back to us, revealing our reflections in the warped glass.

"Emerald," I said, frowning at my visage. "You told me once that if the Conjury found out about me, there would be repercussions. And in Lower Bound, you indicated that people who could turn invisible were rare. So it's a secret they would want to keep hidden, correct? What would the Conjury do if they found out about this?"

"Conscript the citizens into their service, I imagine." Emerald's mirth vanished. He pulled his legs up onto the bed and lay back against the pillows, gazing down at his sturdy hands in thought. Idly, he let the pad of one thumb drag across his opposite wrist as he spoke. "Test them. I'm sure that the Conjury would take a great deal of interest in the notion of invisible soldiers."

"The town could be ripped apart." That explained my attacker's anger, and also the weaponized seeds of love at its core. "It's a secret someone decided to kill to protect. And if we solve it, won't that mean...?"

"That we finish the work the first scouts started." Emerald nodded in agreement.

"But people have died," I mumbled.

"And more will die if we don't stop the person responsible."

"More may die if we do." It seemed to me that there were no heroes here. "And in a town of people who can turn invisible, how will I determine which single person is the one to blame?"

"An excellent question," Emerald agreed.

"I can't exactly tell them to strip down for me, that would be sacrilegious to their beliefs."

Emerald nodded. "If those beliefs are real."

"And the whole town could be in on it." I took another step toward my reflection in the window. "Shale, Parian, Nechtan... they might all be working together. We don't even know how they *turn* invisible."

"No, we don't." Emerald's eyes glowed in the lamplight. "But Tincrown told me a story. I was hoping that we could verify it together."

"You and him?"

"*You* and me," he corrected. "Tonight. If you're willing."

I turned to face him. "What exactly is your plan?"

"We can't very well wrestle the robes off of everyone and town without causing an uproar." Emerald nodded to an object in the corner of the room, one which I had failed to notice in that very moment. "Tell me, Crimson, do you think it's sacrreli-gious to defile a grave?"

I stared at the shovel. Judging by the worn handle, it had seen some use before. "You cannot be serious," I exclaimed.

"Can't I?" Emerald reached for the handle and lifted it onto his shoulder. "Why don't we find out?"

Chapter Twenty-One

I knelt beside the edge of the grave, watching Emerald labor to unearth the casket of the oldest headstone in the cemetery, that of Throop of Dunmore, dead for nearly three centuries.

"Isn't there an easier way of doing this?" I asked.

"I'm open to suggestion," Emerald grunted, heaving another shovelful of wet soil onto the pile that he'd already amassed.

"You know how to use the *aidea*. Can't you just... magic the soil out of the way?" I waved my hands at random to encompass the slowly growing mound of grave dirt.

Emerald stopped long enough to lean on his shovel, wipe a mixture of rain and sweat from his brow, and glare at me. "Yes, Crimson, I could. Why didn't I think of that?"

My shoulders drooped. "You can't, can you?"

"I'm a lightweaver, Crim. That's not how this works. Now, be quiet for a bit, and let me shovel."

"Are you going to explain what you know?"

"All in good time."

I dropped back on my bottom, taking secret delight in the fact that the mud would stain neither my palms nor my dress. I pretended to cough. *"Dramatic."*

"Nothing wrong with a bit of, *huuh!*, showmanship." Emerald tossed another shovelful of dirt. "Do you remember when you asked about, *huuh!*, whether people could turn invisible?"

"Back in Lower Bound?" I pulled my knees in toward my chest and watched him work. He'd set his shirt and jacket aside, under the awning of the church where they would be protected from the rain. His bare arms and strong back were on full display, as were the marks that scarred his forearms from his wrist all the way to his elbow. I rested my chin on my knees. "Yes, I remember. You told me that there hadn't been a wizard who could turn invisible in centuries, and that he'd—well, that he'd disappeared. So to speak. Run off, I think you said?"

"Quite right. About three hundred years ago." Emerald paused again and took a few deep breaths. "Does that spark anything?"

"The only thing sparking at this exact moment is my curiosity. Why haven't you invited Tincrown to your little show? I think he might enjoy the view." I tried to send Emerald an image of himself through our mental link, wondering if that would work.

Apparently it did, although not with the effect I had intended. He immediately hunched over in an attempt to make himself smaller, and covered the scars on his left arm with his right hand. "It's not like that," he mumbled. "He hasn't seen... We only talk."

My first impulse was to apologize and change the subject as I had in the past, but instead I held my tongue until I found more constructive words. "I haven't talked to Tincrown as much as you have, but I suspect that if you *did* show him, he would be kind. You might consider it, since you seem reluctant to discuss certain topics with me."

Emerald shuffled around to face me. His eyes were wide and almost frightened. In his shrunken posture, he looked very much like a frightened little boy, and my heart broke for him.

"As for the wizard," I said, "is that how the people of Dyrne learned to turn invisible? Because he came here?"

Emerald's stillness lasted the span of a few breaths, and with each inhalation he stood a little more upright, like a fiddlehead uncoiling into a mature fern. "Not quite. But you're close, Crim."

He dug a little more while I rifled through the contents of my memory. I had seen some residents in town more than once. Davina had failed to don her hood on several occasions. Parian had only agreed to wear the robes in the last day. Others I had not seen at all.

I rolled to my feet and padded over the grass. The last time that I had set foot in the church, I had been driven by Emerald's will. This time, when I entered the holy ground, I alone chose my course.

The lowest line of the family tree bore dozens of familiar names. Parian, with no mark beside his name. Aindreas, with an x. Shieling, with one slash. Dun, with an x. Lidia, with an x. Kristine, followed by a slash...

And all those branching limbs intertwining together, binding neighbors and cousins and the occasional outsider, all reaching back, converging upon a single name.

Throop of Dunmore.

He didn't teach *them how to become invisible. They're* born *that way.* I ran my finger beneath the names I knew. The x must indicate invisibility, since Dun bore that mark. No mark at all, judging by Parian's lack thereof, must mean that they were fully visible.

Which left the slash. I let my finger rest beneath Kristine's name.

"He didn't skin her," I murmured. "She was naked—and only parts of her can be seen."

Which meant that the answers I needed were right in front of me. Whoever's name bore an x beside it was still a suspect. There were plenty of them, but I could safely rule out Lidia. Shale, by default, was no longer a consideration. A dozen new possibilities presented themselves: Vanora's name bore an x beside it, and Oidche, and Moira, along with a few I did not recognize. My fingers skimmed over the names in search of one in particular.

I found it at last, two lines from the bottom, marked with an incriminating x.

Nechtan.

I backed away a step and rotated on the spot, wary of being watched. Emerald was outside, with no one to watch his back, or warn him if someone attacked. I might not be able to help if someone struck him, but at the very least I could scream my head off until help arrived.

And who would help you, in this town, if Nechtan decided to strike Emerald's head from his shoulders? Or bury him alive in that freshly-dug grave?

Tincrown would, I decided. If anything happened, I could alert the doctor.

I hurried back outside to where Emerald was hauling open the lid of the casket.

"Have you figured it out?" he asked.

"I believe so." I passed through Throop's headstone and stood on the lip of the grave, staring down into what appeared to be an empty wooden box. "He was invisible. These murders are his legacy."

Emerald lifted a handful of wet soil and tossed it into the casket. Instead of splattering against the empty box, it clung to what appeared to be thin air, outlining an unseen skeletal ribcage.

"And there you have it," Emerald said. "Proof."

"All these people were killed to protect the secrets of the town. To keep the Conjury out, and to allow Nechtan to maintain his control of the villagers." I closed my eyes, torn between disgust and pity. If the priest had acted out of anger alone, or out of greed, it would have been easy to revile him, but I had felt the emotions that plagued his heart for myself. Greed and the lust for power were not among them. He only wanted to protect the people of Dyrne, but in the process, he had allowed himself to become twisted into something else, something altogether monstrous.

"Is everyone in the town in on it?" I murmured.

"I worried about that, too." Emerald closed the lid of the casket. "But Tincrown disagrees. He believes the best of most of the villagers. They're secretive, certainly, but all they want is to be left alone. Only one man is to blame for all of this."

"They won't like it if we arrest him," I said.

"No, not if they believe we are acting against them. But I believe that it is possible to take action without alienating everyone else, so long as people understand that we're not the enemy."

I ran my fingers over my lips. "So you intend to arrest Nechtan, but leave the rest of the town in peace?"

Emerald let the lid of the coffin drop closed and began to shovel the dirt back into place. "I believe," he said carefully, "that every terrible thing we have seen was born out of a desire to protect the people of Dyrne. We shall arrest our killer, and once he sees that the people have turned against him, he will accept that murdering everyone who crosses his path will not lead to peace. He had sacrificed so many other lives to achieve his ends. Faced with the option of betraying his kinsfolk, or offering himself up as a martyr, I believe he will make the right choice. The Conjury will have their man, and Dyrne will find a way to survive."

"How do you propose to make all of this happen?" I asked.

Emerald sent an image back to me, a memory of me circling Coirpre at the inn, revealing his crimes to the merchants of Lower Bound until they saw him as he truly was and turned against him.

"Easy, Crimson. We're going to unmask him in public and reveal his crimes to the people."

"We are?"

Emerald's eyes glittered in the darkness. "I misspoke. *We* aren't going to do all that. *You* are."

"Me?" I squeaked.

Emerald's cocky smile only widened. "Do you know the meaning of your name? Your *real* name?"

"Crimson, you mean?" I gestured to my hair. "Seems obvious. You like colors."

"I created you to make you flashy. To make you *bright*. All style, no substance. You are the great Crimson Smoke, the fog that fills the room and draws the eye. And I am the Emerald Flame: the source of all that style and flash, working behind the scenes while you draw everyone's attention."

"You make it sound as if I am *still* all style and no substance," I complained. "As if I, a mere illusion, cannot hold a candle to the great *Emerald Flame*."

"That's what you were," he pointed out, heaving another clod of clay over the coffin.

"Not anymore," I insisted.

"So you keep telling me." Emerald's low laugh echoed back to us from the tombstones and the church walls. "And tomorrow, you're going to get a chance to prove it once and for all."

Chapter Twenty-Two

It was well after midnight by the time Emerald finished washing up and lay down in his bed at the inn. I stood by the window to watch the last trickle of rain run down the windowpane. The clouds parted eventually. By and by, a few stars appeared, and their reflections glimmered against the rain-slick cobblestones of the street.

"Can't sleep?" I asked. "Are you worried that I'll make a mess of things tomorrow?"

Emerald didn't answer right away. When the silence stretched uncomfortably thin, I abandoned my post and turned back to the bed.

He was not biding his time or considering his response. His eyes were closed, and his solid chest rose and fell beneath the thin sheet.

He was asleep.

I walked to the bedside and sat on the edge of the mattress. There was plenty of room, and when he did not stir, I lifted my legs onto the bed and made every appearance of lying down beside him.

Every other time that Emerald had fallen asleep, I had vanished. Perhaps he was only half-asleep, or faking. On closer inspection, however, his eyes darted back and forth beneath his eyelids, and he stirred and snuffled from time to time.

And still, I lingered.

I rolled over, so that I lay on my side, memorizing the contours and planes of his sleeping face. I had never observed him in a position which rendered him so relaxed. All the tension and wariness that ruled his waking posture had disappeared.

One of his hands lay on the pillow beside him, arm extended, leaving the pin-straight scars thereon exposed to the night air. I reached out toward them.

I want to help him. If I let myself into his dreams, for only a moment, I might learn more. I might be able to understand him better than before. I might come to understand exactly what I am, and what my purpose is. It was the same logic that I had employed when peering through the walls of Dun's house. The means justified the end.

Or so I'd told myself.

My hand stopped a few inches from his, and I could force it no further. Yes, I had the best of intentions—just as his had been when he steered me into the church. Tonight, he had made it quite clear that I was the only one who was allowed to see him as he was. He had also admitted that he *finally* believed that I was essentially autonomous.

He trusted me. Peeking into his sleeping psyche would be a violation of that trust.

I slipped back to my feet and put some distance between us to rid myself of the temptation to spy on his dreams. My internal debate raised another question, however: the same night that Emerald had admitted that I was 'real' was also the first night where I did not vanish while he slept.

Did his belief that I am real somehow make me more powerful? If so, what happens if he changes his mind?

The sun had stained the sky in shades of rose and fuschia by the time Emerald awoke. He yawned and sat up, rubbing his eyes. Only then did he spot me sitting on the floor in front of the mirror.

"Crimson?" The second yawn fighting to reach his face lost the battle to the shock of seeing me there. "How are you already here? Also, what in *every hell* are you *wearing?*"

I caught his eyes in the mirror. "I can explain."

He swung one leg out of bed and gawped at me. "Is that *Coirpre's outfit?*"

"Here's the thing." I spun around to face him. "I didn't disappear last night. So rather than watch you sleep, like *Dun* would probably do, I figured that I might as well experiment." I got to my feet and held out my arms, examining the green suit I had conjured for myself. "It took me hours to work out how to do it, but I think I've managed. Only, were his buttons silver? Or gold?"

"Brass." Emerald shook his head in bewilderment. "Crimson, you're *Simon* right now. How...?"

"That's the *other* thing." I straightened my new green capelet. "I tried to change my appearance. I can make small alterations. Earrings, for example. I can change the cut and style of my hair, but not the color. And I can change from Simon to Simone, but I can't alter anything else. Is that normal?"

"Nothing about this is normal." Emerald rubbed his palms against his eyes. "And I detest that suit. Green isn't your color."

"It's Coirpre's color, which is the only reason you hate it," I argued. "I distinctly recall you telling me to shut up and wear green when *you* picked the outfit."

"Doesn't sound like me." He scratched his head and stifled another yawn. "You say that you can change yourself now? Show me."

"Absolutely." I examined my profile in the mirror. "One question, though. What sort of outfit would people expect someone to wear while making an arrest?"

"Something formal, I suppose. Mostly black? Something somber?"

I recalled the very first outfit that Emerald had chosen for me when I was first Simon. Black boots, black trousers, and a cape. I would have to be Simone today, in order to play my assigned role, but an outfit like that, with a bit of feminine flair, would do nicely.

I stood in front of the mirror, watching my reflection intently, and *rearranged* myself. It was easier, now that I'd had a bit of time to practice. Slipping between Simon and Simone was the easy part; the clothes were the tricky bit, especially since I'd never seen the outfit I had in mind.

My reflection blurred, and when it resolved, I was Simone again, wearing high leather boots, tight black breeks, and a long white tunic cinched around the middle with a thick black belt sporting a distinctive silver buckle. My new capelet was shot through with silver embroidery, my hair was held back from my face by a trio of thick braids.

"Better?" I asked, examining my reflection. "Not a speck of green to be found."

Emerald choked. "How did you *do* that?"

"Excellent question," I replied. "Force of will, I expect."

Emerald reached into the pocket of his vest, which he'd hung on a peg on the wall. He produced the green stone, which he turned over in his fingers a few times. "I wonder. Hm. I want to try something. I'm going to dissolve the illusion. Let's see what happens."

"Wa—" I began.

"—it." I choked on the word a few times and shook the fog out of my head. "Hold on. What did you just do?"

"I told you, I dissolved the illusion." Emerald had been standing beside the bed an instant before; now, he was sitting in the chair, with his hair combed, fully dressed for the day. "I waited about fifteen minutes to see if you would reappear on your own, but you didn't. What happened to you?"

"Nothing." I rubbed my forehead and examined my reflection. "I didn't realize that any time had passed." Sure enough, the sky beyond the window was now crystal blue.

"So you can alter your own appearance, within certain limits, and the illusion sustains even while I'm asleep, but you can't cast yourself." Unless I was very much mistaken, Emerald found that news to be a great relief.

That made one of us. "So it would seem."

"Out of curiosity..." Emerald opened his palm to cast the illusion of a small flame, as he had done inside the church. It burned bright against his palm. He smothered it, then turned to an empty patch of floor and gazed at it intently, clutching the stone in one hand and making strange gestures with the other. The general outline of a person appeared, but even as it became more solid, I began to thin.

"Don't do that!" I squeaked, lifting my translucent hands.

He stopped at once, and the shadow vanished, while I became opaque once more. "Interesting. So even when I don't have to actively summon you, I can only cast one large illusion at a time. Pity." He flipped the stone over in his fingers. "Imagine how much ground we could cover as a group of three."

I clapped my hands in delight, although my palms made no sound when they met. "Ooh, imagine if there were *two* of me!"

"Hell after hell." Emerald gagged. "I can only begin to imagine. At the very least, you're here now, and you look the part of a Conjury representative. I believe it is time to unmask our killer. What do you say?"

"I say that unmasking him would make it easier for him to get away. I can only hope that you're right about how the people of this town will react."

Emerald grunted and picked up the goggles that I had noticed earlier. "Only one way to find out."

I took one last look at my reflection. I was exactly as dashing as I had been before, but I could not muster a cocky grin. I had not, it seemed, broken entirely free. I was still dependent on Emerald to conjure me into being, and likely still bound by the tether that kept me within reach.

Nechtan had decided on a whim who lived and died. If Emerald ever dismissed me and failed to summon me back, he would not be tried for murder. I only existed so long as Emerald *wanted* me to exist.

Just focus on the case, Crimson. You can tackle your existential dread later.

"Alright," I said. "Let the show begin."

I had wondered how we would gather the citizens of Dyrne together, but in the end, it was far easier than I had imagined.

When we descended into the dining room of the inn, there was no sign of Cait or any of the other familiar robed figures. Only Errol sat at a table, swinging his stubby legs high above the floor as he pored over a small book of what appeared to be recipes.

"Where is everyone?" I asked.

The lambkin smiled in greeting. "Oh, good morning, Miss Simone. There won't be breakfast until midmorning, I'm afraid. The Church of Dathan considers the dark of the four moons a High Holy Day. All the townsfolk left before the sun came up, and they won't be out for another hour or so. Don't worry, Cait will be back before too long."

[Oh, good,] I grumbled to Emerald. *[We're going to arrest the high priest right after he and his partially visible flock pay homage to their god. Lovely.]*

[It will all work out for us. Have faith.] Emerald chuckled aloud, but I had a feeling there was a double meaning to his joke. "Actually, Errol, we'll be going out. It's time to let the people of Dyrne know that we've done what we came here to do."

"You know who's been killing people?" Errol's eyes widened. "That's ala-a-arming. And you'll announce your findings after Dark Moon Mass?"

"That's our intention," I agreed. *[Because we've gone quite mad, apparently.]*

[We solved everything as quickly as we could,] Emerald

reminded me. *[And justice waits for no man.]*

"Might I join you?" Errol asked.

I nodded. "By all means. It's a public event." *[And it might be nice to have someone else there who isn't indoctrinated into the faith.]*

[Oh, yes.] Emerald smirked. *[Master Errol strikes me as a born fighter.]*

[Very funny. You do realize that, if the crowd turns on us, you'll be the one in danger?]

[The thought has occurred to me.] For a man who was about to thrust himself into harm's way, Emerald struck me as remarkably calm.

[And you have some plan to defend yourself against the mob?]

[I do.]

Emerald did not elaborate, so we waited in silence for Errol to close his book, tuck it into the small cloth satchel at his side, and hop down from the chair.

"Lead the way, good folk." Errol bowed to us and gestured to the door.

That was how we came to be accompanied to the Church of Dathan with only a lambkin to watch our backs. I stuck close to Emerald in the hopes of finding some way to help him if trouble arrived early; Errol did the same, although I suspected that the lambkin's reasons were somewhat more self-interested in nature. Emerald was a reassuringly solid wall of flesh.

That would not be enough to protect him, if trouble came. I had felt the full force of Nechtan's murderous emotions, and the only comparable hatred I had ever felt from *Emerald* was for himself. If Nechtan attacked him, I was not sure that Emerald's desire to survive the encounter would be any match for Nechtan's desire to end his life.

There was already a lone figure waiting outside the church, a familiar slight form in ill-fitting clothes with wild black hair.

"Doctor?" Errol asked. "What are you doing here?"

Tincrown turned to us, keeping his arms wrapped around his

chest, and offered a small smile. "I'm here to see how all this ends."

[He doesn't know the identity of our killer,] Emerald said. **[I want to trust him, but I can't be sure that his conscience would allow him to keep silent. He loves this town and its inhabitants.]**

Tincrown moved to meet us in the street. *I'm not the only one who feels tethered to Emerald... and the citizens of Dyrne aren't the only ones Tincrown cares about.* I'd experienced my fair share of jealousy when it came to the doctor, but in truth, I was glad that he'd decided to join us. Emerald might not have sufficient will to defend his own life, but I knew from being in his own head that he'd do whatever it took to protect the people he loved.

"Are you ready?" Tincrown asked.

Emerald reached into his pocket and produced the goggles. The lenses flickered with a glittering light that reminded me of the gloves Tincrown had used to investigate Bilk's death. Their lenses were dark green, held together by a leather casing inscribed with unfamiliar symbols.

"*Aidea*," Errol breathed. "What are those?"

"They're called Dawyd-goggles." Emerald put them on and adjusted them a few times. The leather strap had not been designed for someone with such a large head, and I felt the pinch of too-tight leather over my own nose. Whatever had changed between us last night had not severed our connection entirely.

"What do they do?" The name was familiar, but I could not think where I'd heard it before. Dawyd, of course, was the longest-lived of the Conjury scouts, but who had mentioned goggles before?

Emerald's cryptic reply was for Errol's benefit alone. "They make it easier to see the truth of things." To me, he added, **[They reveal the invisible. The fully concealed citizens of Dyrne are still flesh and blood. They have heartbeats like anyone else. The lenses make it possible to see such things.]**

Another piece of the puzzle fell into place. When I was a

bird, I had seen Oidche go to Vanora and request the Dawyd-goggles. The tracker had wanted to make it easier to find Livia.

[And what do you see when you look at me?] I asked.

The lenses winked in my direction, but Emerald held his tongue, which was answer enough. According to that particular branch of the *aidea,* I did not exist.

Tincrown laid a slender hand on Emerald's shoulder. "So you know who did it?"

"I do," Emerald replied.

"*We* do," I corrected. I did not want Tincrown getting it into his head that I was just an extension of Emerald.

Emerald grunted again, but did not comment.

[So you didn't use your in with the doctor to cheat and solve the mystery?] I teased.

[No. I only confirmed my suspicions about the local residents' invisibility, and convinced him to let me borrow the goggles. I still haven't told him who did it, just in case.]

"Alright." Tincrown swallowed, and his hand tightened on Emerald's left shoulder. My own shoulder prickled with what felt like a shower of sparks. "I have your back. You know that, don't you?"

Emerald patted the doctor's hand before shrugging it off. "Stay back for now. If things go badly, I don't want you to be caught in the line of fire."

Tincrown nodded and withdrew a pace. "Very well. Errol and I will watch from the steps of the church, won't we, Master Lambkin?"

Errol nodded. "I'll be gla-a-a-ad to see the end of all this bloodshed."

[Let us hope it does not end in more,] I grumbled to Emerald. *[Watch your back.]*

Emerald tapped one fingertip against the casing of the goggles and bared the shorn-off roots of his tusks in a wry grin.

The Church of Dathan had stood silent all the while, but from within came a sudden swell of voices and the tramp of feet. The hinges of the great door creaked.

[Alright, Crim.] Emerald rubbed his hands together and withdrew toward the outer wall of the church, pressing his back to the weathered, mossy stones of the oldest building in Dyrne. *[This is it. The moment of truth.]*

I clenched my hands into fists as the mighty doors swung open, revealing the gold-and-violet robes of the high priest, backed by a whole town of faithful followers.

From my left, Tincrown nodded to me; from my right, Emerald did the same.

[Very well.] I straightened my shoulders and lifted my chin, willing my black capelet to stir in an imagined breeze. *[Time to prove to you that I'm just as much substance as style.]*

Chapter Twenty-Three

From the top of the church steps, the high priest lifted a bandaged hand in greeting. "Good morning, Simone of the Road. May the gods keep you."

Of course he would throw that line back in my face. Those very words marked the spot of Cassandra of Wishwind's final moments in the mortal world. He had attacked me the day before alongside that inscription. Clever of him, to use what should have been a prayer for safety as a threat against my life.

Or, more accurately, Emerald's life. The high priest already knew what I was, and what I was not.

"Same to you," I replied.

"What brings you here?" As Nechtan spoke, a handful of curious faces peered over his shoulder. I recognized Kristine's robes, as well as Vanora's. Behind them, a host of indistinguishable figures milled about in the shadows of the church.

"We've worked out who's responsible for the deaths of the scouts, and the boss at the mining encampment." I kept my eyes fixed on Nechtan's. He might be invisible. For all I knew, with his wrappings removed, there would be nothing at all to see beneath the heavy layers of cloth. Even so, I was certain that I could detect a glimmer of cruel intellect where his eyes should be.

Nechtan held his place, but a wiry, liver-spotted figure elbowed past him. Mayor Reade blotted his forehead with a cotton kerchief. "Perhaps we ought to discuss this in private."

"I think it best that people see for themselves what's happening." I tossed my braided hair, never looking away from Nechtan. He might disappear at any moment. "After all, aren't there enough secrets in Dyrne? Isn't that the source of all this trouble to begin with?"

Reade turned to Nechtan for confirmation, but the high priest remained fixated on me. He descended the steps, and the faithful came after him, overflowing between the ancient doors.

"Let her speak, Mayor," the priest intoned. "She is right. We have turned a blind eye to the problems in our midst. The two of us have been unable to put an end to our troubles. Let us hear what she has to say."

"I know how much you love this town." I bared my teeth in the facsimile of a smile. I was not certain that Nechtan knew that I had been able to read his emotions during our altercation, but in case he did, I wanted him to know what *I* knew. Let him embarrass himself in front of our audience, just has Coirpre had done in the tavern.

"That I do," Nechtan said. "More than you can know."

"I have a *sense* of it," I retorted. At last, I lifted my gaze toward the people waiting on the steps. "I know how much this place means to all of you. I know that sometimes hiding what you are can be the last, best form of self-defense."

A murmur rippled through the crowd, and something flickered through my connection to Emerald. **[You're right about that,]** he said, but there was a fuzzy quality to the thought that suggested he had not meant for me to hear it.

"What are you getting at?" Reade demanded.

Nechtan answered for me. "She knows."

"I do indeed know," I said. I raised one hand to the crowd. "I know that some of you are invisible. I know that others are only partly so. I know that you are desperate to keep this fact secret from the Conjury—and that one of you was desperate enough to kill for it."

Kristine sobbed and clung to her mother, and a few of the children whimpered, grabbing at their parents' robes.

"What do you intend to do?" Davina asked.

I held up both hands. "I know what you think of the Conjury. I understand why keeping this secret is so important to you. But it has gone too far. Even if you turn on us, others will come to investigate until the matter of these murders is resolved. You've drawn too much attention and spilled too much blood."

"So we are all to pay for the crimes of a few?" Parian snapped. He took a step forward, shrugging his mother's hand off of his shoulder, and dragged the ceremonial hood off of his head. "You know how I feel about the Church of Dathan. Everyone here does. I *hate* the fact that we have to hide!"

"And yet you will hide, when the lives of the ones you love depend upon it," I countered.

Parian gripped the thin material of his hood in one fist, but he stopped in his tracks and turned back to look at his mother and Kristine. "You're right," he said. "I will."

"I'm not asking you all to sacrifice your safety. Only one person should pay." I held out my hands. "One person, who is responsible for all of this. Who killed Bilk Deepvein, to keep him from blackmailing the town. Who killed Maximilien, when he fled Dyrne after discovering the truth. Who killed Cassandra, after one of your own revealed your secrets. Who killed Trotter of Shantytown for no greater crime than bearing witness. He meant to protect you, but instead, his actions threaten to bring the wrath of the Conjury down on each and every member of this community."

As I spoke, I drew even with Nechtan, who held his ground throughout my diatribe. The priest stood still as a stone on the cliffside, never flinching from my accusations.

"That person is the source of all your present troubles," I

insisted. "And that person is..." I swept out my arm, and so doing, the tips of my fingers passed through Nechtan's shoulder.

It was only a brief touch, one that I might have avoided if I had been looking at him rather than at the assembly, but it left me reeling.

The high priest's mind was filled by a myriad of emotions: fear, resignation, frustration, despair, hope, and love. It was a mind populated with shadows and pockmarked with secrets, some of which were buried so deeply that a single brush with him wasn't enough to make sense of them all.

What it did tell me, however, was that I had leapt to the wrong conclusion once again. Nechtan was not our man.

I froze, scrambling through the flurry of my thoughts. Everything had pointed to Nechtan. He was invisible, he had motive and means, and he had rubbed me the wrong way at every turn.

[It isn't Nechtan,] I thought.

Emerald's reply was, of course, patently infuriating. *[I know.]*

Somehow, I had gotten it wrong. The eyes of Dyrne were all on me, and I stood, prepared to accuse their high priest... who was *innocent.* Emerald had warned me about what would happen if I pointed fingers at the wrong man without proof. And yet I'd *had* proof. All the evidence indicated that Nechtan was our killer —all the evidence except for a handful of griffin feathers meant to frame Shale.

But it wasn't just the griffin feathers that pointed to the dwarf, was it? Someone tried to point me in the direction of the merchant. Someone who knew that the evidence pointed to a person and not a beast.

Someone who mentioned griffins even before Bilk was killed.

Someone skilled in tracking, who could move silently, and who could easily bring a babblebird down with a well-timed stone.

Someone who had fabricated his whereabouts during the time that Maximilian was killed, and lied about where he was when the mining camp was attacked.

Someone invisible.

Someone I had never suspected.

"...Aindreas," I said aloud.

"How *dare* you!" Parian exploded, rushing down the steps toward me. Before he could close the distance, Vanora leapt after him, catching him by the wrist and pulling him off-balance. Parian pinwheeled his arms, and they both toppled to the ground at the foot of the church stairs.

"Vanora!" Kade emerged from the crowd and leapt after his wife.

"No, no, no, no." The woman clung to Parian with an iron grip even as he tried to struggle to his feet. "No, leave it, leave *her*. I won't lose you both."

"Mother?" Parian asked. "What are you saying?"

Whatever words Vanora was about to say were lost in the bellow of rage that issued from Emerald. He fell with a grunt, landing on his hands and knees, grappling with empty air.

"Aindreas of Dyrne, you are hereby under arrest in the name of the Conjury! The gods grant you the right to—*oof.*" My companion was thrown backward toward the black iron fence of the churchyard gate. The Dawyd-goggles were knocked from his head and skittered away across the cobbles.

"Emerald!" Tincrown was already moving, but he'd vastly underestimated the fighting prowess of my associate. The half-Jotunn lifted both hands and made a complicated gesture, muttering under his breath as he did so. A burst of what looked like indigo paint splattered outward. Just as the muddy grave dirt had done the day before, his illusion snagged on the planes and contours of Aindreas's body. I felt the same *thinning* as I had before when Emerald tried to cast a second illusion, but the spray of glittering purple light did not require enough of his energy to dispel me.

I had never laid eyes on the man, but when the apparition cried out a curse to the gods, it did so in Aindreas's voice.

"Scourge!" Aindreas bellowed. "Enemy of Dathan! *Half-breed lapdog!*" He threw himself at Emerald again, but now that his naked and muscular body was partly visible, Emerald grinned.

He redoubled his attack on the invisible man, swinging his mighty fists as he regained ground that he'd lost to his attacker.

"Aindreas, please!" Vanora wailed. "You will make it that much worse for yourself."

Aindreas might have relied on invisibility in most instances, but he was clearly a skilled fighter. He ducked beneath Emerald's fists and swiped his legs under Emerald. My friend did not anticipate the attack, and he landed with a ground-shaking thud, smacking his head on the pathstones.

Aindreas was on him in an instant, hauling Emerald to his feet, with one arm wrapped around my companion's sturdy neck.

"Aindreas, please." Vanora pulled Parian even closer. "*Please.*"

"Please, what?" Aindreas spat. "Please lie still and allow the Conjury to grind its heels against our throats? Please submit to the will of a governing body who doesn't give a Teguan's shit about our well-being?"

Emerald gagged and struggled to get a grip on Aindreas's arm. *[Help. Air...]*

"Are you all such cowards that you would allow that?" Aindreas's voice rose to a howl. There was not a doubt in my mind that he was the one who had attacked me with such blind hatred. The skin around Emerald's eyelids turned red as Aindreas tightened his arm again my friend's throat.

"You understand, don't you, Parian?" Aindreas growled. "Tell her. Tell her that we will not go quietly."

Parian, who had made a great show of his sullen adulthood, recoiled into Vanora's arms. He was nothing more than a frightened little boy.

"*Tell her, Parian!*" Aindreas insisted. "If you were not such cowards, any of you would have done the same!"

[Aster's sake... Air... Air...] Emerald thrashed, trying and failing to knock Aindreas off of his feet. I watched, helpless to act. The people of Dyrne did the same.

They are all culpable, each and every one. They might not have known who was at fault, but they knew why, and they did nothing to stop it. They worried only about their safety, and spared no thought for the lives of others who would die to protect their secrets.

Fortunately, the audience was not composed only of stunned villagers and one helpless illusion. In the time I had known him, Tincrown had only ever been gentle and kind, but apparently he was capable of action when the moment called for it. He collided with Aindreas, knocking the distracted murderer off of his feet.

Emerald fell to all fours, gasping for air, as another small figure launched its attack on Aindreas.

"For the King of Apple Boughs!" Errol bleated. "No fear!" He landed square in the middle of Aindreas's back and pummeled the rough vicinity of his shoulderblades with his tiny fists.

"Get off me, you abomination!" Aindreas tried to catch Errol's leg, but the lambkin was surprisingly nimble. He darted out of Aindreas's grasp.

The Dyrnian thrashed his way to his feet, but Emerald got there first. Aindreas rose just in time to find himself nose-to-knuckle with Emerald's right fist.

My associate was many things at different times: an arrogant prick, an accomplished detective, an awkward flirt, an empath, an intellectual, and a consummate pain in the ass. Anyone who looked at him and saw him as nothing more than a wall of muscle missed out on a great deal of the best he had to offer.

That said, he *was* strong. Under one mighty blow from him, Aindreas dropped to the earth in a limp heap and did not rise.

Emerald stood above him, breathing hard. **[And that,]** he told me, **[is how you put on a show.]**

Chapter Twenty-Four

"Hold still," Tincrown said as he examined Emerald's scrapes. My friend sat in the front pew of the Church of Dathan, watched intently by the silent congregation.

Nechtan hovered over us; Reade had left with Errol and Shale, along with a few others, to imprison Aindreas.

"I hope that Aindreas has caused you no lasting harm," the high priest said. "As for his words, know that he does not speak for all of us."

A row away, Vanora sobbed against her husband's shoulder. They sat in isolation. Even Parian had put distance between himself and his parents. He sat beside Kristine and Davina, staring straight ahead with unfocused eyes.

"He acted alone, didn't he?" Tincrown asked the priest.

"I had no part in it, certainly." Nechtan sighed. "No direct part, anyway—although I won't deny that I did little to stop it until it was too late. I did not look too closely at the evidence, I'm afraid. How did you discover him?"

Emerald nodded to me, and I glanced down at my boots before responding. "He lied to us about where he'd been. When we were at Sheiling's store, he told us that he'd been traveling with Oidche for two weeks, but Oidche later said that he'd gone after Lidia more than once in the past week. He needed an excuse for why he'd been out of town, because he'd been in Lower Bound chasing Maximilien. He also tried to frame Shale for Bilk's death. Although I'm still not certain why he left the rag in Bilk's mouth?"

"To make it obvious that griffins *weren't* responsible," Emerald said. "I'll bet you two bottles of Shine of the Moon that he wanted to make sure that we knew a person was involved. He did his best to tie Shale to the killing from both directions."

"Why Shale?" I asked. "Because he overheard us talking to him outside the shop?"

"It is more than that." In the pews, Davina removed her hood, so that we could see her lovely face once again. "I only married Shale because he found out about our town's secrets many years ago. He threatened to expose the town unless I agreed to be his bride."

"No, Mai-mai!" Kristine exclaimed.

"It's true." Davina hugged her daughter's shoulders. "There has never been much love lost between us." Her blue eyes flicked toward me and Emerald. "He can be an unpleasant man, and he made a miserable husband, but he loves our daughter as much as I do. He will always be an outsider, but he will never betray our trust, because he knows what it would cost him. Show them, my darling."

Kristine whimpered and turned to Nechtan, who nodded his agreement. With a trembling gloved hand, she removed her hood.

Emerald flinched, and even though I was prepared for the sight of a flayed girl, I could not quite smother my shock. Beside her striking mother, the horror of her condition was all the more obvious. Her eyes, just as blue as Davina's, were perfectly round in their socket. In some places, the musculature of her face was visible, while in others it was possible to see down to the bone.

Kristine sniffled and began to cry. "I don't want to look like this, Father Nechtan." She raised one gloved hand to her face, trying to stave off our disbelieving stares.

To my surprise, it was Parian who took her arm, then leaned in to kiss the skin of her cheek. His lips stopped short of the muscle. She *had* skin, then, even if we could not see it.

"How many times do I have to tell you?" He placed one hand on the far side of her head and leaned his forehead against her temple. "You're beautiful, Kristine. You have nothing to be ashamed of. We shouldn't *have* to hide."

"I wish that were true." Nechtan sighed heavily. "But the world outside cannot accept us, Parian. They would use us, and our children. We would be hunted and reviled."

Several other members of the audience stirred. One by one, they began to remove their hoods. People with ordinary faces sat alongside those who appeared to be nothing more than headless bodies. Others still seemed as strange to my eye as Kristine did. Sheiling's face was visible in patches, with a shock of black hair standing upright from what I could see of his forehead, and a single blue eye overflowing with tears. Next to him sat a person who appeared to be made of nothing but nerves. Through some faces, it was possible to see the pulse of veins, or bare bones. With each exposed face, my horror shrank, until it disappeared entirely.

They were only people, after all.

At last, Nechtan lifted his own elaborate headdress and set it on the altar, beneath an amorphous statue. "Dathan sees us as we are, and he does not judge us. I cannot say the same for the outside world. Thanks to our progenitor, Throop of Dunmore, the children of Dyrne are born invisible. Over time, some of us grow into our visibility. Others never do—and we must not judge ourselves for what others see." He said this last part with an air of stern affection that only made Kristine sob harder.

[Ah,] I thought. *[That explains Shale's habit of yelling at ghosts, and the sand on Sheiling's shop floor.]*

[An effective countermeasure against small thieves in search of sweets,] Emerald agreed. *[And why we've encoun-*

***tered so few children. Their parents must have kept them
inside to avoid them making any mistakes while we were
present.]***

I remembered my flight into Parian's room. Was Aindreas
watching me in the garden, wondering how I had managed that
little trick? Small children were not the only ones who slipped
up and revealed things to the wrong people.

"Shale was not the first outsider to discover our secrets,"
Nechtan explained. "Dawyd of Sailor's Reprieve did so when I
was still training, and he is the reason we were able to acquire—"

"The Dawyd-goggles!" I yelped, and instantly bit my tongue.

"Indeed." Nechtan gestured to Emerald. He still wore his
bandages, but without the headdress, he seemed less imposing
than before. "He was a fellow native of the island, even if he
wasn't from our village. He worked for the Conjury, but he
understood how their interference could impact our way of life.
For the duration of his decades as a scout, he hid the truth of
our circumstances. He even commissioned the goggles. You
cannot possibly imagine how difficult it is to help an invisible
woman give birth to an invisible babe." He chuckled, and a few
others did the same, although Vanora's quiet weeping never
ceased.

"Yes, Dawyd was a good man," Nechtan went on. "And we
found other good people. Tincrown being one of them."

The doctor dipped his head modestly. "I doubt that I would
have been much help without Dawyd's contributions."

"Be that as it may, you have not judged us for what we are,
and we are grateful for it." Nechtan bowed his head, and a
murmur of assent rose from the crowd of the faithful.

"But then Dawyd died," Emerald prompted. "And you
weren't sure that you could trust the new scouts."

Nechtan slumped back against the altar. "Dathan help me,
but I allowed myself to believe that Trotter's death was an accident. And then Sheiling tried to take Cassandra into our confidence. I truly believe that she would have kept our secret. She
was a good woman. But then she died, and I thought, *The road*

can be treacherous, and she was new to the area. I convinced myself that it was an accident."

"And then Maximilien fled," I said. "He made it all the way to Lower Bound."

"Indeed. I didn't know about his passing until you two arrived." Nechtan stared out into the crowd. "Only then did I allow myself to see the truth. This is a small town, tightly-knit. To think any of us capable of such a thing is a horror. Now, Simone of the Road, our fate lies in your hands. What will the two of you do with us?"

I shifted uncomfortably beneath the town's collective gaze. "I don't believe I'm qualified to make that decision. I must leave that question in the hands of my mentor."

[Mentor?] Emerald echoed. *[Doesn't that strike you as a bit sycophantic?]*

[Seems pretty accurate to me. You taught me everything I know, but you haven't prepared me for something like this.]

Emerald puffed out his cheeks and got to his feet, leaving Tincrown sitting on the pew. He folded his large hands behind his back, covering the bruised knuckles of his right hand.

A lesser man would have remembered the cruel words hurled his way, the little digs and jibes of the villagers. Such a man would have relish the fact that he now held total power over their futures.

But Emerald's love was without malice, and his sense of justice was the same.

"If I turn Aindreas over to the Conjury," he said, "life as you know it will end. What would you do then?"

"Leave this place." The high priest passed a bandaged hand across his brow. "Go our separate ways. Do our best to hide in twos and threes."

Emerald shook his head. "You know that won't work. Sooner or later, someone will find you. What would happen, then, if I left Aindreas here? What would you do with him?"

"With us?" Nechtan seemed surprised, but I was not. I had

sensed the question brewing in Emerald's mind long before he spoke. "We could rehabilitate him, I suppose. If such a thing is even possible. Otherwise, we would be forced to keep him imprisoned."

"That wouldn't solve the problem of the Conjury, though." Emerald ran the pad of his thumb over his lips. "Even if I can convince them to let the matter lie, they will eventually send another scout."

"You speak as if you are considering it." Nechtan wrung his hands.

Emerald gazed upon the assembled villagers. Parian's jaw twitched, but others seemed more hopeful.

[It would be an awful lot of lives to ruin,] I told him. *[Surely the great Emerald Flame can come up with something a bit more merciful?]*

Emerald snorted. *[Now I know you're being a sycophant.]* Aloud, he said, "I can only see one way to proceed. The town of Dyrne must vanish."

Kristine wailed, and Vanora fell to her knees.

"I misspoke," Emerald added hastily. He lifted both hands to pacify the crowd. "What I mean to say is, the town of Dyrne must *appear* to vanish. We will need the help of the dwarves, but I'm sure it can be done."

"How?" asked a chorus of voices.

Emerald turned to me and bit his lip. "Let me confer with my associates first," he said.

I puffed up my chest. *[Asking for my advice after all, eh?]*

Rather than smiling, my friend's expression only turned more grim. *[Not advice. Permission.]*

Emerald, Tincrown, and I withdrew to the silent chamber at the back of the church. It was my third time inside, but the first time I had entered by invitation.

"Have they let you back here before?" I asked Tincrown.

The doctor nodded toward the wall inscribed with all those

generations-worth of names. "Nechtan brought me here when he was trying to explain the town's circumstances. Dawyd was here, too. He was the one that suggested I come to Dyrne in the first place. Apparently he found me trustworthy enough to make that decision on behalf of the locals." Tincrown smiled fondly. "I'm so glad he did. I don't know how to explain it, but I'm certain that I'm right where Ardus wants me."

"It seems that you're good at drawing people into your confidence." I lifted one scarlet eyebrow in Emerald's direction.

"Evidently," the doctor agreed. "But it might surprise you how good I am at keeping secrets from all but the right people."

"He knows what you are, Crim," Emerald clarified. He stood with his back to me, staring up at the family tree inscribed upon the wall.

"Come on, then. Out with it. Let us hear your spectacular plan for protecting the people of this town." I moved toward him until we stood shoulder to shoulder.

"If we can get Carthan Deepvein to agree, we could send him back to Sailor's Reprieve with the news that the mining operations below the town caused an avalanche when the mountain peak was disturbed. It might involve selling them the mining rights, or at least a portion of them." Emerald spoke slowly, but there was little doubt in my mind that he could see the whole thing plainly, coming together just as he described it. "The road coming into town is treacherous. It wouldn't take much to make it appear that it had been buried under a heap of rubble. If the Conjury sends scouts to follow up on these reports, they'll see exactly what the dwarves describe. Perhaps we can weave in some explanation about Maximilien's death. Make it out to be an accident, just like the other two."

"You mean that you'll create an illusion large enough to convince the scouts?" I whistled. "That sounds like quite a feat. Can you manage it?"

Emerald's head whipped toward me, and he narrowed his moss-colored eyes. "I can make an illusion with a mind of its own. You don't think I can lightweave a pile of *rocks?*"

"I'm sure you can," Tincrown said soothingly.

"But?" I prompted. "There's going to be a '*but*,' I can feel it."

Emerald nibbled his bottom lip.

"I've had enough histrionics for one day," I snapped. "Out with it."

"I can't do both," he admitted.

"Both what?" I asked. "Both a sentient illusion *and* a pile of rocks?"

"Exactly. I can either protect this village, or I can keep casting you, but it's one or the other." Emerald scratched the back of his neck. "I can *try,* given how you've changed lately, but I've never been able to do it in the past, and this would be a massive, mind-straining illusion to sustain all that time. I'd likely have to teach someone else how it's done, which, in itself, will require me to split my attention, and will take awhile. So—Crimson? Crimson, are you listening?"

I was not. Not attentively, at any rate. Instead, I stared up at the wall of names.

What is your little half-life compared to the lives of all these people? Not only the ones who are alive now, but their future descendants? You have the potential to make a small sacrifice with a long-lasting legacy. Six months of consciousness. You've only been alive a week. You're still a baby, and have gone the whole span of the universe before *that without existing. Six months? That's nothing.*

And yet, I was standing in the very room where I had watched Emerald summon that small flame on the night when he'd forced me through the wall, only to watch him smother it again. I remembered what I'd thought then: *When Emerald has no more use for that little flame, he will snuff it out and think no more about it.*

I was more than I had been, but I was still entirely at his mercy. If Emerald ever decided to be rid of me, it would be effortless.

"I'll summon you again, when the work is done." He held one hand out to me. "See my intentions for yourself, if you want."

I stood there for a moment, turning the matter over in my

mind. After a pause, I shook my head. "I don't need to do that," I said. "I believe you."

Emerald smiled at me and lowered his hand. "I'm glad. And I mean it, Crim. I'll try to weave both, but even if I can't, I'll bring you back as soon as Dyrne is safe."

[I do have one condition,] I added silently. *[You have to tell Tincrown.]*

Emerald's brow wrinkled. *[Tell him what?]*

[Whatever it is that you won't tell me.]

Emerald shuddered. *[Crim—]*

[You're asking me to give up part of myself to protect these near-strangers. I'm asking you to do this to protect yourself. After all, if I'm not here to look out for you, someone ought to be.]

Both of us glanced over our shoulders at Tincrown, who shuffled his feet and smiled awkwardly. "Are you doing that thing where you can talk to each other in your heads?" he asked.

"Yup," I said.

"It's a bit uncanny, to be honest." He backed away. "But by all means, don't let me intrude."

"I think we're done here," I said, then turned to Emerald for confirmation. "Do we have a deal?"

"We do," he agreed.

"Then we should tell everyone what you have in mind and see what *they* think." I waved toward the door. "Let's see how they feel about it. Go on then, Em. What are you waiting for?"

The citizens of Dyrne followed us in a mute procession toward the pass outside of town. Vanora was still sobbing against her husband's shoulder, and I wondered how many skeptical expressions sat on the faces of the invisible or near-invisible residents of the village. I found Kristine, who walked with her head uncovered, hard to read. Parian, however, looked utterly content.

It was strange to me that a man who had been so unkind to

Emerald would find it so easy to love someone who looked the way Kristine did. I found her far more unsettling to gaze upon than my companion, although I supposed that if she'd been the first face I ever laid eyes upon, I might have felt differently.

I glanced once more toward Emerald. Certainly, he was no great beauty, but in his moments of compassion he had the *kindest* face I'd ever seen, barring perhaps Tincrown's.

I fell back a few paces until I walked alongside the doctor. "You had better take care of him," I hissed. "He needs minding."

"I shall do my best," Tincrown said. To my surprise, he didn't seem amused by my request. Perhaps he saw Emerald's quiet hurt as clearly as I did.

I was glad, at least, that someone saw my friend as clearly as Parian saw his lover.

The sky was overcast when we reached the pass, and the gray solemnity of the occasion settled over the assembly like a shroud. I left Tincrown behind and approached Emerald once again as he ran his blunt-knuckled fingers over the inscription marking the place where Cassandra of Wishwind spent her final moments among the living. What had she felt when Aindreas put his hands on her? Had she felt his hatred as deeply as I had? Or had she only been aware of standing on solid ground one moment and falling the next?

"I'm sorry," Emerald murmured.

I tilted my head. "For what?"

[For not getting here sooner. If we'd solved the mystery of Dyrne before any of the scouts died, we might have been able to help them all without bloodshed. That's the trouble with solving mysteries... most of the time, you arrive when the disaster's already over and done.] He sighed heavily and stood upright once more. ***[Are you ready?]***

I braced to be banished. "Very well," I said aloud. If these were to be the last words I ever spoke, I wanted them to exist somewhere outside of Emerald's mind. "I shall see you after the fall equinox at the latest."

My companion tugged on the bright chain about his neck,

and the emerald pendant emerged from the neckline of his shirt. I had never seen him in the act of lightweaving before, not when the effort involved was more than rudimentary. A handful of fire here or a bowl of fruit there seemed to require no real finesse on his part, but this was to be a much larger act.

The citizens of Dyrne and I watched in breathless wonder—admittedly, an easy state for me to accomplish given my lack of lungs—as Emerald held the pendant on one palm and made a strange sign with his free hand. His lips formed a word, one that I could not quite make out, and his eyes began to glow with an inner fire brighter than any star.

I felt myself growing thin, and for a moment I was little more than a shadow of myself, peering down a long, dark hallway into an endless night. As the illusion of a landslide rose around us, Emerald's eyes blaze bright as firelight, and I *became* the stones. I tried to call out for my friend, to tell him to stop, to beg for a little more time until I was swept under by a tidal wave of entropy.

For a long time, I was nothing and nowhere, and I did not have it in me to be afraid.

Chapter Twenty-Five

In the blink of an eye, spring was over, and summer too. One moment, I was standing in the Church of Dathan while Emerald explained his plan. The next, I was in a familiar cozy kitchen littered with pressed flowers and dog-eared tomes. Tincrown sat on the small couch, his boyish chin obscured by a rather scruffy mass of facial hair that took me by surprise, while Emerald stood facing me. He looked much the same as he had before, aside from his easy smile and the rolled-up sleeves of his shirt.

"Did it work?" I asked.

Emerald lowered his hands. "The autumn equinox was yesterday. Two scouts came by, but when they saw the state of the 'ruined' pass, they turned back."

"It was magnificent," Tincrown added dreamily, staring at Emerald with lovestruck eyes.

"Good to know that my time away was so *productive*," I observed drily.

"I haven't been idle." Emerald leaned against the kitchen table, which protested with a wooden squeak but managed to support his sturdy frame. "I've spent the last six months teaching Nechtan how to energize the spell that will hide the village. He's no lightweaver, and it took me *ages* to imbue an inscription he can actually use, but on the bright side, it only needs to be renewed every few days. Even though he's not actively weaving it, the spell will hold."

"Dyrne is safe, thanks to Emerald." Tincrown smiled at him, then turned his eyes on me. "And thanks to you."

"What happens now?" I asked.

Emerald and Tincrown exchanged a knowing glance.

[Not fair,] I griped. ***[Have you learned how to read each other's minds while I was away?]***

[Still a brat, I see.] Aloud, Emerald said, "For the moment, I'm planning to stay in Dyrne. As far as the Conjury knows, I was killed in a landslide along with everyone else, and you were nothing more than a lightweaving I had license to cast as part of my work. Nobody will notice if we linger here for a while."

"What else have I missed?" I wandered over to the window and peered through the pane into the street. "Has Nechtan made any progress with Aindreas?" It was strange to think of six whole months passing in the time I'd been away. Though to call it sleep would be a misnomer. Dreamless nothing? My week of consciousness had been so eventful, and now I had more than *twenty times* that much to catch up on and did not want to wait even a moment longer.

Emerald grunted. "I wouldn't say that."

"Why don't we let her see for herself?" Tincrown suggested.

"Oh, please?" I spun to them and clasped my hands together. "Since I had to be away, the least you can do is assure me that all my lost time didn't go to waste."

Emerald clicked his tongue. "*Fine.* Just try not to cause a scene this time, please?"

I made him no promises.

The walk from Tincrown's house through Dyrne could not have been more different from any of the other times I had walked through the streets. Instead of grim silence, we were surrounded by the lively chatter of neighbors. The people around us no longer wore their hoods, and many of them had eschewed gloves as well. Parian, wearing a new set of robes that fitted him properly, walked hand-in-hand with Kristine. This time, the sight of her seemingly flayed body didn't alarm me. Sheiling and Shale were having an argument of some kind outside the general store, and Davina sat outside the schoolhouse relishing the golden autumn sunlight, surrounded by an array of what appeared to be undersized, empty robes and the disembodied chatter of high childish voices. Vanora and Dun were outside, squabbling over an indifferent pair of goats who appeared to be better-fed than ever.

"You made all of this possible," Tincrown told us as we headed toward the church.

"Don't say things like that," Emerald complained. "She'll get a big head."

"Or she'll recognize how much she's appreciated," Tincrown pointed out, slipping one of his hands into Emerald's as we went.

Emerald smiled, my own hand tingled as though I had brought it too close to a fire, or caught the air after a lightning bolt had scored it.

[Six months, and he's not tired of you yet?] I feigned a yawn. *[Despite your stodgy attitude?]*

The old Emerald might have taken offense, but now he only replied, *[Not yet.]*

I resigned myself then and there to an eternity of watching them fawn over one another, and was only half annoyed.

"How is it that Shale can still bring supplies to the village?" I asked, hoping to move on from the subject of their happily ever after.

Tincrown was the one who answered. "Mayor Reade cut a deal with Carthan Deepvein. The dwarves got their mining rights, with a few caveats, and Shale brings supplies for both the encampment and the village. Since he never told anyone else on the island that he lives here, nobody seems to have picked up on the ruse."

"Considering what happened to Bilk, I imagine it required some tactful negotiation."

"Em interceded," the doctor replied. "They get all the minerals from the mountain without having to pay for the rights and we get to keep a lifeline to the outer world."

"So Dyrne is hidden, without being entirely cut off from the rest of the world," I mused. "Aindreas got what he wanted after all."

"I didn't do this for Aindreas's sake," Emerald observed. His grip tightened on the doctor's hand. "But we do seem to have solved the problem without further bloodshed."

"All it took was that big brain of yours." Tincrown nudged Emerald with one elbow.

I pretended to gag.

"He's only doing this because he knows it will get a rise out of you," Emerald grumbled, although his green-tinted cheeks had darkened like fresh moss in a rain.

"You're adorable, and it's sickening. I'm going to talk to Aindreas. Is he——?" I gestured toward the church.

"Nechtan has him confined in the back room of the tower," Emerald said. "We can get him to accompany you."

"No need." I left the two of them to their canoodling and pushed off from the ground, sailing above the roofline toward the buttress at the back. If the citizens of Dyrne now felt free to be themselves, then surely I could do the same.

[Showoff,] Emerald thought.

I seeped between the bricks of the buttress just shy of the uppermost room and hesitated on the steps. I had not yet decided what to say to him, or what to ask him. Any of the questions I might have wished to pose now seemed irrelevant. His words to Emerald outside the church had told me everything that I needed to know.

Aindreas was the worst kind of monster, the one who could blend in among ordinary people. His invisibility helped, but it was his aptitude for social niceties that most disturbed me. I had genuinely liked him until I understood his capacity for violence and cruelty.

Steeling myself for another encounter with the man who'd reduced me to tears the night of his attack, I forced myself upward and through the locked einwood door above.

The room was anything but spare. Texts and tomes filled shelves that covered nearly every inch of the wall, an inviting bed draped in handmade blankets stood beneath one iron-barred window, and a well-stocked writing desk below the other. Nechtan had created a little scholar's paradise.

My first impulse was fury. Why should a killer like Aindreas be allowed to enjoy such a pleasant room? A dank cell swarming with rats would be too good for him. But then again, Nechtan had promised to *rehabilitate* him. Locking Aindreas up for the rest of his life was unlikely to cure his mind. Perhaps the high priest was onto something.

I was still standing with my back to the door when a raw voice whispered in my ear, "Have you come to spy on me, little lightweaving?"

I flinched away from the source of the voice. "Aindreas?"

"Welcome back, Simone. I've missed you." His voice was deeper now, either as the result of misuse or out of some misguided attempt to frighten me. "We played a fun little game, didn't we? But you think you won." Bare feet slapped against the stone floor, and the chair in front of the writing desk slid out and spun to face me. The legs screeched against stone as Aindreas sat down. "Have you come to laugh in my face? To flaunt your perceived triumph? How petty of you."

"I'm not here to celebrate." I straightened up again and lifted my chin to show that I was not afraid. Confidence was as free as my tailoring, and I wanted Aindreas to know that I had an abundance of it. "I wanted to know how you've changed now that Dyrne is safe."

"Safe?" He scoffed. "For now, hidden by a mountain of fake pebbles. Subterfuge has never served us."

"It's kept you safe from the Conjury," I pointed out. "And

now your brother and his lover can walk in the street without shame."

"They are still *hiding!*" Aindreas hissed. "While that putrid half-breed flaunts his affections high and low, as if the sight of him is not enough to turn our stomachs."

I glanced toward the windows. They were set too high on the walls to allow Aindreas to watch the comings and goings of pedestrians below. "How do you know what Emerald does with his time?"

Aindreas let out a bark of bitter laughter. "A *little bird* told me."

My mouth snapped shut.

"Oh, yes, so it was you." The chair squeaked again as Aindreas rose. "Little redwing blackbird, little shapeshifting web of light, you think you're safe now that I'm trapped in here? You think the dangerous element has been stripped away and Dyrne is a safe place for you now? You cannot truly believe that I am the only one who thinks this way. I have ways of finding out what occurs beyond these walls. Not everyone has turned their backs on me."

"Parian?" I asked, and wished at once that the high note of worry in my voice had not betrayed me.

"Parian is besotted. He casts your mutt as a *savior.* His edges have been blunted by small kindnesses, but no. There are others like me." He was close now, close enough that I would have felt his breath on my skin, if I'd had any. "Others who resent the fact that our futures rest in the hand of an inhuman abomination."

"Emerald is a better man than you'll ever be," I muttered.

"He is not a *man.* The doctor defiles himself by association, but never mind. Tincrown was never one of us. Those who accepted him will see him clearly, now that he makes no secret of lying down with an *animal.*"

If I'd had fists and knuckles, I would have swung, just as Emerald did the day Aindreas was arrested. I could not strike the shade that lingered beside me, or deliver a blow to the mouth from which his hideous lies spilled.

As it happened, I had other weapons.

I was not sure exactly where Aindreas stood, but a rough estimate was all that was required. I swept my arms toward him, as if to pull him into an embrace. The moment I passed through the limits of his unseen skin, I pushed myself forward, so that we overlapped entirely. I had never done anything like that before, and the result was instantaneous and sickening. I reached into him, just as he had once reached into me unknowingly. Instead of being overcome with *his* love and *his* self-righteous anger, it was his turn to be overcome with mine.

Oh, how I longed to hurt him, to injure him in some way that would leave a mark as a reminder of my anger. But the thought of little marks on bare skin reminded me of Emerald's self-loathing, and even if I could, Aindreas I did not want to become the sort of creature that answered pain with pain. To let him feel it was enough.

We were more alike than I had reckoned. At its most potent, love made monsters of us both.

Aindreas cried out and stumbled, overbalancing in his haste to get away. He tried to catch himself and only succeeded in grasping at a blanket before hitting the ground. The quilt slithered to the floor beside him, although I could clearly see the place where his hand clenched the material for all he was worth.

I crouched beside him, baring my teeth and bringing my face close to where his must have been. Let him try to lay a hand on me again. Blessed Aster, let him *try*.

"It's not a matter of being invisible," I told him. "It's a matter of what's in your heart, and your heart is *rotten*. Leave my friend alone, and if you are in touch with other *like-minded individuals* in this town, tell them to do the same. If anyone lays a hand on him, or speaks to him as you have just spoken to me, I swear by all eighty of the gods that I will find you again, and I will enter your mind as I have done just now, and I will *never leave*. Do I make myself clear? I will inhabit you. I will wreck you. You are nothing, Aindreas of Dyrne, and if you harm my friend, I will make sure that you remember it in vivid detail every day for the rest of your worthless, petty, miserable life."

Aindreas whimpered.

"Say it," I commanded.

"I understand," he rasped.

"I'm glad to hear it." I rose to my feet, glaring down at the empty air where he lay. "Remember this covenant of ours, Aindreas, because *I* will not forget."

With that, I strode to the stone wall of the buttress, tipped forward, and soared out into the sunlight once more.

Tincrown and Emerald walked me back to the doctor's house, chatting easily as we went. They did not ask me what the imprisoned man had said, and I did not offer any information. Instead, I trailed behind them, staring at my hands.

I had not known that I was capable of that kind of anger. I had swelled with self-righteousness in the moment, but now I felt dirty. Tainted, almost. And yet, I could not truthfully say that I regretted it.

Emerald startled me out of my reverie. ***[You're awfully quiet back there. Are you broken?]***

"No," I said aloud.

Tincrown turned back to me. "Did you say something, Simone?"

I shook my head.

[What's the matter? Don't want to let me into your head?] Emerald asked.

"No," I said again.

"My mistake," Tincrown said and continued walking.

[Crimson, if Aindreas did something, you know that you can tell me, right?]

[And what if I did something?]

Emerald turned to address me, but Tincrown tugged on his hand. "Is that a babblebird?" he asked.

Sure enough, one of the squat, pudgy birds sat on Tincrown's stoop, jabbing its fat beak against the seeded head of a drooping sunflower, one of dozens that surrounded the house.

All three of us stopped in our tracks.

"If everyone thinks that Dyrne has been destroyed," Tincrown murmured, "who would send us a message? They would have had to say 'go to Tincrown's house in Dyrne' to get it here."

"Unless word of the village's destruction hasn't spread yet," Emerald said.

I added my two coppers. "Or the Conjury is doing its due diligence, and sending a babblebird to ferret out whether or not we're in hiding."

"Good point." Emerald frowned. "How do we make it go away?"

"Depends who it's from," Tincrown said. "What if it's a message from my family?"

Emerald pressed his palms together in front of his face. "So we ascertain who the message is *for,* and who it's *from,* and then go from there?"

"I think that would be best," Tincrown said.

We tiptoed forward together, as if the bird was liable to explode if we made any sudden moves.

When it saw us, the babblebird swiveled its head to one side to fix us with one beady eye. Tincrown squatted down beside the steps. "Hello there," he said. "I'm Tincrown of Swoop Oasis. Do you have a message for me?"

The babblebird only stared.

"Hm." The doctor rubbed the thick hair that covered his chin. "Who is it for, then?"

The babblebird twisted its head to the other side and continued its inspection. "Crimson Smoke and the Emerald Flame," it said in a familiar female voice.

"Oh, hell after hell," Emerald groaned.

"Hold on." I shuffled forward. "Is it me, or does it sound just like Amaya? The Auger from Lower Bound?"

The babblebird whipped its head toward me. "Crimson Smoke," it repeated. Yes, that was definitely Amaya's voice.

"Um, yes, that's me." I knelt beside Tincrown. "Did you have something to tell me?"

The babblebird made a noise like a burp. "*Harpax sends greetings. Your employers will be speaking to his good friend as soon as possible. If you are available, come around for tea at your earliest convenience. Reply preferred.*"

Emerald groaned and pressed his hands to the top of his head.

"Who's Harpax?" Tincrown asked.

"Maximilien's horse," I said. "Which means—"

"That the Conjury doesn't consider the matter closed," Emerald snapped.

The illusion of the rockslide might have fooled the scouts, but forces beyond our control were still in play. I had overestimated the success of our ruse. Dyrne and everyone who lived there was still in danger of being discovered.

Little did I know that our troubles had only begun.

⚜

We hope you enjoyed this Heavenfall novel. Book two of the Crimson Smoke and the Emerald Flame is available here: Tale of the Swamp Song.

Become part of our reader group here for free novellas and other swag by signing up here!

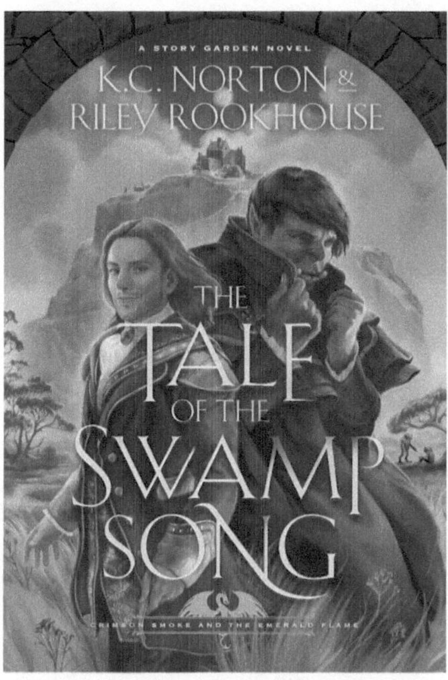

Finding a murderer should be easy when you can ask the corpse who killed them.

Every few nights, a swamp at the edge of civilization gives back its dead. When a victim returns to demand justice from beyond a watery grave, the renowned Emerald Flame douses himself in spirits, leaving his partner to wade through their pool of suspects alone.

Upper Bound is full of swindlers, frauds, and misanthropes: a lord who never fails to be the life of the party. A minstrel with more charisma than talent. The head of the city's criminal underbelly. A vagrant who claims to be a landless king.

Crimson Smoke has never failed to puzzle out a mystery, but if they can't solve one murder faster than they can cover up another, the lives of an entire town could be at stake.

And Crimson is starting to believe that the city's restless dead aren't the only thing that the bog has brought back to life.

Acknowledgments

K.C. Norton: This book, and what comes after, means more to me than I could have imagined when we first discussed the premise. I started out a visitor in the world that Jordan had been kicking around for a long time, and now it's something entirely different than what either of us would have imagined alone. Jordan, thank you for trusting me enough to let me steer the ship a little. There's so much of myself in these characters, and it means the world to me that you let me follow my gut on that. Don't you dare hang up your quill the way you're always threatening, or Diane and I will be forced to write a strongly worded letter. My thanks also to the assortment of strangers who joined me in haranguing Jordan's (lack of) Ren Faire garb. Talk about a peak experience.

Thank you to the Crimsons in my life, the people who have managed to get into my head enough to smack some sense into me: AJ and Ami, Katie and Katie, Brant, Thomas, Liz, Harrow, and Callie. Of course, most of all, to Dawn—imagine a gender-fluid protagonist with a flair for the dramatic who loves to perform for an audience. *Imagine.*

To my Allies and Assassins, always, espccially the Birches.

Thank you to one Tia for extended discussions about gender

identity, even the ones that cut us both a little too close to the bone. And for another Tia, if you're reading this, please know that all future Coirpre escapades have been heavily influenced by that spectacular Florence concert. Next one's on me. ♥

Riley Rookhouse: I'd like to give thanks to all the usual suspects: Amy and Ami for our long bouts of plotting—I owe them so much; Diane Callahan, Story Garden's lead editor; and the Zanesville crew who inspired Heavenfall in the first place.

We have an amazing team over here at Story Garden. I couldn't ask for a more creative and reliable writer than K. C. Norton, who turned an idea I had decades ago into reality, creating characters with such depth that they have become living, breathing people in my mind. I often say that K.C. opened up an emotional vein and bled this story onto the page. You can see it in every word she crafted and every wound she exposed to make these characters more than the sum of their parts.

We're grateful for Angela Traficante's thorough copy editing. Our compliments also go out to the book cover illustrator Hannah Elizabeth who can finally add this cover to her portfolio. As well as letterer James T. Egan of Bookfly Design for his assistance on the cover.

We can't wait to share the rest of the stories in the Crimson Smoke and the Emerald Flame series. And thank you, dear reader, for reading until the very last line.